U0057529

Effective Business Communication
商用英文

By Ted Knoy
柯泰德

Illustrated by Ming-Jay Chen
插圖：陳銘杰

Ted Knoy is also the author of the following books in the Chinese Technical Writers' Series（科技英文寫作系列叢書）*and the Chinese Professional Writers' Series*（應用英文寫作系列叢書）：

An English Style Approach for Chinese Technical Writers
《精通科技論文寫作》

English Oral Presentations for Chinese Technical Writers
《做好英文會議簡報》

A Correspondence Manual for Chinese Writers
《英文信函參考手冊》

An Editing Workbook for Chinese Technical Writers
《科技英文編修訓練手冊》

Advanced Copyediting Practice for Chinese Technical Writers
《科技英文編修訓練手冊進階篇》

Writing Effective Study Plans
《有效撰寫讀書計畫》

Writing Effective Work Proposals
《有效撰寫英文工作提案》

Writing Effective Employment Application Statements
《有效撰寫求職英文自傳》

Writing Effective Career Statements
《有效撰寫英文職涯經歷》

Effectively Communicating Online
《有效撰寫專業英文電子郵件》

Writing Effective Marketing Promotional Materials
《有效撰寫行銷英文》

Effective Management Communication
《管理英文》

This book is dedicated to my wife, Hwang Li Wen.

Table of Contents

· Describe the general setting for developing a particular product or service.

描述產品或服務研發的流程配置

· Introduce the main problem(s) that managers face in developing that product or service.

描述產品或服務研發主要的問題點

· State the implications or consequences of the problem(s) remaining unresolved.

描述不解決問點的後果

· Introduce the objective of a project.

方案目標介紹

· Describe the methodology of the project.

方法論介紹

· State the main results of the project.

描述方案實行後會產生的主要成果

· Describe the main contribution of the project to a particular field or sector.

描述對特定領域或部門的貢獻

Table of Contents

Foreword

Professional writing is essential to the international recognition of Taiwan's commercial and technological achievements. *The Chinese Professional Writers' Series* seeks to provide a sound English writing curriculum and, on a more practical level, to provide Chinese speaking professionals with valuable reference guides. The series supports professional writers in the following areas:

Writing style

The books seek to transform old ways of writing into a more active and direct writing style that better conveys an author's main ideas.

Structure

The series addresses the organization and content of reports and other common forms of writing.

Quality

Inevitably, writers prepare reports to meet the expectations of editors and referees/reviewers, as well as to satisfy the requirements of journals. The books in this series are prepared with these specific needs in mind.

Effective Business Communication is the eighth book in *The Chinese Professional Writers' Series*.

"*Effective Business Communication*"（《商用英文》）爲「應用英文寫作系列」（*The Chinese Professional Writers' Series*）之第八本書，本書中練習題部分主要是幫助國人糾正常犯的寫作錯誤，由反覆練習中熟能生巧，進而提升有關英文商業策略的寫作能力。

　　「應用英文寫作系列」將針對以下內容，逐步協助國人解決在英文寫作上所遭遇之各項問題：

A.寫作形式：把往昔習於抄襲的寫作方法轉換成更積極主動的寫作方式，俾使讀者所欲表達的主題意念更加清楚。更進一步糾正國人寫作口語習慣。

B.方法形式：指出國內寫作者從事英文寫作或英文翻譯時常遇到的文法問題。

C.內容結構：將寫作的內容以下面的方式結構化：目標、一般動機、個人動機。並了解不同的目的和動機可以影響報告的結構，由此，獲得最適當的報告內容。

D.內容品質：以編輯、審查委員的要求來寫作此一系列之書籍，以滿足讀者的英文要求。

Introduction

This handbook orients business professionals on the essentials of written communication in the workplace. First, how to make inferences from statistics is introduced, including how to briefly introduce a market trend, use statistics that reflect this market trend and its impact, state the implications of those statistics and make a recommendation based on those statistics. How to describe organizational or technical needs is then introduced, including how to briefly introduce a technology sector or market niche, describe an external or internal factor affecting that sector or niche, introduce a specific problem that hinders development of that sector or niche and state the technical or marketing need that must be addressed to resolve this problem. Next, how to explain difficulties in developing a product or service is outlined, including how to describe the general setting for developing a particular product or service, introduce the main problem(s) that managers face in developing that product or service and state the implications or consequence of the problem(s) remaining unresolved. Additionally, how to summarize the results of a project is described, including how to introduce the objective of a project, describe the methodology for the project, state the main results of the project and describe the main contribution of the project to a particular field or sector. Moreover, how to describe recent technical accomplishments in a company is introduced, including how to briefly describe the role of a company in a particular sector, describe a unique feature of the organization in developing a particular technology, cite an example of a recent endeavor and summarize the technical accomplishments of the organization in a particular sector. Furthermore, how to cite examples of product/service commercialization is explained, including how to introduce the main emphases of a sector or industry, cite specific applications, including examples of commercialization, describe the mid-term or long term benefits of such commercialization to a particular field of technology and describe the mid-term or long term benefits of such commercialization for practical purposes. Finally, how to identify future directions and challenges in developing a product or service is described, including how to introduce a sector or industry concerned with the development of a specific product or service, describe product or service development in detail, cite a specific application and describe future directions or potential applications of this product or service.

Each unit begins and ends with three visually represented situations that provide essential information to help students to write a specific part of a business strategy. Additional oral practice, listening comprehension, reading comprehension and writing activities, relating to those three situations, help students to understand how the visual representation relates to the ultimate goal of writing an effective business strategy. An Answer Key makes this book ideal for classroom use. For instance, to test a student's listening comprehension, a teacher can first read the text that describes the situations for a particular unit. Either individually or in small groups, students can work through the exercises to produce concise and well-structured business strategies.

簡 介

　　本手冊主要訓練商業專業人才撰寫符合工作場合需要的書面英文。書中內容包括：

1. 統計結果的推論及應用：包括如何運用統計結果來觀察市場趨勢及其造成的衝擊，並進一步運用統計結果做成因應市場趨勢的建議。
2. 描述組織或科技需求：包括簡述一個科技部門或市場利基及其受內外部影響的因素。並找出一個阻礙科技部門或市場利基發展的問題。並說明必須解決這個問題的科技或市場需求。
3. 描述產業所面臨的困境：描述研發產品或服務時遇到的困難。包括描述產品或服務研發的流程配置，及主要的問題點，及若不解決問點的後果。
4. 方案結果的總結：包括方案目標介紹，方法論介紹，並描述方案實行後會產生的主要成果及對特定領域或部門的貢獻。
5. 描述公司最新的科技成就：包括描述公司在特定領域或部門的角色，並舉最近的實例說明公司研發的特殊科技對特定領域的貢獻。
6. 產品／服務銷售實例：描述如何把產品／服務商品化。包括特定部門或產業所強調的主要重點。舉特定實例說明產品／服務商品化後對特定領域或部門的中長期利益及實際運用成效。
7. 產品／服務開發的未來動向及挑戰：描述如何預測特定產品／服務未來的方向及挑戰。針對特定產品／服務的發展詳細說明，並舉特定運用實例說明未來的發展方向及其發展潛能。

　　書中的每個單元呈現三個視覺化的情境，經由以全民英語檢定為標準而設計的口說訓練、聽力、閱讀及寫作四種不同功能，來強化英文總體能力。此外，書中所附的解答使得本書也非常適合在課堂上使用，教師可以先描述單元情境，讓學生藉由書中練習循序在短期內完成。不論是小組或個人皆可由書中的練習，寫出更精確的英文商業策略。

Unit One

Making Inferences from Statistics

統計結果的推論及應用

1. Briefly introduce a market trend.
   簡述市場趨勢
2. Use statistics that reflect this market trend and its impact.
   運用反映市場趨勢的統計結果及其影響
3. State the implications of those statistics.
   統計結果的運用
4. Make a recommendation based on those statistics.
   根據統計結果做成建議

Vocabulary and related expressions

global production value	全球性生產價值
strengthening its market position	強化其市場地位
aligning	使密切合作
tremendous potential for expansion	擴張的潛能
aggressive policies	積極的策略
mature market	成熟的市場
reflecting public concern	反映大眾的關心
governmental subsidies	政府補助金
unique situation	獨特的情形
irrelevant	無關係的
Taiwan's national health insurance scheme	全民健保
global aging phenomenon	全世界的人口老化現象
market demand perspective	市場需求觀點
enormous growth potential	巨大的成長潛能
stymie future growth	妨礙將來成長
medical expenditures	醫療消費
impetus	推動力
administrative operations	行政營運
pricing strategies	定價策略
increasing societal acceptance	增加社會的接受度
a wide array of fields	廣闊的範圍
abundance of	豐富
existing patent laws	現行的專利法
breakthroughs	突破性進展
gain a competitive edge	得到競爭優越條件
unique market niche	獨特的市場利基
pervasive use of	普遍的使用
boost consumer spending	推動客戶消費
economic recession	經濟的衰退
stalled personal income growth	個人所得的延遲成長

Situation 1

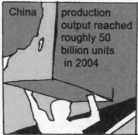

Situation 2

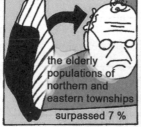

Situation 3

A

Write down the key points of the situations on the preceding page, while the instructor reads aloud the script from the Answer Key. Alternatively, students can listen online at www.chineseowl.idv.tw

Situation 1

_____

_____

Situation 2

_____

_____

Situation 3

_____

_____

B Oral practice I

Based on the three situations in this unit, write three questions beginning with **When**, and answer them. The questions do not need to come directly from these situations.

Examples

When did the global production value of LEDs and LED displays grow by 78%?

between 2004 and 2008

When did production output in China reach roughly 50 billion units?

in 2004

1. _____

   _____

2. _____

   _____

3. _____

   _____

C

Based on the three situations in this unit, write three questions beginning with *How*, and answer them. The questions do not need to come directly from these situations.

Examples

How does the World Health Organization define a country as an aging society?

when 7% of the population exceeds 65 years old

How do most industrialized countries try to ensure the welfare of the elderly?

by implementing aggressive policies

1. _____

_____

2. _____

_____

3. _____

_____

D

Based on the three situations in this unit, write three questions beginning with **Why**, and answer them. The questions do not need to come directly from these situations.

Examples

Why is Taiwan's hospital sector unique?

It includes private, non-profit and government-owned facilities.

Why have medical institutions often cited difficulty in continuing operations?

increasing competition in the health sector

1. _____

_____

2. _____

_____

3. _____

_____

E Write questions that match the answers provided.

1. _____

_____

China

2. _____

_____

1/3

3. _____

_____

The unemployment rate and per capita income of the local population

F Listening Comprehension I

Situation 1

1. Why is the production output of LEDs and LED displays in China expected to reach a record 65 billion units in 2006 or 2007?

    A. manufacturers with production bases in the Asia Pacific region

    B. large-scale governmental initiatives

    C. 30 manufacturers in Taiwan that comprise the supplier base

2. Who leads the global production of HB LEDs?

    A. Hong Kong

    B. China

    C. Taiwan

3. What are Chinese and Taiwanese manufacturers aligning their chip LED production to?

    A. the Industrial Technology Research Institute

    B. the strong market demand from the portable devices sector

    C. HB LEDs

4. What percentage do China and Taiwan account for in the global production of LED and LED displays?

    A. over 25%

    B. over 20%

    C. over 15%

5. Why is the production of LEDs and LED displays in China, Hong Kong and Taiwan expected to rise markedly in the next few years?

    A. mainly owing to portable electronic devices

    B. mainly owing to Taiwan's market position in the global LED industry

    C. mainly owing to the influx of overseas LED manufacturers

Situation 2

1. What percentage of Taipei's population will become elderly in the next two to three decades?

    A. 1/2

    B. 1/4

    C. 1/3

2. When did Taiwan become an aging society?

    A. in 1990

    B. in 1992

    C. in 1993

3. What is the World Health Organization's definition of an aging society?

    A. when 7% of the country's population exceeds 60 years old

    B. when 7% of the country's population exceeds 65 years old

    C. when 5% of the country's population exceeds 65 years old

4. Why have private enterprises in Taiwan significantly expanded investments into the senior citizen housing sector?

    A. effective marketing policies

    B. aggressive governmental policies to ensure the welfare of the elderly

    C. increased demand for elderly care and tax incentive policies

5. What does Taiwan lack in comparison with other industrialized countries?

    A. clear legislation and policies to ensure the welfare of the elderly

    B. strong market growth for senior citizen housing and acceptance by consumers of this trend

    C. a widely anticipated surge in the elderly population

Situation 3

1. What can accurately predict whether a hospital will close?

    A. its geographical position

    B. the unemployment rate and per capita income of the local population

    C. the global aging phenomenon

2. Why could selecting the wrong location for a new hospital significantly increase operational costs and stymie future growth?

    A. because a reduction in hospitals will negatively affect the medical sector

    B. because of the saturated and fiercely competitive medical service sector

    C. because Taiwan officially became a "rapidly aging society" in 1993

3. Why is Taiwan's hospital sector unique?

    A. It includes private, non-profit and government-owned facilities that occasionally compete for the same patients.

    B. It develops strategic models that resemble those applied in industry.

    C. Its hospitals are not distributed uniformly around the island.

4. What do hospitals fiercely compete with clinics for?

    A. growth potential

    B. governmental subsidies

    C. patients

5. What evidence is there of Taiwan's enormous growth potential?

    A. the fact that patients account for only 5% of revenue in the health care sector

    B. the financial accountability of hospitals

    C. the establishment of many hospitals and increasing competitiveness in the medical care sector

G Reading Comprehension I

Select the word or expression whose meaning is closest to the meaning of the underlined word or expression in the following passages.

Situation 1

1. According to market <u>forecasts</u> by Communications Industry Researchers and iSuppli, the global production value of LEDs and LED displays grew 78% between 2004 and 2008.

    A. recall

    B. prognostications

    C. retrieve

2. China and Taiwan will probably <u>pave the way</u> as manufacturers with production bases in the Asia Pacific region, as evidenced by the fact that China and Taiwan account for over 25% of the global production of LED and LED displays, with output in the former expected to reach 65 billion units by 2007.

    A. retrograde

    B. revert

    C. innovate

3. Production in China, Hong Kong and Taiwan is expected to rise markedly in the next few years, <u>driven</u> mainly by portable electronic devices, such as mobile phones, PDAs, digital cameras, as well as applications in indoor and outdoor lighting and illumination, automotive electronics, navigation, aviation, railway and traffic systems.

    A. impelled

    B. dissuaded

    C. deterred

4. In China alone, production output reached roughly 50 billion units in 2004. <u>Spurred on</u> by large-scale governmental initiatives, output is expected to reach a record 65 billion units in 2006 or 2007.

  A. Forestalled

  B. Encouraged

  C. Precluded

5. Meanwhile, Taiwan is <u>strengthening</u> its market position in the global LED industry.

  A. fortifying

  B. debasing

  C. subverting

6. According to the Industrial Technology Research Institute, the Asia Pacific region's global market share for LEDs <u>increased</u> to 25% - second only to that of Japan at 50%.

  A. attenuated

  B. ablated

  C. accrued

7. HB LEDs used in the automotive industry are more cost efficient and <u>longer lasting</u> than fluorescent lights.

  A. perishable

  B. durable

  C. putrefiable

8. While Chinese, Taiwanese and Hong Kong companies can produce HB LEDs, Taiwan <u>leads</u> global production, followed by China and Japan.

  A. abases

  B. induces

  C. aggravates

9. However, given the <u>influx</u> of overseas LED manufacturers, China is widely expected to become the global leader, with nearly 30% of global production.

　A. emergence

　B. withdrawal

　C. regression

10. HB LEDs already account for 1/3 of LEDs produced by Chinese manufacturers, and are used particularly for backlighting, and in <u>portable</u> devices and automobiles.

　A. immutable

　B. static

　C. mobile

11. Moreover, Chinese and Taiwanese manufacturers are <u>aligning</u> their chip LED production to the strong market demand from the portable devices sector.

　A. differentiating with

　B. secernating

　C. corresponding to

12. The production of LEDs and LED displays is also <u>concentrated</u> in Jiangsu, Zhejiang, Shandong, Shanghai, Fujian and Guangdong.

　A. dispersed

　B. centralized

　C. dissipated

13. In 2004, while <u>domestic</u> suppliers produced 25 billion of the LEDs and LED displays produced in China, overseas companies that were operating locally produced at least 20 billion units.

　A. internal

　B. external

　C. international

14. In contrast, 30 manufacturers in Taiwan comprise the supplier base, reflecting a tremendous potential for <u>expansion</u> given the above statistics and trends.

    A. contraction

    B. miniaturization

    C. amplification

Situation 2

1. The World Health Organization defines a country as an aging society when 7% of the population <u>exceeds</u> 65 years old.

    A. transcends

    B. specifies

    C. limits

2. With most industrialized countries having attained this status, <u>aggressive</u> policies have been implemented to ensure the welfare of the elderly.

    A. pugnacious

    B. timid

    C. trepid

3. Having become an aging society in 1993, Taiwan lacks <u>clear</u> legislation and policies to ensure the welfare of the elderly, by comparison with other industrialized countries.

    A. turbid

    B. murky

    C. transparent

4. According to population trend estimates from Taiwan's Council for Economic Planning and Development and the Ministry of the Interior, a widely anticipated <u>surge</u> in the elderly population will increase the demand for care.

    A. regression

B. uprising

C. retroversion

5. In 1990, the <u>elderly</u> populations of northern and eastern townships in Taiwan outside of central business districts surpassed 7%, as they did in some western townships in 1996 and in some southern townships in 2001.

A. geriatric

B. adolescent

C. infantile

6. <u>Consistent with</u> this trend, senior citizen housing was one of the ten leading building structures in 2003.

A. resistant to

B. contradicting

C. complying with

7. Already a <u>mature</u> market, senior citizen housing in the United States is estimated to be able to expand in the next two decades.

A. callow

B. puerile

C. autumnal

8. Given increased demand for elderly care and tax incentive policies, private enterprises in Taiwan have significantly expanded investments into the senior citizen housing sector, <u>reflecting</u> public concern over meeting the accommodation and special needs of this population.

A. manifesting

B. obviating

C. distracting

9. <u>Effective</u> marketing policies are an effective means of forecasting trends in this housing market.

A. inefficacious

B. competent

C. obsolete

10. The above statistics reflect not only strong market growth for senior citizen housing and <u>acceptance</u> by consumers of this trend, but also the importance of product, price, promotion and place to marketing strategies in this area.

A. dismissal

B. reception

C. refutation

Situation 3

1. Taiwan's hospital sector is <u>unique</u> in that it includes private, non-profit and government-owned facilities - all occasionally competing for the same patients.

A. demotic

B. incomparable

C. grassroots

2. While patients account for only 5% of revenue in the health care sector, governmental <u>subsidies</u> through the National Health Insurance Scheme (54%) and private insurers (34%) account for the majority of revenues, with 7% from other sources.

A. penalties

B. fines

C. compensations

3. This unique situation requires that the hospital sector develop strategic models that <u>resemble</u> those applied in industry.

A. correspond to

B. deflect

C. misalign

4. Empirical evidence suggests that some environmental issues normally considered in analyzing organizations are irrelevant to analyzing the financial accountability of hospitals, while others are very <u>relevant</u>.

   A. unconnected

   B. dissimilar

   C. pertinent

5. For instance, the unemployment rate and per capita <u>income</u> of the local population can accurately predict whether a hospital will close.

   A. interest

   B. deficit

   C. revenues

6. Other environmental <u>factors</u> only slightly affect hospital performance.

   A. expendables

   B. considerations

   C. luxuries

7. Since the implementation of Taiwan's national health insurance scheme in 1995, medical institutions have often cited difficulty in <u>continuing</u> operations, given increasing competition in the health sector.

   A. prolonging

   B. intermittent

   C. infrequent

8. In particular, the Taiwanese healthcare market <u>faces</u> several challenges. (1) The average size of hospitals has increased.

   A. averts

   B. disavows

   C. confronts

9. The geographical positions of hospitals are not distributed <u>uniformly</u> around the island.

    A. consistently

    B. sporadically

    C. periodically

10. Hospitals <u>fiercely</u> compete with clinics for patients.

    A. passively

    B. inactively

    C. vehemently

11. Medical organizations are either extremely small or large. According to the Department of Health, Executive Yuan, Taiwan (DOH), the number of hospitals in Taiwan <u>declined</u> by 231 or 29.35%, from 787 in 1989 to 556 in 2004.

    A. augmented

    B. diminished

    C. magnified

12. Additionally, the number of public hospitals declined by five or 5.38%, from 93 in 1989 to 88 in 2004; correspondingly, the number of <u>private</u> hospitals declined by 126 or 32.56%, from 694 in 1989 to 468 in 2004 (DOH, 2005).

    A. unrestricted

    B. cloistered

    C. national

13. Obviously, this reduction in hospitals will <u>negatively</u> affect the medical sector.

    A. affirmative

    B. constructive

    C. adversely

14. Additionally, the global aging phenomenon is <u>evident</u> in Taiwan, with the island officially becoming a "rapidly aging society" in 1993, as defined by the World Health Organization.

   A. murky

   B. ambiguous

   C. discernible

15. Therefore, from a market demand perspective, Taiwan has enormous growth <u>potential</u>, as evidenced by the establishment of many hospitals and increasing competitiveness in the medical care sector.

   A. breach

   B. latency

   C. squander

16. Given the <u>saturated</u> and fiercely competitive medical service sector, selecting the wrong location for a new hospital could significantly increase operational costs and stymie future growth.

   A. diffused

   B. dispersed

   C. concentrated

17. Selecting the location of a hospital to maximize competitiveness involves <u>devising</u> appropriate evaluation criteria.

   A. contriving

   B. eradicating

   C. decimating

H

Common elements in making inferences from statistics統計結果的推論及應用 include the following elements:

1. Briefly introduce a market trend. 簡述市場趨勢
2. Use statistics that reflect this market trend and its impact.運用反映市場趨勢的統計結果及其影響
3. State the implications of those statistics. 統計結果的運用
4. Make a recommendation based on those statistics. 根據統計結果做成建議

1. Briefly introduce a market trend. 簡述市場趨勢

◎ Electronic 3C products have rapidly emerged in the new century, accelerating the rate at which consumers receive information. Of those products, Taiwanese consumers highly regard the Apple ipod mini among available mp3 walkman products given its cool appearance and multi-functions.

◎ Physically challenged elderly individuals frequently require a diverse array of services, including assistance with daily living tasks, nursing care, physical therapy and nutritional consultation. Industrialized countries have struggled with how to effectively coordinate such services given the rapid rise in the number of elderly residents.

◎ Recent societal advances have spurred domestic consumption in Taiwan of luxury items, with cosmetics no exception. Many female consumers view cosmetics as a daily necessity, as reflected by the wide array of cosmetic brands in the intensely competitive market sector. Given the enormous consumer demand and stringent competition, manufacturers must thoroughly understand the purchasing behavior of consumers in this market niche.

2. Use statistics that reflect this market trend and its impact. 運用反映市場趨勢的統計結果及其影響

◎ While promoting the product slogan, "If you buy it, you will own the Mac + pc", the

Apple Computer Company announced retail sales of more than 800,000 ipod units sold during one season, with 4,580,000 units sold last year.

◎ While Taiwan's elderly individuals over 65 years old in 2003 comprised 9.2% of the entire population, this figure will increase to 15.9% by 2021.

◎ Although the United States accounts for the largest market worldwide, France is the largest exporter of cosmetic products. However, market growth has shifted from industrialized countries to developing ones in South America, Eastern Europe and Asia (especially China), with the compound annual growth rate exceeding 10.4% over the past five years. Despite a global economic turndown, the cosmetics and fragrance sector continues to perform well, i.e., an average growth rate of nearly 5%.

3. State the implications of those statistics. 統計結果的運用

◎ Given its commercial success, product design research is underway to combine the ipod with wireless Internet and cellular phone functions normally associated with 3C products; this is commonly referred to as "digit space-time". The Internet is an excellent medium to educate consumers on the latest developments in 3C products. More specifically, the 4P based marketing strategy that emphasizes product, price, promotion and place is an effective means of promoting 3C products.

◎ To effectively respond to this population shift, policy makers and various health care professionals are concerned with how to coordinate available resources effectively.

◎ Having profoundly impacted the cosmetics manufacturing sector, the biotechnology industry has developed innovative products that have strengthened the competitiveness of this newly emerging sector. As evidence of governmental support, the Executive Yuan of the Republic of China, i.e., the highest administrative organization in Taiwan, prioritized biotechnology cosmetics as a target item in its National Developmental Strategy for 2008. Cosmetic manufacturers in the biotechnology industry especially focus on female consumers, who form a vital niche in the market, given the strong desire to appear as youthful as possible.

4. Make a recommendation based on those statistics. 根據統計結果做成建議

◎ The GM (1,1) model can be used to determine product demand and supply manipulation. Data acquired from the GM (1,1) model can be useful in forecasting the sales volume and market demand for the apple ipod, as well as photo image telecommunication and related 3C products such as the widely anticipated "digit space-time" ones. Adopting appropriate statistical methods such as the GM (1,1) model can optimize the effectiveness of 4P strategies for 3C products.

◎ In doing so, effective healthcare management can combat various chronic diseases by integrating the efforts of multi-disciplinary healthcare professionals, which is desperately needed as long term healthcare management in Taiwan is still in its developmental stages. In addition to the need for qualified healthcare management professionals, the government should help establish and closely monitor a standard means of payment for long term healthcare services.

◎ As the cosmetics sector continuously develops innovative products, the life cycle for these products is extremely short. Manufacturers must therefore optimally allocate marketing strategies to ensure that the product delivery cycle is shortened as much as possible without sacrificing product quality.

In the space below, make inferences from statistics on the development of a particular product or service.

_____

_____

_____

_____

_____

_____

_____

_____

_____

Look at the following examples of making inferences from statistics.

Taiwan's electronics industry has significantly impacted the island's economic growth. In particular, the IC industry will continuously expand in this decade, with its output value in 1999 reaching NT$479.6 billion. The IC industry comprises the foundry wafer, IC package, IC fabrication, as well as diode and transistor sectors. According to the Industrial Technology Research Institute (ITRI) in Taiwan, IC fabrication for computer components continued to lead in revenues among product category items in 1999, i.e. a nearly 5% increase in generated revenues over the previous year. Correspondingly, the IC packaging sector recorded revenues of NT$155.825 billion, or 32.49% of the total output, i.e. a 14.3% increase over the previous year. The foundry wafer sector generated revenues of NT$114.306 billion, i.e. a 57.6% increase over the previous year. An exception to the other growth sectors is the diode and transistor sector, while representing only 4.26% of all revenues, declined in profits over the previous year. As is widely anticipated, continuous development of the information technology sector will further spur growth of the IC industry. According to forecasting model estimates, the 2005 output value of the foundry wafer, IC packaging, IC fabrication, diode and transistor sectors will reach NT$403.648 billion, NT$374.607 billion, NT$470.685 billion, NT$19.695 billion, NT$7.644 billion and NT$1 276.279 trillion, respectively. As the growth rate of the IC industry greatly surpasses that of other local industries, Taiwan employs highly qualified personnel and adopts advanced technologies to ensure sustained growth. Governmental authorities must draft further incentive policies to help the IC industry remain globally competitive.

●

Technological advances and the increased promulgation of information have made digital life a reality for many individuals. The Internet service provider YAM recently released results of an Internet-based investigation in Taiwan. According to those results, the number of female Internet users has gradually increased over the past three years. Additionally, on-line messenger services have become the third major network application service after the Internet and e-mail. Moreover, more than 66% of all Internet users use on-line messenger software regularly. Furthermore, on-line purchases are steadily increasing, with 18% of all 25 year-old Internet users purchasing financial services and real estate frequently. Based on these results, YAM asserted that Taiwanese are increasingly drawn to purchasing hi-tech products, which should further advance this industry. As for consumer behavior, in 2004, over 32% of all Internet users used on-line messenger software. Furthermore, 7% of all users think that blogs are of significant importance. Such trends are worth noting. Furthermore, 55%, 26%, 11% and 17% of all Internet users have a flash disk, MP3, IP phone and GPS, respectively. Such results reflect the strong demand for digital products island wide. WLAN use has also grown from 33% to 42% from 2003-2004. Digital life is definitely a reality for many. As for on-line shopping, growth will increase steadily. According to the YAM study, Internet users pay close attention to brand name (38%), price (44%) and quality (52%) of the products purchased online, further demonstrating the tremendous market potential for online shopping.

●

The World Health Organization (WHO) defines an aging society as one in which 7% of a country's population is over 65 years old. Under this definition, Taiwan became an aging society in September 1993, with its elderly population reaching 1,470,000. Moreover, the island's growth rate of the aging population exceeds that of European and North American countries. According to the Executive Yuan of the Republic of China (1999), the elderly age population accounts for more than 14% of the entire population of all industrialized countries. Peterson (2000) attributed this trend to the following factors: (a) advances in medicine, public health as well as related infrastructure, nutrition and safety; (b) the gradual aging of the baby boom population, which has now reached middle age; and (c) the continuously declining birthrate. In line with these trends, Taiwan formally became an "aging society" in 1993. However, European and North American countries have had significantly more time to respond to this challenge than Taiwan has. The Executive Yuan indicated that while Taiwan's advanced age population will quickly account for 21.65% of the entire population by 2036, European and North American countries will not reach this high level for approximately five to eight decades. Therefore, immense pressure from the significant demand for long-term care of the continuously aging population must be addressed immediately. Furthermore, governmental authorities should continue to raise concern over the long-term care insurance legislation introduced in the Legislative Yuan in recent years.

Situation 4

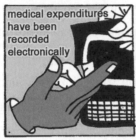
medical expenditures have been recorded electronically

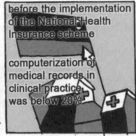
before the implementation of the National Health Insurance scheme

computerization of medical records in clinical practice was below 20%

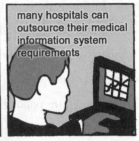
many hospitals can outsource their medical information system requirements

Situation 5

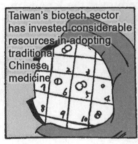
Taiwan's biotech sector has invested considerable resources in adopting traditional Chinese medicine

195 Taiwanese manufacturers' developing traditional Chinese medicine

experts across many disciplines to develop Chinese herbal medicine

Situation 6

the Taiwanese government relaxed financial market regulations in 1980 for overseas firms

Taiwan is becoming a more credit-based than cash-based society in terms of purchasing habits

boost consumer spending, ultimately generating bank revenues

I

Write down the key points of the situations on the preceding page, while the instructor reads aloud the script from the Answer Key. Alternatively, students can listen online at www.chineseowl.idv.tw

Situation 4

_____

_____

_____

Situation 5

_____

_____

_____

Situation 6

_____

_____

_____

J Oral practice II

Based on the three situations in this unit, write three questions beginning with **Why**, and answer them. The questions do not need to come directly from these situations.

Examples

Why is it possible to record medical expenditures electronically?

Because the Taiwanese government has promoted the use of the National Health Information Network (HIN)

Why have medical institutions island wide been able to make data accessible and transparent in digital form?

Use of the National Health Information Network (HIN)

1. _____

   _____

2. _____

   _____

3. _____

   _____

K

Based on the three situations in this unit, write three questions beginning with ***How***, and answer them. The questions do not need to come directly from these situations.

Examples

How has Taiwan's biotech sector invested considerable resources in adopting traditional Chinese medicine?

In a diverse array of health-oriented products

How is the increasing societal acceptance of traditional Chinese medicine reflected?

In forecasted revenues of $US 30.5 billion by 2006

1. _____

_____

2. _____

_____

3. _____

_____

L

Based on the three situations in this unit, write three questions beginning with **What** and answer them. The questions do not need to come directly from these situations.

Examples

What has enhanced the overall quality of financial services island wide?

Relaxation of financial market regulations in 1980 for overseas firms

What does each bank develop to gain a competitive edge?

Unique financial services

1. _____

   _____

2. _____

   _____

3. _____

   _____

M Write questions that match the answers provided.

_____

_____

The National Health Insurance Journal

_____

_____

195

_____

_____

In terms of purchasing habits

N Listening Comprehension II

Situation 4

1. What percentage of all clinics in Taiwan computerized their operations by 1997?

    A. 54.9%

    B. 84.6%

    C. 76.3%

2. What has the Taiwanese government promoted the use of since the National Health Insurance scheme was established in 1995?

   A. reimbursement of service processing

   B. the National Health Information Network

   C. clinical software sources

3. What did a hospital survey of computerization and on-line impetus groups in 1996 note?

   A. a rapid increase in the number of clinics that were computerized

   B. the status of computerization in clinical practice

   C. a desire to provide computer education and training

4. What have advances in information systems greatly facilitated?

   A. data accessible and transparent in digital form

   B. changes in National Health Insurance laws

   C. administrative operations, pricing strategies and bookkeeping

5. When did computerization in Taiwanese hospitals increase from 28% to 57%?

   A. From 1992-1994

   B. from 1994-1996

   C. from 1996-1998

Situation 5

1. What reflects the increasing societal acceptance of traditional Chinese medicine?

   A. the growing number of technology transfers from research institutes

   B. a global development strategy

   C. a forecasted $US 30.5 billion by 2006

2. Why is further evaluation of existing patent laws and scope of application necessary?

   A. to adopt traditional Chinese medicine in a diverse array of health-oriented products

B. to understand the clinical curative effect of components in traditional Chinese medicine

C. to involve experts across many disciplines

3. Why are breakthroughs in Chinese herbal medicine widely anticipated in the near future?

A. because of the growing number of technology transfers

B. because domestic output will probably exceed 4 billion New Taiwanese (NT) dollars

C. because of the implementation of a a global development strategy

4. How many individuals does the traditional Chinese medicine sector employ?

A. nearly 4,000

B. more than 5,000

C. more than 4,000

5. What must the Chinese herbal medicine sector effectively address?

A. a wide array of fields on a relatively small scale

B. a diverse array of health-oriented products

C. the abundance of low-quality Chinese herbal medicine

Situation 6

1. What is the result of the Taiwanese government relaxing financial market regulations in 1980 for overseas firms?

A. current low interest rates

B. extended credit through the pervasive use of credit cards

C. the establishment of 16 new banks

2. What is market growth driven by?

A. competition with other lending institutions

B. the large number of credit card-issuing banks

C. consumer demand

3. How many credit card holders did Chinatrust have by March of 2002?

A. approximately 3 million

B. approximately 6 million

C. approximately 5 million

4. What is evidence of Taiwan's near saturation of the credit card market?

A. unique financial services

B. the large number of credit card-issuing banks

C. potential risks that lending banks face

5. What is Taiwan becoming?

A. a more credit-based than cash-based society in terms of purchasing habits

B. more frugal and less concerned with cultivating personal tastes

C. less competitive marketwise

O Reading Comprehension II

Select the word or expression whose meaning is closest to the meaning of the underlined word or expression in the following passages.

Situation 4

1. Since the National Health Insurance scheme was established in 1995, medical expenditures have been recorded electronically as the Taiwanese government has promoted the use of the National Health Information Network (HIN), which enables medical institutions island wide to make data accessible and transparent in digital form.

A. lucid

B. invisible

C. concealed

2. In 1996, *The National Health Insurance Journal* addressed the status of computerization in clinical practice, revealing that before the <u>implementation</u> of the National Health Insurance scheme, computerization of medical records in clinical practice was below 20%.

A. curtailment

B. cessation

C. promulgation

3. However, according to current statistics, this proportion now <u>exceeds</u> 60%.

A. transcends

B. miniaturizes

C. recoils

4. In 1996, a hospital survey of computerization and on-line <u>impetus</u> groups noted a rapid increase in the number of clinics that were computerized.

A. impedance

B. hindrance

C. incentive

5. From 1994-1996, computerization increased from 28% to 57%. In 1997, 76.3% (6977) of all clinics had computerized their operations, <u>representing</u> a significant increase of 25.7% (4666) in 1994 and 54.9% (6509) in 1996.

A. assailing

B. desecrating

C. symbolizing

6. Moreover, 92.9% of all hospitals in Taiwan that applied to the National Health insurance for <u>reimbursement</u> of service processing had computerized their

operations.

A. levy

B. refund

C. imposition

7. According to the results of an analysis of <u>clinical</u> software sources, software represented approximately 84.6% of purchases from contracted information vendors.

A. medical

B. administrative

C. civil service

8. 35.3% of all hospitals had invested under $100,000 in computers for clinical use; 32% had invested $100,000-$200,000, and 25.1% had invested above $200,000; 7.5% did not <u>reply</u>.

A. retort

B. connive at

C. neglect

9. As most hospitals experience difficulty in adjusting to changes in National Health Insurance laws, 8.7% of them expressed a <u>desire</u> to provide computer education and training.

A. apathy

B. lassitude

C. appetence

10. Many hospitals can outsource their medical information system requirements, reduce the costs of developing medical software, as well as those of <u>maintenance</u> and personnel, receive governmental subsidies for medical expenses and, in doing so, increase the efficiency and effectiveness of staff.

A. renunciation

B. demission

C. sustenance

11. Thus, advances in information systems have greatly <u>facilitated</u> administrative operations, pricing strategies and bookkeeping.

A. constrained

B. expedited

C. inhibited

Situation 5

1. Taiwan's biotech sector has invested <u>considerable</u> resources in adopting traditional Chinese medicine in a diverse array of health-oriented products.

A. negligible

B. monumental

C. remote

2. Globally, traditional Chinese medicine <u>generated</u> revenues of $US 15 billion in 1997.

A. forfeited

B. effectuatcd

C. abdicated

3. A forecasted $US 30.5 billion by 2006 reflects its increasing societal <u>acceptance</u>.

A. acquiescence

B. disallowance

C. turndown

4. With 195 Taiwanese manufacturers' developing traditional Chinese medicine, domestic <u>output</u> probably exceeds 4 billion New Taiwanese (NT) dollars.

A. shortfall

B. paucity

C. yield

5. This sector employs more than 4,000 individuals, and products are sold in a <u>wide</u> array of fields on a relatively small scale.

A. capacious

B. confined

C. parochial

6. Despite an <u>abundance</u> of pharmaceutical firms that manufacture Chinese herbal medicines, the sector lacks a global development strategy.

A. deficiency

B. plenitude

C. scantiness

7. More important than developing new medicine and pricing competitively, the sector must effectively address the abundance of <u>low-quality</u> Chinese herbal medicine.

A. blue-ribbon

B. shabby

C. banner

8. The clinical <u>curative</u> effect of components in traditional Chinese medicine requires further evaluation of existing patent laws and scope of application.

A. antidote

B. debilitating

C. enervating

9. Notably, several <u>collaborative</u> efforts are being made by experts across many disciplines to develop Chinese herbal medicine, as evidenced by the growing number of technology transfers from research institutes, teaching hospitals and clinical testing centers to local industry for commercialization.

A. autonomous

B. sovereign

C. synergistic

10. Given these efforts, <u>breakthroughs</u> are widely anticipated in the near future.

A. advances

B. retrogression

C. reversion

Situation 6

1. The Taiwanese government <u>relaxed</u> financial market regulations in 1980 for overseas firms, resulting in the establishment of 16 new banks, each with its own approach to improving customer service.

A. taut

B. slack

C. stringent

2. Such measures have not only enhanced the overall quality of financial services island wide, but have also led to <u>strong</u> market competition.

A. feeble

B. decrepit

C. puissant

3. While <u>striving</u> to gain customer loyalty, each bank develops unique financial services to gain a competitive edge.

A. aspiring

B. relinquishing

C. renouncing

4. However, lending services are often offered via more established banks, and new banks are confronted with the challenge of creating their own unique market niche to provide <u>innovative</u> financial services.

A. archaic

B. antiquated

C. unprecedented

5. Current low interest rates, increased local consumption and extended credit through the <u>pervasive</u> use of credit cards have dramatically transformed consumption trends - as individuals have become less frugal and are concerned with cultivating personal tastes.

A. intermittent

B. permeating

C. sporadic

6. In summary, Taiwan is becoming a more <u>credit</u>-based than cash-based society in terms of purchasing habits.

A. incumbrance

B. promissory note

C. tab

7. Given such changes in local purchasing habits, the credit card market has become almost <u>saturated</u>, as evidenced by the large number of credit card-issuing banks.

A. imbued

B. void

C. shunned

8. For instance, Taiwanese banks such as Fubon Bank and Chinatrust Commercial Bank aggressively strive to build upon their existing market share with <u>numerous</u> customer-tailored services.

A. paltry

B. copious

C. scant

9. While Fubon increased its number of <u>issued</u> credit cards by 50% in 2002,

Chinatrust had approximately 5 million card holders by March of the same year.

A. appropriate

B. promulgated

C. shanghai

10. Such consumer trends appear to be positive: more credit cards in the market will <u>boost</u> consumer spending, ultimately generating bank revenues.

A. aggrandize

B. contract

C. depreciate

11. However, such an assumption does not consider some of the potential <u>risks</u> that lending banks face.

A. certitude

B. credence

C. prospects

12. Whereas market growth is driven by competition with other lending institutions rather than by consumer demand, an economic recession or <u>stalled</u> personal income growth could lead to high defaulted credit card debt if banks lack adequate credit rating standards and qualified lending practices.

A. stonewalled

B. forge ahead

C. accelerate

Unit Two

Describing Organizational or Technical Needs

描述組織或科技需求

1. Briefly introduce a technology sector or market niche.
   簡述一個科技部門或市場利基

2. Describe an external or internal factor affecting that sector or niche.
   內外部影響科技部門或市場利基的因素

3. Introduce a specific problem that hinders development of that sector or niche.
   描述一個阻礙科技部門或市場利基發展的問題

4. State the technical or marketing need that must be addressed to resolve this problem
   說明必須解決這個問題的科技或市場需求

Vocabulary and related expressions

as evidenced by	由……證明
remain abreast of	朝同一方向並列
lure new customers	吸引新客戶
long term loyalty	長期的忠誠度
market liberalization	市場自由化
multinational corporations	多國經營的公司
create employment opportunities	增加就業機會
external trade	外部貿易
profit margin	利潤幅度
stagnant	蕭條的
cope with	合作
adversely affected	不利地影響
contradictory political policies	對立的政策
exacerbated	使惡化
dire consequences	悲慘的結果
strict governmental controls	嚴格的政府控管
tremendous amounts of capital	極大的成本
infrastructure	公共建設
a budgetary balance	預算的平衡
increasingly fierce competition	日增的猛烈競爭
scrutinize closely	詳細檢查
personnel layoffs	人員的解雇
operational cost reductions	營運成本的減少
outsourcing to companies	外包工作給其他公司
global semiconductor market	全球半導體市場
highly volatile business cycle	高度易變的商業週期
quantitative and qualitative means	測量定量及定性的工具
capital expenditure	成本支出
economies of scale in production	生產經濟規模
pursuit of cultural interests	追求文化利益
strong health consciousness	強烈的健康意識
play a vital role in	扮演極其重要的角色

Situation 1

Situation 2

Situation 3

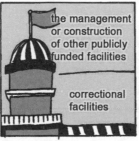

A

Write down the key points of the situations on the preceding page, while the instructor reads aloud the script from the Answer Key. Alternatively, students can listen online at www.chineseowl.idv.tw

Situation 1

_____

_____

_____

Situation 2

_____

_____

_____

Situation 3

_____

_____

B Oral practice I

Based on the three situations in this unit, write three questions beginning with **Why**, and answer them. The questions do not need to come directly from these situations.

Examples

Why must banks identify those success factors that are essential to retaining customers and identifying new ones?

To increase their competitive advantage

Why are customers able to remain abreast of the latest market trends and opportunities?

Because of the availability of Internet-based financial data

1. _____

_____

2. _____

_____

3. _____

_____

C

Based on the three situations in this unit, write three questions beginning with *How*, and answer them. The questions do not need to come directly from these situations.

Examples

How have globalization trends encouraged foreign direct investment?

Many multinational corporations intend to move some of their operations to China.

How can international business centers increase domestic and international trade?

By creating employment opportunities and promoting economic growth

1. _____

   _____

2. _____

   _____

3. _____

   _____

D

Based on the three situations in this unit, write three questions beginning with *What*, and answer them. The questions do not need to come directly from these situations.

Examples

What factors have led to a high prisoner population in Taiwan?
Growing crime rates and related convictions

What has adversely affected Taiwan in terms of lost production and loss of foreign investment?
The accelerating growth of China

1. _____

_____

2. _____

_____

3. _____

_____

E Write questions that match the answers provided.

1. _____

_____

Distinguishing their financial services from those of well-established banks

2. _____

_____

By nearly 15%

3. _____

_____

The conventional means of locating correctional facilities

F Listening Comprehension I

Situation 1

1. Why is there a slow growth rate of 5% among individual banks?

    A. tremendous changes in the finance sector in Taiwan in recent years

    B. a gradual increase in consumer demand

    C. the large number of banks in Taiwan

2. What is a complex task?

 A. analyzing transaction data

 B. devising organizational strategies of banks

 C. remaining abreast of the latest market trends and opportunities in Taiwan's finance sector

3. What are Taiwanese banks actively promoting?

 A. the availability of Internet-based financial data

 B. the lifetime value of consumers and long-term transaction fees

 C. wealth management banking

4. What has enabled customers to remain abreast of the latest market trends and opportunities?

 A. the relative inflexibility of strategies that banks offer

 B. the potential contribution of wealth management practices to bank revenues

 C. the availability of Internet-based financial data

5. What do many newly established banks have difficulty in doing?

 A. retaining loyal customers

 B. distinguishing their financial services from those of well-established banks

 C. devising promotional strategies to lure new customers

Situation 2

1. How does an international business center in China typically disseminate information to attract foreign investment?

 A. through the World Trade Organization

 B. through local governmental regulations

 C. through the mass media

2. What is vital to commercial success?

 A. identifying the factors that influence the location of an international business center

B. selecting sites where overseas firms can operate

C. reducing operational costs and exchanging information

3. What will increase operating costs and reduce the profit margin?

    A. the inability to provide information on such topics as food, clothing and lifestyle

    B. uncertainty of the investment climate and laws

    C. the inability to locate an international business center efficiently

4. What factors have enabled China's economy to grow at an annual rate of more than 9%, with external trade increasing by nearly 15% annually?

    A. market liberalization and export-oriented markets

    B. foreign direct investment and many multinational corporations

    C. overseas investors and governmental officials

5. Why do many multinational corporations intend to move some of their operations to China?

    A. because overseas firms are unfamiliar with the local language and constraints on capital

    B. because globalization trends encourage foreign direct investment

    C. because selecting sites where overseas firms can operate can be a complex task

Situation 3

1. What factors have contributed to growing crime rates and related convictions in Taiwan?

    A. often contradictory political policies

    B. the stagnant Taiwanese economy and increasing unemployment in recent years

    C. overburdened governmental finances

2. Why must the government spend tremendous amounts of capital to maintain correctional facilities and prevent crime when adopting the conventional approach?

    A. since a conventionally chosen location is not close to service providers

    B. since such a dangerous imbalance makes effective management almost impossible

    C. since increasing unemployment and lost production have continuously reduced tax revenues

3. What will ultimately overburden governmental finances?

    A. lost production and loss of foreign investment

    B. hesitancy among the general population to live near such high-risk facilities

    C. The inability to solve this problem in Taiwan's correctional facilities will extract many unforeseen societal costs in the future.

4. What often involves high handling costs?

    A. high incarceration rates

    B. the expansion of, or maintenance of materials for, correctional facilities

    C. a limited number of service providers that can deliver

5. What is partially responsible for high incarceration rates in Taiwan?

    A. the dangerously low ratio of correctional facility staff to prisoners

    B. insufficient resources to prevent prison rebellions

    C. transition from a manufacturing-based economy to a knowledge-based one

G Reading Comprehension I

Select the word or expression whose meaning is closest to the meaning of the underlined word or expression in the following passages.

Situation 1

1. The finance sector in Taiwan has undergone tremendous changes in recent years, as evidenced by the availability of Internet-based financial data that enable customers to <u>remain abreast</u> of the latest market trends and opportunities.

   A. displace

   B. keep in touch with

   C. squander

2. Given the gradual increase in consumer demand for such information, customer relationship management (CRM) has been greatly <u>emphasized</u> in the organizational strategies of banks to increase their competitiveness.

   A. brushed aside

   B. accentuated

   C. scorned

3. While banking is a traditional business, many newly established banks have difficulty in <u>distinguishing</u> their financial services from those of well-established banks.

   A. corresponding to

   B. assimilating

   C. diverging

4. To increase their competitive advantage, banks must identify those success factors that are essential to <u>retaining</u> customers and identifying new ones.

   A. sustaining

   B. ousting

   C. squandering

5. Analyzing transaction data is a <u>complex</u> task, and obtaining such data is difficult.

   A. rudimentary

   B. facile

C. heterogeneous

6. Nevertheless, such an analysis can help banks to draw up guidelines and promotional strategies to <u>lure</u> new customers.

   A. rebuff

   B. coax

   C. traverse

7. For instance, Taiwanese banks actively <u>promote</u> wealth management banking.

   A. espouse

   B. demean

   C. relegate

8. Given the relative <u>inflexibility</u> of strategies that banks offer in this area, each bank must highlight the unique features of its program to strengthen its competitiveness by encouraging customer loyalty and seeking new clients.

   A. pliability

   B. affability

   C. asperity

9. With a lack of research on wealth management practices in the banking sector, major success factors have not been identified nor has its potential contribution to bank revenues been determined, limiting the <u>scope</u> of not only banking management strategies but also available services.

   A. immenseness

   B. radius

   C. vastness

10. The large number of banks in Taiwan explains the <u>slow</u> growth rate of 5% among individual banks.

    A. expeditious

    B. torpid

C. fleeting

11. Given the emphasis the lifetime value of consumers and long-term transaction fees, banks <u>fiercely</u> compete with each other in the wealth management market.

    A. convivially

    B. irenic

    C. malevolently

12. Financial specialists must not only be able to attract new customers, but also provide <u>satisfactory</u> wealth management strategies that are consistent with banking practices.

    A. vexing

    B. cogent

    C. disconcerting

13. In the intensely competitive financial market, financial specialists must carefully <u>balance</u> effective marketing strategies with efforts to earn the long-term loyalty of customers.

    A. parity

    B. divergence

    C. dissimilitude

14. The inability of banks to adopt CRM and employ <u>effective</u> financial planners negatively affects their competitive edge in the wealth management market.

    A. innocuous

    B. nugatory

    C. trenchant

Situation 2

1. Market liberalization since the 1980s has increased <u>commercial</u> activity between China and Taiwan.

A. altruistic

B. mercantile

C. magnanimous

2. China's accession to the World Trade Organization in 2002 and its hosting of the 2008 Olympic Games have further <u>spurred</u> economic growth.

A. mired

B. encumbered

C. catalyzed

3. Moreover, as globalization trends encourage foreign direct investment, many multinational corporations <u>intend</u> to move some of their operations to China.

A. connote

B. appall

C. unnerve

4. With increasing <u>direct</u> investment in China by overseas companies in recent years, international business centers offer overseas investor resources such as hardware and software and, in doing so, comply with global economic trends.

A. duplicitous

B. sinuous

C. explicit

5. While helping small and medium-sized overseas firms to invest in China and increase the level of their investments, international business centers can increase domestic and international trade, create employment <u>opportunities</u> and promote economic growth.

A. obstructions

B. contingencies

C. vicissitude

6. Market liberalization and export-oriented markets have enabled China's economy to <u>grow</u> at an annual rate of more than 9%, with external trade increasing by nearly 15% annually.

A. wane

B. germinate

C. atrophy

7. International business centers help small and medium-sized overseas firms that are uncertain of the investment climate and laws, and are unfamiliar with the local language and <u>constraints</u> on capital.

A. latitude

B. leeway

C. coercion

8. International business centers can arrange transportation, hold business functions, help expatriates adjust to daily life and provide business premises for rent; they can also help companies reduce operational costs, exchange information, hire secretarial staff and contribute to the development of <u>emerging</u> markets.

A. radiation

B. curtailment

C. deflation

9. An international business center in China typically <u>disseminates</u> information through the mass media to attract foreign investment, acts as a liaison between the overseas investor and governmental officials, helps overseas investors to adjust to Chinese culture by providing information on such topics as food, clothing and lifestyle.

A. kibosh

B. censures

C. dissipates

10. While performing these functions, an international business center must <u>adhere to</u> local governmental regulations.

    A. abstain from

    B. thwart

    C. comply with

11. Identifying the factors that influence the location of an international business center is <u>vital</u> to commercial success.

    A. evanescent

    B. indispensable

    C. frivolous

12. Selecting sites where overseas firms can operate can be a complex task. Selecting a site model to meet investors' <u>concerns</u> is especially important.

    A. truancy

    B. intercourse

    C. no show

13. The inability to locate an international business center <u>efficiently</u> will increase operating costs and reduce the profit margin.

    A. ineptly

    B. incompetently

    C. dexterously

14. Therefore, the factors that influence the choice of location model to be adopted by an international business center must be <u>identified</u> using the decision making statistical method of AHP.

    A. mussed

    B. disheveled

    C. pegged

Situation 3

1. Given the <u>stagnant</u> Taiwanese economy and increasing unemployment in recent
   years, growing crime rates and related convictions have led to a high prisoner
   population on the island.

   A. mutable

   B. inert

   C. protean

2. As individuals strive to cope with the rapidly transforming global economy, the
   <u>accelerating</u> growth of China has adversely affected Taiwan in terms of lost
   production and loss of foreign investment.

   A. avant-garde

   B. staved off

   C. protracted

3. The unemployment rate in Taiwan stands at 5.5%. Often contradictory political
   policies have sought to remedy this negative trend, only to have <u>exacerbated</u> the
   situation.

   A. surpassing

   B. exceptional

   C. piqued

4. Increasing unemployment and lost production have <u>continuously</u> reduced tax
   revenues, necessitating that the government reduce funding for public projects.

   A. intermittently

   B. spasmodically

   C. perpetually

5. Consequently, loss of employment has had <u>dire</u> consequences for many families,
   as Taiwan finds itself in transition from a manufacturing-based economy to a
   knowledge-based one, and has been partially responsible for high incarceration

rates.

A. sporadic

B. pressing

C. scant

6. However, the conventional means of locating correctional facilities is not objective, and depends often on the <u>subjective</u> judgment of decision makers.

A. even-handed

B. dispassionate

C. biased

7. The conventional approach is associated with high public funding, especially for <u>long-term</u> prisoners in correctional facilities.

A. indelible

B. ephemeral

C. fleeting

8. Despite <u>strict</u> governmental controls on the management or construction of other publicly funded facilities, such measures have been ineffective for correctional facilities.

A. derelict

B. lenient

C. puritanical

9. However, doing so often requires that the government spend <u>tremendous</u> amounts of capital to maintain the facilities and prevent crime since a conventionally chosen location is not close to service providers.

A. trifling

B. prodigious

C. feeble

10. The <u>expansion</u> of, or maintenance of materials for, correctional facilities often involves high handling costs.

    A. elision

    B. abridgement

    C. distension

11. <u>Hesitancy</u> among the general population to live near such high-risk facilities, often referred to as not-in-my-backyard (or NIMBY), results in increased operational costs and societal unease.

    A. procrastination

    B. exhilaration

    C. impetuosity

12. For instance, the number of inmates in the 53 correctional facilities in Taiwan increased from 37,000 to 43,000 from September, 2005 until now, with that figure <u>continually</u> increasing.

    A. momentarily

    B. perpetually

    C. finitely

13. Moreover, the ratio of correctional facility staff to prisoners is a dangerously low 1 : 20, far below the <u>prescribed</u> standard.

    A. indeterminate

    B. mandated

    C. precarious

14. Such a dangerous <u>imbalance</u> makes effective management almost impossible, as evidenced by the recent jail rioting in Brazil.

    A. equivalence

    B. symmetry

    C. disparity

15. Regaining control and repairing that facility cost the government enormously in capital and human resources.

    A. sapping

    B. redressing

    C. ravaging

16. Not only Brazil, but many industrialized countries devote considerable resources to preventing prison rebellions.

    A. consign

    B. censure

    C. berate

17. The inability to solve this problem in Taiwan's correctional facilities will extract many unforeseen societal costs in the future, ultimately overburdening governmental finances.

    A. imbibe

    B. amalgamate

    C. siphon

18. Additionally, the location of such facilities affects the convenience of the supply of materials and services; a limited number of service providers that can deliver severely restrict the ability of administrators to control the prisoner population.

    A. vexation

    B. succor

    C. exasperation

19. Therefore, factors that affect the infrastructure and safety of correctional facilities in Taiwan must be identified via the analytic hierarchy process (AHP) to optimize the target population and location of such facilities.

    A. augment

    B. deprecate

    C. miniaturize

H

Common elements in describing organizational or technical needs 描述組織或科技需求 include the following:

1. Briefly introduce a technology sector or market niche. 簡述一個科技部門或市場利基
2. Describe an external or internal factor affecting that sector or niche.. 內外部影響科技部門或市場利基的因素
3. Introduce a specific problem(s) that hinders development of that sector or niche. 描述一個阻礙科技部門或市場利基發展的問題
4. State the technical or marketing need that must be addressed to resolve this problem. 說明必須解決這個問題的科技或市場需求

1. Briefly introduce a technology sector or market niche. 簡述一個科技部門或市場利基

◎ More than just settling accounts and placing new products on view for purchase, further development of the bedding sector in Taiwan requires professional sales personnel to understand consumer preferences and more fully service their needs.

◎ As the 21st century is widely regarded as the era of biotechnology, the biopharmaceutical sector is one of the fastest technology growth areas worldwide, with medical and scientific discoveries widely anticipated to transform daily life: from combating diseases to job creation and economic growth.

◎ Given the critical role of therapeutic equipment in radiation therapy, quality assurance is essential in daily operations to ensure precision. Various tests are required for specific conditions, e.g., location of infrared radiation, dose distribution and frequency.

2. Describe an external or internal factor affecting that sector or niche. 內外部影響科技部門或市場利基的因素

◎ This explains why an increasing number of bedding franchises imitate the one-stop shopping business model of Elsa and Bed World Corporations, in which customers can purchase all of their bedding-related needs when visiting their outlets.

◎ Well aware of the potential impact of the global biotechnology sector, the Taiwanese government has aggressively encouraged local industry through heavy investment and other incentives. Most local biotechnology firms focus on developing therapeutic products, diagnostic procedures, medicinal applications through plant extracts, agricultural production and even genetic testing approaches.

◎ Therapeutic equipment manufacturers in Taiwan not only strive to cater to customers' specific needs, but also facilitate communication between the local market sector and overseas counterparts. However, Taiwan relies on imported therapeutic equipment such as linear accelerators and CO-60 therapeutic machinery, including the maintenance parts required for continuous use.

3. Introduce a specific problem(s) that hinders development of that sector or niche. 描述一個阻礙科技部門或市場利基發展的問題

◎ Still, the bedding sector faces several obstacles, such as the reluctance of customers to spend more than $5,000 New Taiwanese (NT) dollars on a mattress. Alternatively, local repair companies often fix spring beds or purchase old mattresses to recycle their parts. Although economically attractive, the repair and recycling processes are often environmentally unfriendly. Also, many consumers complain of discomfort after sleeping on a spring bed mattress. Therefore, many companies find it difficult to sell higher priced mattresses although superior in quality to traditionally used spring bed mattresses. Given advances in bed manufacturing technology, increased costs in manufacturing equipment and a larger portion in advertising expenditures to establish product brand recognition, consumers pay more than previously when purchasing a bed.

◎ While requiring highly skilled personnel to advance biotechnology product applications, biomedical companies are especially concerned with the shortage of qualified staff with adequate skills to remain abreast of the latest developments. Education, training and information alone are insufficient to keep Taiwanese biotechnology firms in pace with technology-driven changes in the workplace.

◎ Over reliance on appliance parts from Germany, Japan and the United States indirectly affects the quality of patient care and creates a costly financial burden for local hospitals. Despite the island's numerous engineering and computer science talents, Taiwan still lacks the manufacturing capabilities to produce therapeutic equipment for radiation therapy purposes.

4. State the technical or marketing need that must be addressed to resolve this problem. 說明必須解決這個問題的科技或市場需求

◎ Although incapable of reducing the retail price, Elsa Bedding Franchise should add product value to its mattresses in several ways. First, Elsa should customize its products by measuring the physical dimensions of the user to ensure maximum comfort. Recently, Elsa has incorporated the use of anion and bamboo additives in its mattresses. Having spent considerable resources in researching the efficacy of anion and bamboo in product technology, the Industrial Technology Research Institute (ITRI) analyzes the health benefits of bamboo, which is valuable information for adding softer comfort zones in mattresses and cleaning the cloth cover. Elsa and ITRI signed a collaborative agreement recently, with the commercial products to be featured in a sales exhibition in the Science Park Life Hub in Hsinchu Science-based Industrial Park. Moreover, a patent for use of nanotechnology in bamboo-related products has been filed recently. Moreover, in the near future, Elsa will collaborate with retailer RT-Mart in marketing its products.

◎ Therefore, in addition to enhanced training of research and managerial personnel in specific fields, local biotechnology and medical organizations are exploring ways to integrate other innovative fields, including bioinformatics and genomics, into their research scope and product line.

◎ Given the rapid pace of technological advances, an increasing number of therapeutic instruments can achieve better irradiation quality with respect to a more precise location and enhanced dose distribution. The ability of local manufacturers to collaborate with overseas partners will determine whether Taiwan can provide quality assurance treatment for ailing patients.

In the space below, describe an organizational or technical need with respect to developing or promoting a particular product or service.

_____

_____

_____

_____

_____

_____

_____

_____

_____

_____

_____

_____

Look at the following examples of describing organizational or technical needs 描述組織或科技需求 with respect to developing or promoting a particular product or service.

Computer tomography (CT) plays a prominent role in diagnosing medical ailments owing to its ability to achieve precise treatment without unnecessarily high radiation levels that would harm patients. Restated, while effective in therapeutic treatment, CT can not be used during a routine examination. Efforts to integrate CT into routine examinations is thus of priority concern. Although medical images are normally taken through conventional x-ray procedures, such procedures are limited in that while confined to capturing three-dimensional objects, many organs overlap each other, making it impossible to distinguish between them. In conventional inspection procedures, medical treatment involves closely inspecting the form of the disease. However, given the large number of spoke beams, conventional inspection procedures lead to further radiation damage owing to limited available information. Conversely, CT can not only detect diseases in their early stages, but also treat diseases more effectively. Nevertheless, CT is not adopted in routine examinations owing to its higher radiation dose than in normal examinations. Conventional medical imagery procedures emit a low radiation dose owing to the limited exposure time. For instance, in a normal chest x-ray examination, a radiation dosage of only 0.5mGy poses a relatively low risk to the human body. However, a CT examination may contain ten to twenty times higher dosage levels than a conventional x-ray examination would owing to the longer exposure time, possibly causing human injury. Despite the advantages of CT images over those of conventional x-ray images, the inability to reduce its radiation dose to a safe level makes it impossible to detect and subsequently treat cancer in its early stages. The feasibility of accelerating the scanning time during a CT examination must be examined, thus reducing radiation dose levels.

●

Since Taiwan implemented the National Health Insurance scheme in 1995, many hospitals have eliminated the use of medical waste disposal equipment on their premises to upgrade sanitary conditions and attract new patients concerned with a hygienic environment. In practice, hygienic equipment was commonly used in Taiwanese hospitals for disinfecting purposes. However, many hospitals have opted out of using such medical hygiene equipment, leading to an increase in medical waste and rise in expenses in order to cope with this growing amount of waste. According to statistics from the Department of Health of the Republic of China, as of 2003, the number of medical organizations island wide amounted to 18,777, while the number of sick beds in hospitals reached 136,331, which are the primary source of medical waste. According to the Environmental Protection Administration of the Republic of China, around 300 metric tons of medical waste are generated annually, with 42.4 metric tons considered infectious, i.e., an amount increasing annually. Environmental regulations stipulate that medical organizations can contract publicly owned or private disposal firms to handle medical waste. To effectively handle infectious medical wastes, around 62.5% of all public hospitals and 75.8% of all private hospitals outsource this work to disposal firms. Therefore, given the inevitability of growing expenditures in handling medical waste, medical organizations strive to minimize costs, maintain high quality medical services and dispose of infectious wastes legally. Such concerns highlight the importance of selecting qualified medical waste disposal firms during outsourcing. In sum, given the trend to eliminate the use of medical waste disposal equipment on their premises, hospitals must cope with increasing amounts of medical waste and rising treatment costs, as well as comply with environmental regulations, medical organizations commonly outsource their medical waste treatment to disposal firms. While many hospitals select waste disposal firms, hospital management often selects a disposal firm based on its professional experience and a competitive bid. However, such a decision process lacks objectivity and a quantitative means of evaluating outsourcing candidates, not necessarily ensuring that the most appropriate disposal firm is selected.

●

Taiwan's elderly population of roughly 1,900,000 explains the serious demand for long-term care of this segment. According to World Health Organization (WHO) statistics, Taiwan has been an "aging society" since 1993. However, the island's health care sector for long-term care does not have an equitable standard, neither in service nor in service fees despite the tremendous amount of attention paid to this topic. Economic, cultural and other societal problems have made it impossible to achieve a standard level of equitable care among Taiwan's elderly. Moreover, governmental privacy laws severely limit access to long term-care research data, documentation and commercial management practices, which are largely controlled by non-profit organizations involved with organizational management. Non-profit organizations heavily emphasize charity and volunteerism, often resulting in ineffective management and use of available resources that would be viewed as a loss of resources in a commercial enterprise. Adhering to the objectives of governmental law, while remaining aware of its limitations as well as introducing commercial management practices to the long-term health care sector, will help organizations to achieve sustainable management and provide high quality and relatively inexpensive services and products.

Situation 4

 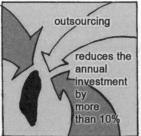 

Situation 5

Situation 6

 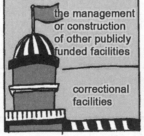 

I

Write down the key points of the situations on the preceding page, while the instructor reads aloud the script from the Answer Key. Alternatively, students can listen online at www.chineseowl.idv.tw

Situation 1

_____

_____

_____

Situation 2

_____

_____

_____

Situation 3

_____

_____

_____

J Oral practice II

Based on the three situations in this unit, write three questions beginning with *What*, and answer them. The questions do not need to come directly from these situations.

Examples

What poses a major challenge for hospitals as they seek to create a budgetary balance in their daily operations?

the Global Budget System implemented by the National Health Insurance Bureau in Taiwan

What have Taiwanese medical administrators focused heavily on?

constructing a deluxe health examination center to outsource diagnosis operations

1. _____

_____

2. _____

_____

3. _____

_____

K

Based on the three situations in this unit, write three questions beginning with *Why*, and answer them. The questions do not need to come directly from these situations.

Examples

Why must suppliers invest heavily in facilities, land and equipment?
because a strong market demand increases industrial output and revenues

Why has the average sales price of integrated circuits decreased?
since the recent construction of mass production facilities has markedly increased the available supply

1. _____

_____

2. _____

_____

3. _____

_____

L

Based on the three situations in this unit, write three questions beginning with *How*, and answer them. The questions do not need to come directly from these situations.

Examples

How have Taiwanese living standards dramatically increased in recent years?
with the availability of consumer goods, the pursuit of cultural interests and a strong health consciousness

How have entrepreneurs been able to promote the health food products market in Taiwan?
by an increase in the popularity of genetically modified foods

1. _____

_____

2. _____

_____

3. _____

_____

M Write questions that match the answers provided.

1. _____

_____

34

2. _____

_____

over the past two decades

3. _____

_____

maintaining one's health and the wide acceptance of nutritional supplements

N Listening Comprehension II

Situation 4

1. What is essential to enhancing the division of both labor and management among specialized departments?

A. enhancing the quality of medical care and competitiveness

B. effectively controlling overhead and, more importantly, establishing a mechanism for sharing in capital and business-related risks

C. generating revenue from such outsourcing under the Global Budget System

2. How many public hospitals operate under the Department of Health?

    A. 25

    B. 46

    C. 34

3. What severely restricts the competitiveness of public hospitals that outsource general operations?

    A. the inability to examine thoroughly the feasibility of generating revenue from such outsourcing

    B. the inability to construct a deluxe health examination center to outsource diagnosis operations

    C. the inability to provide additional budgeting for construction equipment, materials and personnel management

4. How can medical institutions help to maintain the quality of medical treatment without increasing hospital revenues?

    A. by reducing the annual investment by more than 10%

    B. by outsourcing to companies that provide health care

    C. by creating a budgetary balance in daily operations

5. Why do administrators scrutinize closely business models applied to daily operations?

    A. the availability of advanced health examinations that are outsourced to private medical units

    B. operational expenses of a hospital, including investment in equipment, personnel costs and costs of utilities

    C. increasingly fierce competition among hospitals and the need for sustainable development

Situation 5

1. How can Taiwanese firms maintain their competitive advantage?

    A. by forecasting market trends in the global semiconductor industry

    B. by playing a leading role in global production

    C. by investing continuously in research and development

2. What has expanded over the past two decades?

    A. the semiconductor industry in Taiwan

    B. the chipmaking sector

    C. economies of scale in production

3. What causes suppliers to invest heavily in facilities, land and equipment?

    A. increasing industrial output and revenues

    B. economic growth without a clear marketing strategy

    C. a competitive advantage using low-price strategies

4. How can one analyze how global market trends in the semiconductor industry influence the operating performance of Taiwan's semiconductor industry?

    A. based on total capital investment of the industry

    B. based on the ability of administrators to further increase economic growth

    C. based on an index of semiconductor equipment producers in Japan

5. How much has capital expenditure by the Asian semiconductor industry increased?

    A. from 15% in 1999 to 28% in 2003, with a forecasted 30% in 2006

    B. from 25% in 1999 to 38% in 2003, with a forecasted 40% in 2006

    C. from 29% in 1999 to 36% in 2003, with a forecasted 42% in 2006

Situation 6

1. What necessitates that pharmacists remain abreast of marketing and promotional strategies to increase profits?

A. the dramatic increase in Taiwanese living standards in recent years

B. commercial practices and the national health insurance scheme

C. media emphasis on maintaining one＇s health and the wide acceptance of nutritional supplements

2. Why do medical and healthcare expenditures account for an increasing share of household consumption in Taiwan?

A. because of the growth in daily consumption of health food products

B. because of the availability of consumer goods

C. because of the growing number of purchases of health food products at pharmacies

3. What has an increase in the popularity of genetically modified foods promoted?

A. the way for a strong health consciousness

B. the way for continuous changes in retail trends

C. the way for a health food products market

4. What have Taiwanese been able to pursue more in recent years?

A. cultural interests

B. strong health consciousness

C. consumer goods

5. What have local pharmacies played a vital role in?

A. retail trends

B. direct selling channels

C. the island＇s healthcare system

O Reading Comprehension II

Select the word or expression whose meaning is closest to the meaning of the underlined word or expression in the following passages.

Situation 4

1. The Global Budget System implemented by the National Health Insurance Bureau in Taiwan <u>poses</u> a major challenge for hospitals as they seek to create a budgetary balance in their daily operations.

   A. retrogrades

   B. disavows

   C. propounds

2. Increasingly fierce competition among hospitals and the need for sustainable development have forced administrators to <u>scrutinize</u> closely business models applied to daily operations.

   A. dissect

   B. leaf through

   C. thumb through

3. Such <u>initiatives</u> include organizational rearrangement, personnel layoffs, operational cost reductions, lowering of operational risks, outsourcing and the making of investments to enhance the quality of medical care and competitiveness.

   A. crusades

   B. stumbling blocks

   C. confinements

4. Medical administrators have focused heavily on constructing a <u>deluxe</u> health examination center to outsource diagnosis.

   A. paltry

   B. tenuous

   C. posh

5. By outsourcing to companies that provide health care, medical institutions do not require additional budgeting for construction equipment, materials and personnel

management, helping to <u>maintain</u> the quality of medical treatment without increasing hospital revenues.

A. retrench

B. prolong

C. abridge

6. Given the <u>uniqueness</u> of medical operations, outsourcing such operations differs from outsourcing the general affairs of administrative units.

A. vicissitude

B. primitiveness

C. rusticism

7. Effectively controlling overhead and, more importantly, establishing a mechanism for sharing in capital and business-related risks are essential to enhancing the division of both labor and management among specialized departments in order to ensure medical quality and provide a competitive edge over other medical facilities with respect to operations, expanded market share and <u>advanced</u> technologies.

A. embryonic

B. precocious

C. vestigial

8. However, when hospitals examine the feasibility of outsourcing the operations of a medical unit, the analytic hierarchy process and extension theory are <u>seldom</u> applied to evaluate the weights of the assessment criteria and ensure objectivity.

A. recurrently

B. wontedly

C. whimsically

9. Outsourcing reduces <u>expenditure</u> on machines, equipment, medical supplies, renovation and utilities, as well as the numbers of doctors, nurses, medical

technicians and administrators.

A. income

B. dissipation

C. receivable

10. However, the inability of public hospitals that outsource general operations to examine thoroughly the feasibility of generating revenue from such outsourcing under the Global Budget System severely <u>restricts</u> their competitiveness, subsequently increasing operating expenses.

A. demarcates

B. augments

C. amplifies

11. Therefore, the factors influencing the operational <u>expenses</u> of a hospital, including investment in equipment, personnel costs and costs of utilities, must be identified.

A. cache

B. kitty

C. debit

Situation 5

1. The relationship between <u>trends</u> in the global semiconductor market and Taiwan's semiconductor industry has received increasing attention.

A. isolated incidence

B. inclinations

C. episode

2. The electronics industry is an <u>integral</u> part of the Taiwanese economy, and local semiconductor manufacturers play a leading role in global production.

A. nugatory

B. indispensable

C. rinky-dink

3. The revenues of the semiconductor industry have increased in line with economic trends; its business cycle is highly <u>volatile</u> as well.

A. irenic

B. tranquil

C. ephemeral

4. A strong market demand increases industrial output and revenues, causing suppliers to invest <u>heavily</u> in facilities, land and equipment.

A. vigorously

B. marginally

C. imperceptibly

5. As Japan and the United States have gradually lost market share, Taiwan has met strong competition from Asian chipmakers such as those from China and Korea that have gained a <u>competitive</u> advantage by using low-price strategies.

A. collaborative

B. unambitious

C. emulous

6. Although the global billings and bookings (B/B ratio) of North American semiconductor equipment producers are used to forecast market trends in the global semiconductor industry, exactly how such trends are related to Taiwan's semiconductor industry has not been <u>addressed</u>.

A. contemned

B. pontificated

C. spurned

7. Prior to 1998, Europe and the United States accounted for 60% of the semiconductor market, reflecting their previous <u>dominance</u> in this area.

A. enervation

B. languor

C. preponderance

8. Despite previous marketing research to understand how Taiwan's semiconductor industry has contributed to economic growth, administrators find that further increasing economic growth without a clear marketing strategy is almost <u>impossible</u>.

A. preposterous

B. attainable

C. tolerable

9. Taiwanese information technology and electronics firms face <u>fierce</u> competition from multinational corporations when they enter export markets.

A. demulcent

B. poignant

C. negligible

10. Exactly how global market trends in the semiconductor industry influence the operating performance of Taiwan's semiconductor industry can be analyzed based on an <u>index</u> of semiconductor equipment producers in Japan.

A. ostracism

B. exclusion

C. symptom

Situation 6

1. Taiwanese living standards have dramatically increased in recent years, as evidenced by the availability of consumer goods, the <u>pursuit</u> of cultural interests and a strong health consciousness.

A. ebb

B. quest

C. recession

2. Taiwanese living standards have dramatically increased in recent years, as evidenced by the <u>availability</u> of consumer goods, the pursuit of cultural interests and a strong health consciousness.

A. vacancy

B. void

C. dearth

3. Media emphasis on maintaining one's health and the wide <u>acceptance</u> of nutritional supplements have paved the way for a health food products market, which is promoted by an increase in the popularity of genetically modified foods.

A. compliance

B. renunciation

C. rebuff

4. Media emphasis on <u>maintaining</u> one's health and the wide acceptance of nutritional supplements have paved the way for a health food products market, which is promoted by an increase in the popularity of genetically modified foods.

A. derogating

B. perpetuating

C. abasing

5. The growth in daily consumption of health food products explains why, according to governmental statistics, medical and healthcare expenditures account for an increasing share of household <u>consumption</u> in Taiwan and, correspondingly, a rise in the number of recently established local pharmacies.

A. dissipation

B. nest egg

C. hoarding

6. The growth in daily consumption of health food products explains why, according to governmental statistics, medical and healthcare expenditures account for an increasing share of household consumption in Taiwan and, correspondingly, a rise in the number of recently <u>established</u> local pharmacies.

   A. ensconced

   B. disjoined

   C. pieced

7. A recent study of consumer trends in the health food products sector in Taiwan revealed not only that consumers prefer retail outlets over direct selling channels, but also that consumers most often <u>purchase</u> health food products at pharmacies.

   A. peddle

   B. hawk

   C. procure

8. While local pharmacies play a vital role in the island's healthcare system, continuous changes in retail trends, commercial practices and the national health insurance scheme <u>necessitate</u> that pharmacists remain abreast of marketing and promotional strategies to increase profits.

   A. deprecate

   B. impel

   C. vex

9. While local pharmacies play a <u>vital</u> role in the island's healthcare system, continuous changes in retail trends, commercial practices and the national health insurance scheme necessitate that pharmacists remain abreast of marketing and promotional strategies to increase profits.

   A. paltry

   B. requisite

   C. frivolous

Unit Three

Explaining Difficulties in Developing a Product or Service

描述產業所面臨的困境

1. Describe the general setting for developing a particular product or service.
   描述產品或服務研發的流程配置

2. Introduce the main problem(s) that managers face in developing that product or service.
   描述產品或服務研發主要的問題點

3. State the implications or consequences of the problem(s) remaining unresolved.
   描述不解決問題點的後果

Unit Three

Vocabulary and related expressions

poses a major challenge	形成大的挑戰
chronic illnesses	慢性病
academic attainment	學術成就
governmental infrastructure	政府的公共建設
incapacitated	使無能力的
mentally and physically sound	心理及生理健全
evaluative criteria	估計的標準
widespread customer dissatisfaction	客戶全面性的不滿
market liberalization policies	市場自由化政策
sprung up quickly	迅速生長
intensifying market competition	強化市場競爭
adverse effects	反面的效果
dramatic reform measures	引人注目的改革手段
governmental initiatives	政府的倡議
unresolved financial problems	無法解決的財務問題
hospital prescription drugs	醫院處方藥
over-the-counter drug purchases	便利的藥品購買
one-stop shopping	一次購足
empirical analysis	以經驗（或觀察）為依據的分析
consumer purchasing behavior and pricing strategies	客戶購買行為及定價策略
intellectual capital	智慧財產
tangible assets	有形的資產
knowledge-based assets	智慧資產
complex administrative procedures	複雜的行政程序
simplify administrative procedures	簡化行政程序
substantial overhead	實質的經常性花費
suddenly deteriorated	忽然惡化
intensive care unit (ICU)	加護病房

Situation 1

a rapidly growing elderly population poses a major challenge for long-term care management

these workers have no restrictions of age, education or experience

outsourcing firms lack objective criteria in selecting nursing care attendants

Situation 2

credit cooperatives have played a pivotal role as financial institutions

financial organizations draw on their personal experiences to improve their competitiveness

defaulted loans

many credit cooperatives leave behind several unresolved financial problems

Situation 3

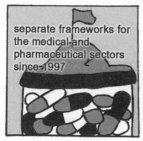
separate frameworks for the medical and pharmaceutical sectors since 1997

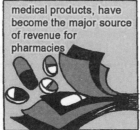
medical products, have become the major source of revenue for pharmacies

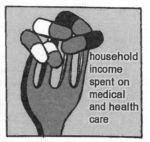
household income spent on medical and health care

A

Write down the key points of the situations on the preceding page, while the instructor reads aloud the script from the Answer Key. Alternatively, students can listen online at www.chineseowl.idv.tw

Situation 1

_____

_____

_____

Situation 2

_____

_____

_____

Situation 3

_____

_____

_____

B Oral practice I

Based on the three situations in this unit, write three questions beginning with **What**, and answer them. The questions do not need to come directly from these situations.

Examples

What poses a major challenge for long-term care management?
a rapidly growing elderly population

What group of professionals does not hold specialized license certification nor has reached a particular level of academic attainment?
nursing care attendants

1. _____

_____

2. _____

_____

3. _____

_____

C

Based on the three situations in this unit, write three questions beginning with *How*, and answer them. The questions do not need to come directly from these situations.

Examples

How has market competition in Taiwan intensified?

with the emergence of several banks and springing up of financial organizations

How has the rapid growth of credit cooperatives been adversely affected?

with banks lowering their criteria for loan approvals to remain competitive

1. _____

   _____

2. _____

   _____

3. _____

   _____

D

Based on the three situations in this unit, write three questions beginning with **Why**, and answer them. The questions do not need to come directly from these situations.

Examples

Why have over-the-counter drug purchases, along with sanitary and other related medical products, become the major source of revenue for pharmacies?
because the Taiwanese government has implemented separate frameworks for the medical and pharmaceutical sectors since 1997, and the rate of hospital prescription drugs filled by pharmacies is extremely low

Why are customers able to purchase a wide array of medical and health food products?
because local pharmacies have adopted a business model of one-stop shopping in recent years

1. _____

_____

2. _____

_____

3. _____

_____

E Write questions that match the answers provided.

1. _____

   _____

   a uniform management approach to ensure the quality of service

2. _____

   _____

   only 30

3. _____

   _____

   since 1997

F Listening Comprehension I

Situation 1

1. What do most nursing care attendants lack?

   A. adequate supervision

   B. adequate evaluative criteria

   C. a uniform management approach to ensure the quality of service

2. What do outsourcing firms lack?

   A. objective criteria in selecting nursing care attendants

    B. a sufficient elderly population

    C. employees with basic healthcare training skills and necessary knowledge of hospital or governmental infrastructure

3. What has led to an emphasis on controlling personnel costs while maintaining high-quality services?

    A. a rapidly growing elderly population

    B. changes in Taiwan's National Health Insurance scheme

    C. changing family structures and the frequency of chronic illnesses

4. What poses a major challenge for long-term care management?

    A. the outsourcing of nursing care attendants

    B. a rapidly growing elderly population

    C. adequate knowledge of hospital or governmental infrastructure

5. What makes it impossible to control the quality of service provided island-wide?

    A. the inability of nursing care attendants to perform their tasks efficiently

    B. the inability of relatives of the patient to select the most appropriate care provider

    C. the lack of standardized training

Situation 2

1. How many credit cooperatives are currently operating in Taiwan?

    A. 72

    B. 35

    C. 30

2. What is at great risk in Taiwan?

    A. the survival of credit cooperatives as governmental initiatives

    B. the survival of credit cooperatives as financial institutions

    C. the survival of credit cooperatives as financial research centers

3. What will create a serious financial crisis domestically?

A. financial organizations drawing on their personal experiences to improve their competitiveness

B. many credit cooperatives leaving behind several unresolved financial problems

C. credit cooperatives playing a pivotal role as financial institutions

4. What has increased the incidence of loan defaults?

A. adverse effects, such as banks' lowering their criteria for loan approvals to remain competitive

B. adverse effects, such as the inability to reform and lower the rate of defaulted loans

C. adverse effects, such as the inability of financial research to directly focus on market developments

5. What is especially prevalent among credit cooperatives?

A. corporate loss among Taiwan's financial organizations

B. turbulent political and economic situations

C. poor investments and subsequent defaulted loans

Situation 3

1. Why have over-the-counter drug purchases, along with sanitary and other related medical products, become the major source of revenue for pharmacies?

A. Local pharmacies have thus adopted a business model of one-stop shopping in recent years.

B. Managers can not analyze market competition accurately.

C. The Taiwanese government has implemented separate frameworks for the medical and pharmaceutical sectors since 1997, and the rate of hospital prescription drugs filled by pharmacies is extremely low.

2. Why is an accurate analysis by managers of market competition and the development of effective strategies almost impossible?

    A. the inability to forecast accurately share of household income spent on medical and health care, or the number of local pharmacies to be established

    B. an insufficient amount of over-the-counter drug purchases

    C. the inability to purchase a wide array of medical and health food products

3. Why are customers able to purchase a wide array of medical and health food products?

    A. Empirical analysis of pharmacies in the field of business management has focused on management strategies.

    B. Local pharmacies have adopted a business model of one-stop shopping in recent years.

    C. Pharmaceutical managers can increase their effectiveness.

4. What has not been developed?

    A. separate frameworks for the medical and pharmaceutical sectors

    B. a forecasting model to help pharmaceutical managers increase their effectiveness

    C. the rate of hospital prescription drugs filled by pharmacies

5. What has empirical analysis of pharmacies in the field of business management focused on?

    A. management strategies

    B. a business model of one-stop shopping

    C. accurate analysis by managers of market competition

G Reading Comprehension I

Select the word or expression whose meaning is closest to the meaning of the underlined word or expression in the following passages.

Situation 1

1. A rapidly growing elderly population poses a major challenge for long-term care management, requiring <u>immediate</u> solutions, given changing family structures and the frequency of chronic illnesses.

   A. elapsed

   B. dilatory

   C. pressing

2. They are members of a sub-specialized field and do not hold <u>specialized</u> license certification nor have reached a particular level of academic attainment.

   A. explicit

   B. prosaic

   C. banal

3. Playing an important role in Taiwanese society, nursing care attendants <u>accompany</u> disabled individuals and help them in their daily activities, such as taking baths and eating meals.

   A. sequestering

   B. quarantine

   C. consort

4. They also <u>monitor</u> urinary or stool specimens, change the posture of incapacitated stroke victims and provide general comfort.

   A. rebuff

   B. affront

C. survey

5. Despite their contributions, most nursing care attendants lack a <u>uniform</u> management approach to ensure the quality of service.

   A. arbitrary

   B. ossified

   C. desultory

6. These workers have no restrictions of age, education or experience, save for their being mentally and physically <u>sound</u>.

   A. vacillating

   B. mutable

   C. virile

7. Despite the <u>abundance</u> of outsourcing agencies for nursing care attendants, the lack of standardized training makes controlling the quality of service provided island wide impossible.

   A. paucity

   B. exiguousness

   C. opulence

8. Moreover, changes in Taiwan's National Health Insurance scheme have led to an emphasis on controlling personnel costs while maintaining high-quality services, further <u>contributing to</u> the outsourcing of nursing care attendants.

   A. proffering

   B. gleaning

   C. eking out

9. Generally, relatives of the patient directly employ nursing care attendants without <u>adequate</u> evaluative criteria to select the most appropriate care provider.

   A. parsimonious

   B. commensurate

C. bush league

10. Additionally, outsourcing firms lack objective criteria in selecting nursing care attendants, leading to <u>widespread</u> customer dissatisfaction and increasing management difficulty.

    A. meager

    B. regnant

    C. scrimpy

Situation 2

1. Credit cooperatives have played a <u>pivotal</u> role as financial institutions in Taiwan's economic development.

    A. focal

    B. inappreciable

    C. trifling

2. The market liberalization policies of the Taiwanese government since 1992 have led to the emergence of several banks, and financial organizations have sprung up quickly, subsequently <u>intensifying</u> market competition.

    A. abridging

    B. elision

    C. augmenting

3. The rapid growth of this market sector has had some <u>adverse</u> effects, such as banks lowering their criteria for loan approvals to remain competitive, increasing the incidence of loan defaults.

    A. auspicious

    B. rosy

    C. inimical

4. Given <u>turbulent</u> political and economic situations worldwide, financial institutions in Taiwan must adopt dramatic reform measures to maintain their competitiveness.

   A. genteel

   B. inclement

   C. urbane

5. Only banks, and not credit cooperatives, have benefited from governmental <u>initiatives</u> such as the nationwide Financial Reform Project, explaining the low competitiveness of the latter in Taiwan's financial market.

   A. retractions

   B. gumptions

   C. repeals

6. Although attempting to <u>reform</u> the financial market, financial research does not directly focus on market developments. In practice, while financial organizations draw on their personal experiences to improve their competitiveness, doing so often leads to poor investments and subsequent defaulted loans.

   A. liberalize

   B. inaugurate

   C. ameliorate

7. This situation is especially <u>prevalent</u> among credit cooperatives, explaining their inability to reform and lower the rate of defaulted loans.

   A. tenuous

   B. ubiquitous

   C. rarefied

8. The survival of credit cooperatives as financial institutions in Taiwan is at great risk, necessitating improved understanding of their <u>importance</u> and unique features.

A. preponderance

B. truism

C. banality

9. The inability of the Experience Rule and financial research to reduce the risk of defaulted loans will lead to further corporate <u>loss</u> among Taiwan's financial organizations.

A. yield

B. dividend

C. insolvency

10. Even following their <u>elimination</u>, many credit cooperatives leave behind several unresolved financial problems, ultimately creating a serious financial crisis domestically.

A. merger

B. annexing

C. repudiation

Situation 3

1. The Taiwanese government has implemented <u>separate</u> frameworks for the medical and pharmaceutical sectors since 1997, and the rate of hospital prescription drugs filled by pharmacies is extremely low.

A. integrated

B. interdependent

C. divergent

2. The Taiwanese government has <u>implemented</u> separate frameworks for the medical and pharmaceutical sectors since 1997, and the rate of hospital prescription drugs filled by pharmacies is extremely low.

A. impeded

B. promulgated

C. obstructed

3. This fact explains why over-the-counter drug purchases, along with <u>sanitary</u> and other related medical products, have become the major source of revenue for pharmacies.

A. disheveled

B. hygienic

C. squalid

4. This fact explains why over-the-counter drug purchases, along with sanitary and other related medical products, have become the major <u>source</u> of revenue for pharmacies.

A. origin

B. bedlam

C. pandemonium

5. Local pharmacies have thus adopted a business model of one-stop shopping in recent years, according to which customers can purchase a wide <u>array</u> of medical and health food products.

A. disorder

B. mess

C. lineup

6. Local pharmacies have thus <u>adopted</u> a business model of one-stop shopping in recent years, according to which customers can purchase a wide array of medical and health food products.

A. vacated

B. abdicated

C. utilized

7. Although empirical analysis of pharmacies in the field of business management has focused on management strategies, the <u>orientation</u> of pharmacists toward marketing practices, consumer purchasing behavior and pricing strategies, studies have not developed a forecasting model to help pharmaceutical managers increase their effectiveness.

   A. randomness

   B. acclimatization

   C. aimlessness

8. The <u>inability</u> to forecast accurately either the share of household income spent on medical and health car or the number of local pharmacies to be established makes almost impossible an accurate analysis by managers of market competition and the development of effective strategies.

   A. inaptitude

   B. proficiency

   C. fortitude

9. The inability to forecast accurately either the share of household income spent on medical and health car or the number of local pharmacies to be established makes almost impossible an <u>accurate</u> analysis by managers of market competition and the development of effective strategies.

   A. explicit

   B. vague

   C. ambiguous

H

Common elements in explaining difficulties in developing a product or service 描述 產業所面臨的困境 include the following contents:

1. Describe the general setting for developing a particular product or service. 描述產品或 服務研發的流程配置
2. Introduce the main problem(s) that managers face in developing that product or service. 描述產品或服務研發主要的問題點
3. State the implications or consequences of the problem(s) remaining unresolved. 描述不 解決問點的後果

1. Describe the general setting for developing a particular product or service. 描述產品或服務研發的流程配置

◎ Both the increasing popularity of credit card use and growing number of Internet-based promotional activities in Taiwan have enabled banking institutions to acquire extensive customer data. In addition to helping banking institutions to execute customer management and service management efficiently, thoroughly analyzing such data can optimize marketing management practices. Corporate survival in the future hinges on the ability to know and treat customers well through analysis of pertinent data.

◎ Infarction strokes may occur at any moment in the human life cycle and cause death in middle age and later life. The clinical diagnosis and treatment of stroke, as well as investigations into the underlying pathophysiology of the disease, hinge on inferences from the anatomy of the stroke lesion. Treatment has been directed towards both reestablishment of flow after occlusion and an increase in tissue tolerance to ischemia. MRI affords approximate estimates of stroke topography and size with respect to numerous aspects. Coordinated diffusion and perfusion studies go even further to provide a view of the evolution of stroke contour in relation to a perimeter of relative hypoperfusion.

◎ Cancer has been the leading cause of mortality in Taiwan since 1982. Surgery, radiotherapy and chemical therapy are three conventional means of treating cancer. Among those, radiotherapy is the most effective approach to using radiation for

successful resolution

2. Introduce the main problem(s) that managers face in developing that product or service. 描述產品或服務研發主要的問題點

◎ However, differentiated marketing practices in Taiwan are insufficient, with conventional methods of ranking customers normally based on the bank account balance for each accounting period. This basis alone does not provide a complete customer profile, and seldom incorporates strategies that analyze the commercial transaction data of customers. Insufficient information of unique customer characteristics can obviously not provide specialized services for individuals.

◎ Although quantitative uses at present are limited, MRI is also appropriate for volumetric study of stroke and the brain damaged by a stroke.

◎ Owing to their inability to estimate precisely the dose required for cancer patients, conventional radiotherapy methods normally underestimate or overestimate the actual treatment dose. Therefore, how to evaluate the proper and correct dose exactly and efficiently is of priority concern in radiotherapy. For instance, conventional dose measurement methods depend on thermoluminescence dosimeter (TLD), which is inefficient owing to that six to eight hours are required for reuse.

3. State the implications or consequences of the problem(s) remaining unresolved. 描述不解決問點的後果

◎ Thus, the inability to interact compatibly with customers will cause companies to lose their focus on the product development and promotional strategies.

◎ The conventional means of diagnosing acute cerebral infarctions, in which clinical physicians review the medical history of patients and current condition as well as make a subjective assessment in diagnosing stroke cases subjectively, normally makes it impossible not only to diagnose patients with an acute stroke the first time, but also to identify the type and regional geography of such a stroke accurately.

◎ As is well known, estimating the accurate radiation dose for treatment efficiently is essential during a radiation examination or radiotherapy course. Conventionally used to estimate the radiation dose, a thermoluminescence dosimeter (TLD) spends too much time in annealing for the next measurement period. For one time use, TLD requires approximately six to eight hours in preparation. Thus, the same group of TLDs can only make two counts in one day. The inability to reduce the time that TLD spends in annealing results in an unnecessarily long time in waiting for experimental results.

Explain difficulties in developing a product or service.

_____

_____

_____

_____

_____

_____

_____

_____

_____

_____

Look at the following examples of how to explain difficulties in developing a product or service.

The incidence of breast cancer in Taiwan is increasing, with females having a higher than average prognosis rate globally. With recent innovations in cancer treatment and the trend of modern oncology towards a greater number of differentiated treatment options, assessing the prognostic factors of breast cancer has become increasingly important. Such trends necessitate the need not only to evaluate the prognostic factors of this disease, but also to establish a uniform standard for clinical diagnosis. In most malignant tumors, prognosis is influenced by several variables, along with several interactions of varying strength that occur among the different factors. Thus, prognostic factor research must initially identify those varieties that have an independent influence on outcome. The prognostic factors are defined using TNM/p. As is well known, TNM system and the residual tumor (R) classification are global standards, as established by the International Union Against Cancer (UICC). Based on these standards, many prognostic factors of breast cancer have been evaluated, including age, residence, pathologic T stage, tumor size, grade, lymphatic or vascular invasion and histology. However, well-defined factors for this disease have still not been identified, making it impossible to establish well-defined factors for breast cancer that can elevate the five-year survival rate of those with breast cancer. Such identification could become possible by adopting multivariate biometric methods that also allow us to estimate the relative risks associated with each prognostic factor. For studies of prognostic factors, univariate analysis alone is insufficient; multivariate methods are required as well.

●

Chemotherapy for cancer patients has a strong medicine toxicity, in which an inaccurate dosage could aggravate great potential harm to normal cells. After a

111

lasting dosage is administered, the cancer cell may resist the medicine, subsequently forming multi-drug resistance in tumor cells. Conventional methods have been adopted to aggravate the medicine dosage for patients; otherwise, other medicines are administered to attack the cancer cell. The dosage of chemotherapy medicine is subsequently increased to terminate a larger number of tumor cells. However, the resistance to chemotherapy poses a major obstacle in treating cancer patients. While producing the tumor cell of multi-drug resistance, other drugs may not be able to produce the anticipated drug effect either because these tumor cells do not merely resist the original therapeutic drug, but can already resist other drugs as well. Cancer cells have many mechanisms to withstand the effects of medicine, including defects in the regulation of genes controlling apoptosis, enhanced intracellular drug detoxification, alterations in DNA repair and activation or overexpression of drug export proteins. Importantly, tumor cells can produce p-glyprotein (pgp), i.e., an active transport protein. As long as ATP persists, many drugs can be flushed out of the cell membrane similar to a pumping action. As chemotherapy treatment makes tumor cells gradually resistant to drug dosages, continuously increasing the dosage amount poses a greater threat to humans owing not only to the lack of complementary medicines to lower the dosage of chemotherapy medicine, but also to the inability to protect normal cells during chemotherapy. Furthermore, although cancer cells can aggravate and suppress medicinal effects with a growing dosage, normal cells of the human body are significantly more fragile than cancer cells. Therefore, following successive rounds of chemotherapy medication, normal cells can not withstand the tumor cells, causing serious sequelae.

Given continuous advances in medical science and medical instrumentation, the medical sector in Taiwan has become intensely competitive, necessitating that hospitals provide quality medical services under limited medical resources. With the island's elevated living standards, an increasing health consciousness among the general public has led to a strong societal demand for hospitals to offer high quality medical treatment and services. Generally, rather than concerned with the price of medical treatment, patients are more concerned with the level of treatment. Despite the high quality medical care provided, hospitals often have difficulty in understanding customer's needs. More specifically, conventional statistical methods such as AHP and TOPSIS cannot analyze how patients select a hospital for treatment, making it extremely difficult to devise effective business management strategies. For example, of the nearly 200 patients expressing dissatisfaction with Wanfang Hospital in 2004, 30% resented medical care, 25% felt that medical personnel had poor professional attitudes, 25% were dissatisfied with hardware equipment and the remaining 20% expressed dissatisfaction over a miscellaneous range of items. Given the lost revenues of nearly 25% from governmental subsidized care, Wangfang Hospital finds it nearly impossible to increase revenues generated from patients desiring services or treatment not subsidized by National Health Insurance without clearly analyzing patient satisfaction/dissatisfaction levels.

Situation 4

intellectual capital is a significant resource in creating wealth

on-line gaming companies emphasize the ownership of intellectual capital

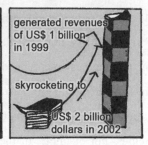

generated revenues of US$ 1 billion in 1999

skyrocketing to US$ 2 billion dollars in 2002

Situation 5

complex administrative procedures associated with Taiwan's National Health Insurance

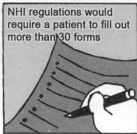

NHI regulations would require a patient to fill out more than 30 forms

staff handling errors and requesting insurers and claimants to correct erroneous information

Situation 6

a young soldier with a high fever brought about by a widespread common cold

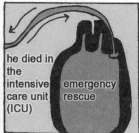

he died in the intensive care unit (ICU) emergency rescue

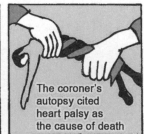

The coroner's autopsy cited heart palsy as the cause of death

I

Write down the key points of the situations on the preceding page, while the instructor reads aloud the script from the Answer Key. Alternatively, students can listen online at www.chineseowl.idv.tw

Situation 4

_____

_____

_____

Situation 5

_____

_____

_____

Situation 6

_____

_____

_____

J Oral practice II

Based on the three situations in this unit, write three questions beginning with ***How***, and answer them. The questions do not need to come directly from these situations.

Examples

How has the relative importance of tangible assets declined?

with the increasing importance of knowledge-based assets

How is a company's value undervalued?

owing to the inability of conventional accounting methods to include knowledge-based assets

1. _____

_____

2. _____

_____

3. _____

_____

K

Based on the three situations in this unit, write three questions beginning with **What**, and answer them. The questions do not need to come directly from these situations.

Examples

What have led to errors in insurance claims and much inefficiency?

complex administrative procedures associated with Taiwan's National Health Insurance (NHI) scheme

What would require a patient to fill out more than 30 forms?

to adhere to all NHI regulations

1. _____

   _____

2. _____

   _____

3. _____

   _____

L

Based on the three situations in this unit, write three questions beginning with *Why*, and answer them. The questions do not need to come directly from these situations.

Examples

Why must medical institutions take responsibility for instilling in physicians a sense of professional ethics?

so that medical professionals can assume responsibility without the assigning of fault to a particular party.

Why is it impossible to apply some management approaches?

because medical treatment involves a degree of risk

1. _____

   _____

2. _____

   _____

3. _____

   _____

M Write questions that match the answers provided.

1. _____

   _____

   533,000,000

2. _____

   _____

   the enormous amount of administrative time and cost involved in handling these errors, as well as its larger implications

3. _____

   _____

   heart palsy as the cause of death

N Listening Comprehension II

Situation 4

1. What do on-line gaming companies emphasize?

   A. the importance of knowledge-based assets

   B. the ownership of intellectual capital

   C. tangible assets

2. How much in revenues did the global online gaming sector generate in 1999?

   A. US$ 1 billion

B. US$ 1.5 billion

C. US$ 2 billion

3. What do conventional accounting methods lack?

   A. the ability to measure the value of tangible assets that can be quantified in a company

   B. knowledge-based assets

   C. the ability to rate a company's value

4. What have previous studies seldom measured?

   A. tangible assets such as property, facilities and equipment

   B. intellectual capital

   C. the value of on-line gaming companies

5. What has declined with the increasing importance of knowledge-based assets?

   A. the relative importance of tangible assets

   B. the relative importance of intellectual capital

   C. the relative importance of scientific and technological advances

Situation 5

1. What does the NHI staff spend much time in doing?

   A. adhering to all NHI regulations

   B. creating substantial overhead

   C. handling errors and requesting insurers and claimants to correct erroneous information

2. Why do errors in insurance claims and much inefficiency occur?

   A. complex administrative procedures associated with Taiwan's National Health Insurance (NHI) scheme

   B. the enormous amount of administrative time and cost involved in handling these errors

C. high operational costs

3. What will lead to higher operational costs?

    A. the inability to fill out more than 30 forms, relating to insurance claims, salary readjustment and the insurer's/claimant's name

    B. the inability to adhere to all NHI regulations

    C. the inability to gradually reduce the amount of human resources involved in handling insurer and claimant errors and simplify administrative procedures as well as NHI forms

4. Why do errors in adhering to all NHI regulations occur?

    A. the increasing time spent by human resources

    B. the enormous amount of administrative time and cost involved

    C. confusion over forms

5. How many forms must a patient fill out to adhere to all NHI regulations?

    A. more than 25

    B. more than 30

    C. more than 40

Situation 6

1. What does medical treatment involve?

    A. a sense of professional ethics

    B. assigning of fault to a particular party

    C. a degree of risk

2. After how many days did the young soldier's condition suddenly deteriorate?

    A. after four days in the sickbay

    B. after six days in the sickbay

    C. after one week in the sickbay

3. What do family members need to complete in terms of procedures in order receive compensation for death incurred from military duty?

 A. the coroner's report

 B. a consensus among all attending physicians on the cause of death

 C. authorization from the chief sickbay administrator

4. How long did emergency rescue procedures undertaken by the medical personnel in the sickbay perform last?

 A. one day

 B. two days

 C. three days

5. Where do professional health care administrators encounter resistance?

 A. from medical consumers

 B. from the military

 C. from the general public

O Reading Comprehension II

Select the word or expression whose meaning is closest to the meaning of the underlined word or expression in the following passages.

Situation 4

1. Intellectual capital is a significant <u>resource</u> in creating wealth.

 A. liability

 B. constraint

 C. recourse

2. Although tangible assets such as property, facilities and equipment continue to play a vital role in the manufacture of products and the provision of services,

their relative importance has <u>declined</u> with the increasing importance of knowledge-based assets.

A. surged

B. waned

C. amplified

3. Although able to measure the value of tangible <u>assets</u> that can be quantified in a company, conventional accounting methods do not include knowledge-based assets, subsequently leading to an underrating of a company's value.

A. impediments

B. resources

C. encumbrances

4. Additionally, scientific and technological advances have increased the <u>importance</u> of intellectual capital.

A. triviality

B. meagerness

C. pertinence

5. For instance, on-line gaming companies <u>emphasize</u> the ownership of intellectual capital rather than tangible assets.

A. obscure

B. accentuate

C. ensconce

6. Accordingly, the value of on-line gaming companies has <u>seldom</u> been measured in previous studies.

A. sporadically

B. frequently

C. often

7. Online gaming is the most important part of the gaming industry, with generated revenues of US$ 1 billion in 1999, <u>skyrocketing</u> to US$ 2 billion dollars in 2002.

A. receding

B. impairing

C. forging ahead

8. The inability to measure the value of companies without <u>incorporating</u> intellectual capital not only leads to an underrating of their value, but also makes impossible an understanding how intellectual capital affects the on-line gaming market.

A. dissipating

B. consolidating

C. diffusing

9. The inability to measure the value of companies without incorporating intellectual capital not only leads to an <u>underrating</u> of their value, but also makes impossible an understanding of how intellectual capital affects the on-line gaming market.

A. exaggeration

B. underestimation

C. overstatement

Situation 5

1. <u>Complex</u> administrative procedures associated with Taiwan's National Health Insurance (NHI) scheme have led to errors in insurance claims and much inefficiency.

A. obvious

B. facile

C. convoluted

2. Complex administrative procedures associated with Taiwan's National Health Insurance (NHI) scheme have led to <u>errors</u> in insurance claims and much inefficiency.

   A. missteps

   B. accuracy

   C. correctness

3. For instance, <u>adhering to</u> all NHI regulations would require a patient to fill out more than 30 forms, relating to insurance claims, salary readjustment and the insurer's/claimant's name.

   A. abstaining from

   B. complying with

   C. refraining from

4. For instance, adhering to all NHI regulations would <u>require</u> a patient to fill out more than 30 forms, relating to insurance claims, salary readjustment and the insurer's/claimant's name.

   A. relinquish

   B. stipulate

   C. abdicate

5. With errors caused by <u>confusion</u> over forms, the NHI staff spends much time in handling errors and requesting insurers and claimants to correct erroneous information.

   A. tidiness

   B. chagrin

   C. systematization

6. With errors caused by confusion over forms, the NHI staff spends much time in handling errors and requesting insurers and claimants to correct <u>erroneous</u> information.

A. spurious

B. valid

C. accurate

7. Despite the enormous amount of administrative time and cost involved in handling these errors, this <u>growing</u> concern and its larger implications have not been addressed in the literature.

    A. receding

    B. mitigating

    C. augmented

8. Despite the enormous amount of administrative time and cost involved in handling these errors, this growing concern and its larger <u>implications</u> have not been addressed in the literature.

    A. speculations

    B. rebuttals

    C. negations

9. The inability to gradually reduce the amount of human resources involved in handling insurer and claimant errors and <u>simplify</u> administrative procedures as well as NHI forms will lead to higher operational costs.

    A. impede

    B. convolute

    C. abridge

10. In practice, telephone, fax or mail is used to correct such errors, subsequently creating <u>substantial</u> overhead and increasing the time spent by human resources.

    A. nugatory

    B. vast

    C. trifling

Situation 6

1. A young soldier with a high fever brought about by a <u>widespread</u> common cold presented himself to a physician, being otherwise physiologically healthy.

   A. finite

   B. hemmed in

   C. pervasive

2. A young soldier with a high fever brought about by a widespread common cold presented himself to a physician, being otherwise physiologically <u>healthy</u>.

   A. tainted

   B. restorative

   C. unwholesome

3. However, after his condition suddenly <u>deteriorated</u> after six days in the sickbay, he died in the intensive care unit (ICU) despite three days of emergency rescue procedures by medical personnel. The coroner's autopsy cited heart palsy as the cause of death.

   A. retrogressed

   B. ameliorated

   C. alleviated

4. However, after his condition suddenly deteriorated after six days in the sickbay, he died in the intensive care unit (ICU) despite three days of emergency rescue procedures by medical personnel. The coroner's autopsy <u>cited</u> heart palsy as the cause of death.

   A. desolated

   B. renounced

   C. exemplified

5. The actual cause of death remains unknown, and the coroner's report is merely a <u>formality</u> for family members in completing procedures to receive compensation

for death incurred from military duty.

    A. abnormality

    B. conventionality

    C. rarity

6. The actual cause of death remains unknown, and the coroner's report is merely a formality for family members in completing procedures to receive <u>compensation</u> for death incurred from military duty.

    A. restitution

    B. mulct

    C. amends

7. Medical institutions must be responsible for <u>instilling</u> in physicians a sense of professional ethics so that medical professionals can assume responsibility without the assigning of fault to a particular party.

    A. siphoning

    B. inseminating

    C. extirpating

8. Moreover, medical treatment involves a degree of <u>risk</u> such that even some management approaches cannot be applied.

    A. shoo-in

    B. prospect

    C. sure bet

9. Professional health care administrators not only encounter <u>resistance</u> from medical consumers, but also pose a potential threat to a patient's rights.

    A. acceptance

    B. receptivity

    C. intransigence

10. Under such circumstances, these administrators must occasionally make choices without <u>conferring</u> with many others.

    A. parleying

    B. sidestepping

    C. evading

Unit Four

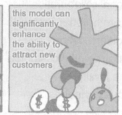

Summarizing the Results of a Project

方案結果的總結

1. Introduce the objective of your project.
   方案目標介紹
2. Describe the methodology of the project.
   方法論介紹
3. State the main results of the project.
   描述方案實行後會產生的主要成果
4. Describe the main contribution of the project to a particular field or sector.
   描述對特定領域或部門的貢獻

Vocabulary and related expressions

semiconductor equipment producers	半導體設備生產者
operating performance	營運表現
regression analysis	回歸分析
global ranking	全球排名
sales growth rate	業務成長率
net profit	淨利
most recent collaboration	最近期的合作
diverse promotional strategies	多變化的促銷策略
market differentiation	市場區別
identifying potential customers	識別潛在客戶
retain the loyalty	保持忠誠度
devise questionnaires	設計意見調查表
on-line gaming companies	線上遊戲公司
perceptions	看法
to grant commercial loan	給予商業貸款
clear guidelines	清楚的指導方針
intangible capital.	無形的資本
identify target customers	區分目標客戶
incurring of debts	陷於債務中
purchasing behavior	購買行為
reduces operating costs	減少營運費用
investment risk model	投資風險模式
SPSS statistical software SPSS	統計軟體
maintain their market competitiveness	保持市場競爭力
initiate timely financial reforms	開始實施適時的財務改革

Situation 1

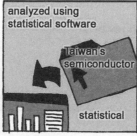

Situation 2

Situation 3

A

Write down the key points of the situations on the preceding page, while the instructor reads aloud the script from the Answer Key. Alternatively, students can listen online at www.chineseowl.idv.tw

Situation 1

_____

_____

_____

Situation 2

_____

_____

_____

Situation 3

_____

_____

_____

B Oral practice I

Based on the three situations in this unit, write three questions beginning with **What**, and answer them. The questions do not need to come directly from these situations.

Examples

What did our recent project analyze?
exactly how global market trends in the semiconductor industry influence the operating performance of Taiwan's semiconductor industry

What were publicly listed Taiwanese semiconductor manufacturers in information technology and electronics industries from 2002 to 2004 selected for?
as the sample in this study

1. _____

_____

2. _____

_____

3. _____

_____

C

Based on the three situations in this unit, write three questions beginning with **Why** and answer them. The questions do not need to come directly from these situations.

Examples

Why did our most recent collaboration develop a customer ranking model?
for analyzing the dynamic purchasing behavior of customers and identifying potential generators of bank revenues

Why was a data mining method, CRISP-DM, employed?
to determine how various purchasing activities are related and how many factors can be used to rank the value of a customer's relationship

1. _____

_____

2. _____

_____

3. _____

_____

D

Based on the three situations in this unit, write three questions beginning with *How*, and answer them. The questions do not need to come directly from these situations.

Examples

How was our recent project able to measure the value of the intellectual capital of on-line gaming companies?

by developing a novel index based on the analytic hierarchy process (AHP)

How was the intangible capital of on-line gaming companies measured?

by sending questionnaires to the managers of those companies and banks to find out which factors should be considered

1. _____

    _____

2. _____

    _____

3. _____

    _____

E Write questions that match the answers provided.

1. _____

_____

by regression analysis

2. _____

_____

to enhance the ability to identify, acquire and retain the loyalty and profitability of customers.

3. _____

_____

criteria to determine their intellectual capital

F Listening Comprehension I

Situation 1

1. How did the study determine the relationships between the B/B ratio and leading indicators of the composite index of Taiwan, the operational performance of the Taiwanese semiconductor industry and the semiconductor sector in Philadelphia?

   A. by factor analysis

   B. by the global B/B ratio

C. by regression analysis

2. How was the operating performance of Taiwan's semiconductor industry analyzed?

    A. using the proposed index

    B. using the B/B ratio on a monthly basis

    C. using statistical software

3. For what years were publicly listed Taiwanese semiconductor manufacturers in information technology and electronics industries selected as the sample in this study?

    A. From 2000 to 2002

    B. from 2002 to 2004

    C. from 2004 to 2006

4. What does the proposed index enable the semiconductor equipment producers in Japan to do?

    A. assess more accurately the global B/B ratio of semiconductor equipment producers in North America

    B. provide a valuable reference for stock market investors

    C. analyze global market trends in the semiconductor industry

5. What strategies can the proposed model help enterprise managers to devise?

    A. those for the operational performance of Taiwan's semiconductor industry

    B. those for an increase in the net profit after tax growth rate

    C. those for various economic cycles

Situation 2

1. Why were factors associated with customer relations and the customer life-cycle combined?

    A. to devise diverse promotional strategies

B. to construct an enhanced management model

C. to achieve market differentiation and effective management of customer relations

2. How was a data mining method, CRISP-DM, employed?

   A. by verifying and adjusting factors of the ranking module

   B. by ensuring that a company continues to provide quality services

   C. by combining the conventional means of data exploration with two mathematical calculations

3. Why can one use the proposed model to verify and adjust factors of the ranking module?

   A. to ensure that a company continues to provide quality services

   B. to identify potential generators of bank revenues

   C. to devise diverse promotional strategies

4. Why can the proposed customer ranking model significantly reduce promotional costs and allow sales staff to concentrate on identifying potential customers?

   A. because it can analyze the dynamic purchasing behavior of customers and identify potential generators of bank revenues\

   B. because it can devise diverse promotional strategies

   C. because it can be adopted to manage effectively customer relations

5. What can the proposed model significantly enhance?

   A. the ability to analyze current customer data

   B. the ability to attract new customers

   C. the ability to achieve market differentiation and effective management of customer relations

Situation 3

1. Why were questionnaires sent to managers of on-line gaming companies and banks?

    A. to measure the actual value of an on-line gaming company

    B. to find out which factors should be considered in measuring the intangible capital of their companies

    C. to understand which factors are deemed most important by them in determining the intellectual capital of on-line gaming companies

2. Why were the results considered based on the criteria applied by banks?

    A. to understand how on-line gaming companies measure their intangible capital

    B. to provide a valuable reference for banks when determining whether to grant commercial loans

    C. to measure the intellectual capital of a business

3. Why was content analysis performed?

    A. to enhance the conventionally used indexes and increase their accuracy

    B. to devise questionnaires on the components of intellectual capital

    C. to measure the value of the intellectual capital of on-line gaming companies

4. How does the proposed index provide a valuable reference for banks when determining whether to grant commercial loans?

    A. by measuring the value of the intellectual capital of on-line gaming companies

    B. by significantly reducing the likelihood of defaulted loans

    C. by providing on-line gaming companies with criteria to determine their intellectual capital

5. What do banking institutions need to understand?

    A. how to enhance the conventionally used indexes and increase their accuracy

    B. how on-line gaming companies measure their intangible capital

    C. how to measure the value of the intellectual capital of on-line gaming companies

G Reading Comprehension I

Select the word or expression whose meaning is closest to the meaning of the underlined word or expression in the following passages.

Situation 1

1. Based on an index of semiconductor equipment producers in Japan, our recent project <u>analyzed</u> exactly how global market trends in the semiconductor industry influence the operating performance of Taiwan's semiconductor industry.

   A. scanned

   B. leafed through

   C. scrutinized

2. Semiconductor equipment producers in Japan <u>announce</u> their B/B ratio on a monthly basis.

   A. concealed

   B. propound

   C. suppressed

3. The <u>operating</u> performance of Taiwan's semiconductor industry was then analyzed using statistical software.

   A. functioning

   B. haywire

   C. downtime

4. Next, the operating performance of the Taiwanese semiconductor industry was <u>determined</u> by factor analysis.

   A. protracted

   B. intent on

   C. remanded

5. Additionally, the relationships between the B/B ratio and <u>leading</u> indicators of the composite index of Taiwan, the operational performance of the Taiwanese semiconductor industry and the semiconductor sector in Philadelphia were determined by regression analysis.

A. menial

B. bottom rung

C. stellar

6. The proposed index enables the semiconductor equipment producers in Japan to <u>assess</u> more accurately the global B/B ratio of semiconductor equipment producers in North America based on the operational performance of Taiwan's semiconductor industry.

A. castigate

B. reproach

C. apprise

7. Additionally, the proposed index can determine whether semiconductor equipment producers in Japan can <u>exceed</u> 20% of the global B/B ratio of semiconductor equipment producers in North America.

A. surmount

B. flounder

C. blunder

8. Moreover, in addition to enabling entrepreneurs to understand more thoroughly the global ranking of Taiwan's semiconductor industry, the proposed index can provide a <u>valuable</u> reference not only for stock market investors, but also for enterprise managers who are devising appropriate strategies for various economic cycles.

A. paltry

B. cherished

C. bogus

9. A significantly positive relation between the sales growth rate and the net profit after tax growth rate indicates a significantly positive relationship between management performance and <u>fluctuations</u> of the business cycle in the semiconductor industry.

A. stability

B. uniformity

C. transitions

Situation 2

1. Our most recent collaboration developed a customer ranking model for analyzing the dynamic purchasing behavior of customers and <u>identifying</u> potential generators of bank revenues.

A. obscuring

B. diagnosing

C. enshrouding

2. The behavioral results can be used either to devise <u>diverse</u> promotional strategies or to customize products or services to meet consumer needs, subsequently achieving market differentiation and effective management of customer relations.

A. multifarious

B. parallel

C. conforming

3. Based on numerous available customer data, a data mining method, CRISP-DM, was employed, in which the conventional means of data exploration was combined with two mathematical calculations (decision tree and category nerve) to determine how various purchasing activities are related and how many factors can be used to <u>rank</u> the value of a customer's relationship.

A. disband

B. repel

C. align

4. Factors associated with customer relations and the customer life cycle were then combined to construct an <u>enhanced</u> management model.

A. impaired

B. augmented

C. defiled

5. According to our results, the proposed customer ranking model can be adopted to <u>manage</u> effectively customer relations, significantly reducing promotional costs and allowing sales staff to concentrate on identifying potential customers.

A. bollix

B. superintend

C. agitate

6. By <u>incorporating</u> CRIPS-DM, the proposed model can efficiently analyze current customer data, enabling marketing staff to understand customers more closely; identify potential niche markets and optimize the relationship between the customer and the institution.

A. coalescing

B. dichotomizing

C. sundering

7. The proposed model can be used to <u>verify</u> and adjust factors of the ranking module to ensure that a company continues to provide quality services.

A. disprove

B. invalidate

C. authenticate

8. While the customer's value in the customer relationship management system can be determined, this model can significantly enhance the ability to <u>attract</u> new customers.

A. repulse

B. solicit

C. repel

9. Furthermore, it can be used in other business sectors to enhance the ability to identify, acquire and <u>retain</u> the loyalty and profitability of customers.

A. preserve

B. dissipate

C. intersperse

Situation 3

1. Our recent project developed a novel index based on the analytic hierarchy process (AHP) to measure the value of the <u>intellectual</u> capital of on-line gaming companies.

A. ignoramus

B. illiterate

C. highbrow

2. Content analysis was performed to <u>devise</u> questionnaires on the components of intellectual capital.

A. eradicate

B. decimate

C. contrive

3. The questionnaires were sent to the managers of on-line gaming companies and banks to <u>find out</u> which factors should be considered in measuring the intangible capital of their companies.

A. ensconce

B. distinguish

C. burrow

4. Next, AHP was used to understand which factors are <u>deemed</u> most important by the managers of on-line gaming companies and banks in determining the intellectual capital of on-line gaming companies.

A. detested

B. considered

C. rebuffed

5. By using AHP, the weight (relative importance) of each intellectual capital variable was evaluated based on the <u>perceptions</u> of managers of on-line gaming companies and banks.

A. chasm

B. abyss

C. sensations

6. The results were considered based on the criteria applied by banks to <u>measure</u> the intellectual capital of a business.

A. proliferate

B. manifold

C. calibrate

7. Moreover, exactly how banks and on-line game companies <u>differ</u> when measuring intellectual capital was determined using Principal Component Analysis.

A. deviate

B. jibe

C. coadjute

8. Based on the results, the proposed index provides on-line gaming companies with criteria to determine their intellectual capital, providing a valuable reference for banks when determining whether to <u>grant</u> commercial loans.

A. sign on

B. remonstrate

C. dissent

9. The ability to measure the actual value of an on-line gaming company will significantly reduce the <u>likelihood</u> of defaulted loans.

A. incongruity

B. ludicrousness

C. fighting chance

10. Additionally, on-line gaming companies will have <u>clear</u> guidelines regarding how banks measure intellectual capital, ultimately enhancing their competitiveness.

A. opaque

B. palpable

C. dubious

11. Moreover, the proposed index of intellectual capital in this growth sector can enhance the conventionally used indexes and increase their <u>accuracy</u>.

A. meticulousness

B. imprecision

C. solecism

12. The results of this study provide a valuable reference for banking institutions that need to understand how on-line gaming companies measure their <u>intangible</u> capital.

A. touchable

B. discernible

C. evanescent

H

Common elements in summarizing the results of a project include the following:

1. Introduce the objective of your project. 方案目標介紹
2. Describe the methodology of the project. 方法論介紹
3. State the main results of the project. 描述方案實行後會產生的主要成果
4. Describe the main contribution of the project to a particular field or sector. 描述對特定領域或部門的貢獻

1. Introduce the objective of your project. 方案目標介紹

◎ Our recent project analyzed the factors that influence operational expenses of a hospital, e.g., equipment investment, peripheral consumptive materials, personnel costs and utilities, by integrating the analytic hierarchy process and extension theory to optimize decision making.

◎ Our most recent project investigated why critically ill patients at regional hospitals in Taiwan transfer to larger medical centers in order to more thoroughly understand the anticipated medical services that their families expect.

◎ Our recent project developed a novel prediction model to identify the turnover rate of customers in the medical sector. More specifically, the proposed model incorporates a novel set of management strategies that emphasize customer retention within the medical sector to strengthen a hospital's competitiveness.

2. Describe the methodology of the project. 方法論介紹

◎ Location-related factors were identified through an exhaustive literature review and consultation with experts in the field. Exactly how these individual factors are related to each other was then identified through use of AHP. Next, a questionnaire was submitted to hospital procurement professionals to examine the correct factors. Additionally, all factors involved in selecting the target population and factories and stores were analyzed using AHP, with the optimal factories and stores chosen based on those factors.

◎ Factors of patient transferal were identified based on statistics from regional hospitals in Taiwan. A questionnaire based on customer relations management (CRM) was then issued to families of critically ill patients to determine anticipated medical services. Based on those results, an APH methodology was formed.

◎ A database containing pertinent hospital patient data was utilized by applying a data mining method to identify the factors associated with customer turnover rate. A data mining approach that incorporates various data analysis tools was also adopted to discover interesting trends and relationships among various data sets. Pertinent literature was then reviewed to confirm the reliability of variables in the database. Next, questionnaires were sent to hospital administrators regarding the level of customer satisfaction. Additionally, distinct consumer groups were identified using cluster analysis to distinguish between all consumer groups. Moreover, neural networks were used to enhance the model accuracy, with those results subsequently analyzed.

3. State the main results of the project. 描述方案實行後會產生的主要成果

◎ Analysis results of this project can be used as a model for selecting the most qualified outsourcing company. Adopting the AHP-based assessment criteria can enable hospitals to generate revenues and save on equipment investment, peripheral consumptive materials, personnel costs and utilities. Decision making based on the AHP criteria can provide a valuable reference for public hospitals that seek outsourcing partners.

◎ According to our results, the proposed CRM-based approach can identify how the medical services anticipated by families of critically ill patients differ from actual ones provided by regional hospitals, with the objective of ultimately reducing this discrepancy and patient transferal rate to larger medical centers.

◎ According to our results, the proposed prediction model can be adopted to design and implement precautionary measures towards customer turnover rates in related fields. In addition to providing the medical sector with more accurate guidelines on patient retention and marketing planning, the proposed model can greatly facilitate hospitals in providing high quality and flexible health care services that will ultimately their public image with markedly improved relations with patients. Additionally, besides identifying the major factors underlying customer turnover rate, the proposed model can offer feasible strategies to cope with this dilemma and achieve management goals.

Moreover, the proposed model can contribute to efforts to maintain customers in the highly competitive medical market sector as well as provide a valuable reference for healthcare managers in enhancing customer relations.

4. Describe the main contribution of the project to a particular field or sector. 描述對特定領域或部門的貢獻

◎ In addition to enabling Department of Health authorities to understand the full implications of outsourcing, the AHP-based assessment criteria can help public hospitals to understand the nature of problems that arise during outsourcing when constructing a deluxe health examination center.

◎ While providing regional hospital administrators with an effective means of determining the anticipated services of critically ill patients and their families, the proposed approach can highlight the importance of medical quality in emergency care, eventually increasing hospital revenues and establishing high quality emergency medical centers among regional hospitals in Taiwan.

◎ Importantly, the customer retention strategy can reduce the operational costs of hospitals and increase the number of overall patients. Increasing the number of overall patients would not only increase subsidized revenues from the National Health Insurance scheme, but also increase their competitive edge in the intensely competitive medical sector..

In the space below, summarize the results of a project in your company aimed at developing or promoting a particular product or service.

_____

_____

_____

_____

_____

_____

_____

_____

Look at the following examples of summarizing the results of a project.

Our recent project developed a novel 4P-based marketing strategy for the local cosmetics sector within Taiwan's biotech industry by considering consumer needs under the principles of product, price, promotion and place. This strategy can enable managers in the cosmetics sector to more thoroughly understand consumer preferences not only by learning how to identify and target potential customers efficiently, but also by establishing a retention strategy to maintain loyal customers and attract new ones. A questionnaire was submitted to cosmetic manufacturers on the most appropriate marketing method, followed by factor analysis of those results associated with such an approach that adopts 4P principles. According to our results, adopting this 4P-based marketing strategy can enable local cosmetic manufacturers to increase their market share in related products and services. The proposed strategy can also provide a more objective outcome for members when making related decisions than conventional approaches can, thus accelerating the marketing process. In addition to demonstrating the feasibility of using the 4P marketing strategy in order to increase consumer satisfaction, the proposed strategy can provide cosmetic manufacturers with valuable information for use in a customer database, thus enabling sales marketing strategies to reach their target audience. In addition to encouraging product innovation, the 4P-based marketing strategy can provide Taiwan's biotech industry with clear guidelines on how to equip management in the local cosmetics sector with appropriate and efficient marketing policies that will ultimately decrease operating costs and enhance competitiveness. Moreover, the proposed method can reveal how the biotechnology industry incorporates 4P concepts, thus clarifying the behavioral patterns of cosmetics customers.

●

Our most recent project developed a flexible and accurate fuzzy theory-based AHP method that applies the fuzzy theory to the business ratings of logistics centers, providing corporate managers with an effective criterion to assess the management practices of logistics centers and the quality of services delivered. In doing so, enterprises can identify the specialties of logistics centers and construct an effective criterion for administrators to evaluate the effectiveness of logistics centers based on a clear criteria. A questionnaire was designed based on interviews with managers of logistics centers. Data obtained from those interviews regarding service quality were then analyzed using the AHP method and fuzzy theory. Next, service quality of logistics centers was determined using AHP-based criteria. Additionally, quality of service was assessed based on the corporate expectations, enabling us to select the best logistics center from available options. Moreover, customer service and other special services were incorporated into efforts to achieve customer satisfaction. According to our results, the proposed fuzzy theory-based AHP method can enable local enterprises to evaluate the effectiveness of logistics centers based on a criterion index, subsequently increasing corporate competitiveness and efficiency by 25% while reducing personnel costs by 10%. Additionally, the proposed method provides an effective means of assessing the quality of services provided by logistics centers, thus offering enterprise managers the ability to enhance the quality of services and enhance management procedures, ultimately enhancing the global competitiveness of Taiwanese enterprises by providing managers with clear guidelines for evaluating their suppliers.

●

Our most recent project developed a feasible forecasting method to estimate the growth of medical and health care expenditures as well as pharmaceutical units in Taiwan. Medical and health care expenditure-related data during the period 1999 to 2002 were obtained from the Central Region Office of the Budget, Accounting and Statistics, Executive Yuan. Data on pharmaceutical units were then obtained from the 2003 Annual Report of the Department of Health. Based on data from those sources, the GM (1, N) model of the Grey theory was applied for forecasting purposes. According to our results, the proposed forecasting method can accurately estimate medical and health care expenditures as well as the number of pharmacies to be established in Taiwan from 2003 to 2005. The proposed method can also identify how the medical and health care share of household consumption is related to the number of pharmacies. The results of this study can provide a valuable reference for both governmental authorities in formulating policies and pharmaceutical managers in developing competitive marketing strategies.

Situation 4

Situation 5

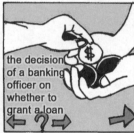

Situation 6

I

Write down the key points of the situations on the preceding page, while the instructor reads aloud the script from the Answer Key. Alternatively, students can listen online at www.chineseowl.idv.tw

Situation 4

_____

_____

_____

Situation 5

_____

_____

_____

Situation 6

_____

_____

_____

J Oral practice II

Based on the three situations in this unit, write three questions beginning with **Why**, and answer them. The questions do not need to come directly from these situations.

Examples

Why did our research group develop a novel evaluation method recently?

to identify target credit card customers

Why was pertinent literature reviewed?

to identify the characteristics of credit card customers and the effect of their lifestyles on their purchasing behavior

1. _____

   _____

2. _____

   _____

3. _____

   _____

K

Based on the three situations in this unit, write three questions beginning with *How*, and answer them. The questions do not need to come directly from these situations.

Examples

How did our most recent project attempt to reduce the defaulted loan burden of small financial institutions?

through developing a credit risk assessment model by analyzing a mass of data or by detecting concealed purchasing models

How were attributes of each customer account identified?

by applying highly *effective data mining approaches*

1. _____

   _____

2. _____

   _____

3. _____

   _____

L

Based on the three situations in this unit, write three questions beginning with *What*, and answer them. The questions do not need to come directly from these situations.

Examples

What is the main feature of the investment risk model that our group developed recently?

It analyzes the features of credit cooperatives in Taiwan.

What was the purpose of designing a questionnaire for loan officers at credit cooperatives?

to accumulate relevant loan information and background information about credit cooperatives

1. _____

_____

2. _____

_____

3. _____

_____

M Write questions that match the answers provided.

1. _____

   _____

   characteristics associated with the lifestyles of such customers and the factors that contribute to their incurring of debts

2. _____

   _____

   for all customers in the bank database

3. _____

   _____

   by directly focusing on market developments that previous financial research neglected

N Listening Comprehension II

Situation 4

1. Where were the questionnaires sent?

   A. to our research group

   B. to banking institutions

   C. to customers

2. How was cluster analysis used?

    A. to lower operating costs and credit risk

    B. to classify credit card customers into different categories

    C. to identify target credit card customers

3. What are banking institutions attempting to do?

    A. identify the characteristics of credit card customers and the effect of their lifestyles on their purchasing behavior

    B. identify target credit card customers

    C. identify desirable credit card customers

4. What does the proposed evaluation method provide a valuable reference for?

    A. the lifestyles of credit card customers and the factors that contribute to their incurring of debts

    B. banking institutions that are attempting to identify desirable credit card customers

    C. efforts to classify credit card customers into different categories

5. What can the evaluation method identify?

    A. a marketing strategy to attract target customers

    B. characteristics associated with the lifestyles of credit card customers

    C. target credit card customers

Situation 5

1. What was established for all customers in the bank database?

    A. the defaulted loan burden of small financial institutions

    B. data mining applications in financial institutions

    C. credit ranking criteria based on a decision tree

2. How were highly effective data mining approaches applied?

    A. to reduce operating costs by enhancing process flow

B. to identify the attributes of each customer account

C. to reduce the defaulted loan burden of small financial institutions

3. How does the credit risk assessment model reduce operating costs?

A. by reducing the defaulted loan burden of small financial institutions

B. by analyzing a mass of data

C. by enhancing process flow

4. What does each customer account include?

A. effective marketing strategies based on acquired data

B. overdraft records, outstanding loans and income level

C. potential data mining applications in financial institutions

5. What is the proposed model highly promising for?

A. concealed purchasing models

B. small financial institutions

C. other industrial applications

Situation 6

1. What have previous studies not addressed?

A. the features of credit cooperatives in Taiwan

B. financial reforms that will enhance the role of cooperatives in the financial market

C. the financial problems of credit cooperatives

2. How can credit cooperatives maintain their market competitiveness?

A. by initiating timely financial reforms

B. by identifying potential defaulted loans

C. by making good loan decisions

3. What does the investment risk model analyze?

A. limitations of previous financial research and the Experience Rule

B. the ability of loan officers in banks and credit cooperatives to identify potentially defaulting loans

C. the features of credit cooperatives in Taiwan

4. How were features of credit cooperatives analyzed?

A. using factor analysis

B. using cluster analysis

C. using MDS

5. What can the proposed investment risk model enable loan officers in banks and credit cooperatives to do?

A. identify potentially defaulting loans

B. initiate timely financial reforms that will enhance the role of cooperatives in the financial market

C. accumulate relevant loan information and background information about credit cooperatives

O Reading Comprehension II

Select the word or expression whose meaning is closest to the meaning of the underlined word or expression in the following passages.

Situation 4

1. Our research group recently developed a <u>novel</u> evaluation method to identify target credit card customers.

A. venerable

B. neoteric

C. patriarchal

2. Our research group recently developed a novel evaluation method to identify target credit card customers.

A. germane

B. impertinent

C. irrelevant

3. The method incorporates characteristics associated with the lifestyles of such customers and the factors that contribute to their incurring of debts.

A. obviates

B. precludes

C. coalesces

4. The method incorporates characteristics associated with the lifestyles of such customers and the factors that contribute to their incurring of debts.

A. ostracizing of

B. proscribing of

C. accumulation of

5. Pertinent literature was reviewed to identify the characteristics of credit card customers and the effect of their lifestyles on their purchasing behavior.

A. extraneous

B. apropos

C. inapplicable

6. Pertinent literature was reviewed to identify the characteristics of credit card customers and the effect of their lifestyles on their purchasing behavior.

A. merchandising

B. procuring

C. peddling

7. Questionnaires were sent to customers to determine their personality and lifestyle, and their relationships to their purchasing behavior.

A. reciprocations

B. retorts

C. queries

8. Questionnaires were sent to customers to determine their personality and lifestyle, and their relationships to their purchasing <u>behavior</u>.

A. demeanor

B. anomaly

C. deviation

9. Based on the results, cluster analysis was performed to <u>classify</u> credit card customers into different categories.

A. dissipate

B. collocate

C. propagate

10. The proposed evaluation method provides a valuable reference for banking institutions that attempt to identify <u>desirable</u> credit card customers, eventually leading not only to the development of a marketing strategy to attract such target customers, but also to the lowering of operating costs and credit risk.

A. repellent

B. odious

C. covetable

Situation 5

1. Our most recent project developed a credit risk assessment model by analyzing a mass of data or by detecting <u>concealed</u> purchasing models, to reduce the defaulted loan burden of small financial institutions.

A. divulged

B. ulterior

C. transpired

2. Our most recent project developed a credit risk assessment model by analyzing a mass of data or by detecting concealed purchasing models, to reduce the defaulted loan <u>burden</u> of small financial institutions.

A. repose

B. equanimity

C. hindrance

3. A database of customer data was constructed, to which highly effective data mining approaches were applied to <u>identify</u> the attributes of each customer account, including overdraft records, outstanding loans and income level.

A. ensconce

B. peg

C. eclipse

4. A database of customer data was constructed, to which highly effective data mining approaches were applied to identify the attributes of each customer account, including overdraft records, <u>outstanding</u> loans and income level.

A. propitious

B. delinquent

C. opportune

5. Credit <u>ranking</u> criteria based on a decision tree were then established for all customers in the bank database.

A. trifling

B. evanescent

C. pecking order

6. Credit ranking criteria based on a decision tree were then <u>established</u> for all customers in the bank database.

A. endowed

B. abrogated

C. eradicated

7. In addition to greatly <u>facilitating</u> the decision of a banking officer on whether to grant a loan, the credit risk assessment model also reduces operating costs by enhancing process flow.

A. contravened

B. hamstringed

C. expedited

8. In addition to greatly facilitating the decision of a banking officer on whether to grant a loan, the credit risk assessment model also reduces operating costs by enhancing process <u>flow</u>.

A. drought

B. desiccation

C. flux

9. Moreover, the proposed model <u>paves the way for</u> other potential data mining applications in financial institutions, such as more thoroughly satisfying customers through more effective marketing strategies based on acquired data.

A. facilitates

B. stonewalls

C. stymies

10. The proposed model is highly <u>promising</u> for other industrial applications.

A. up-and-coming

B. exorbitant

C. restraining

Situation 6

1. Our group recently developed an investment risk model that analyzes the <u>features</u> of credit cooperatives in Taiwan.

   A. vagueness

   B. ambiguities

   C. attributes

2. A questionnaire was designed for loan officers at credit cooperatives to accumulate <u>relevant</u> loan information and background information about credit cooperatives.

   A. congruent

   B. superseded

   C. anachronistic

3. Features of credit cooperatives were then <u>analyzed</u> using factor analysis. Next, factors that influence whether or not financial officers approve loans were analyzed using SPSS statistical software.

   A. disdained

   B. let slide

   C. confabbed

4. Additionally, <u>potential</u> defaulted loans are identified using MDS.

   A. incompetent

   B. quiescent

   C. maladroit

5. Moreover, factors that <u>distinguish</u> credit cooperatives from banks were analyzed using cluster analysis.

   A. muddy

   B. demarcate

   C. obscure

6. According to our results, the proposed investment risk model can enable loan officers in banks and credit cooperatives to identify potentially defaulting loans, since the method is derived by directly focusing on market developments that previous financial research <u>neglected</u>.

A. emblazoned

B. rebuffed

C. showcased

7. Additionally, whereas previous studies have not addressed the financial problems of credit cooperatives, the proposed model can more thoroughly <u>elucidate</u> the features and the role of credit cooperatives by identifying factors that enhance their performance.

A. misconstrue

B. enucleate

C. distort

8. In addition to compensating for <u>limitations</u> of previous financial research and the Experience Rule, the proposed model provides a valuable means of understanding current developments in financial markets, as well as helps credit cooperatives to make good loan decisions to maintain their market competitiveness.

A. protractions

B. elongations

C. impediments

9. In addition to compensating for limitations of previous financial research and the Experience Rule, the proposed model provides a <u>valuable</u> means of understanding current developments in financial markets, as well as helps credit cooperatives to make good loan decisions to maintain their market competitiveness.

A. priceless

B. inutile

C. ignoble

10. Moreover, the proposed method provides a valuable reference for the Taiwanese Government to initiate <u>timely</u> financial reforms that will enhance the role of cooperatives in the financial market.

A. punctual

B. laggard

C. procrastinating

Unit Five

Describing Recent Technical Accomplishments in a Company

描述公司最新的科技成就

1. Briefly describe the role of a company in a particular sector.
   描述公司在特定領域或部門的角色
2. Describe a unique feature of the organization in developing a particular technology.
   描述一個研發特殊科技公司的特色
3. Cite an example of a recent endeavor.
   舉一個最近的實例
4. Summarize the technical accomplishments of the organization in a particular sector.
   總結公司研發的特殊科技對特定領域的貢獻

Vocabulary and related expressions

pioneered the development of	為某發展做先驅
upgrading existing technologies	提升現行的科技
a wealth of experience	經驗豐富
aggressively pursuing its missions	富野心的進行其任務
state-of-the-art facilities	最先進的設施
strong technical capabilities	強有力的科技才能
multidisciplinary approaches	有關各種學問的路徑
technical support services	科技支援服務
technology expertise	科技專門知識
repetitive experiments	反覆的實驗
virtual environment	虛擬的環境
unnecessary medical expenses	不必要的醫療花費
greatly accelerate the rate	大大地加快速率
infringement of their privacy	侵犯他們的隱私
counterfeiting	假冒的
information theft	資訊盜竊
resource recovery	資源重獲
a more secure means of technological innovation	更安全的科技革新方式
difficulty in integrating	使合併的困難
administrative errors	行政錯誤
patient satisfaction	病人滿意
a high success rate	高的成功率
advanced support capabilities	高等的支援能力
reluctance	不情願
teaching and a research facility	教育及研究設備
prescription medicine	處方上開的藥
conveniently accessed by	藉由……而有方便接近的機會

Situation 1

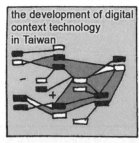

the development of digital context technology in Taiwan

35 employees, 75% have a bachelor's degree or higher

takes multidisciplinary approaches to its technical support services

Situation 2

human factor engineering applications in automotive safety testing

driving simulation systems

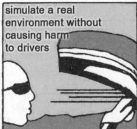

simulate a real environment without causing harm to drivers

the installation of warning or reflective signs along roadways

Situation 3

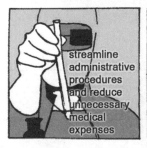

streamline administrative procedures and reduce unnecessary medical expenses

the NHIB strictly protects the confidentiality of patient information

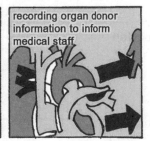

recording organ donor information to inform medical staff

A

Write down the key points of the situations on the preceding page, while the instructor reads aloud the script from the Answer Key. Alternatively, students can listen online at www.chineseowl.idv.tw

Situation 1

_____

_____

_____

Situation 2

_____

_____

_____

Situation 3

_____

_____

_____

B Oral practice I

Based on the three situations in this unit, write three questions beginning with *How*, and answer them. The questions do not need to come directly from these situations.

Examples

How does GameQ strive to enhance on-line games?

by upgrading existing technologies and strengthening its 3D animation skills

How is the company's commitment of 1/4 of its annual operational budget to R&D reflected?

by a wealth of experience that GameQ staff members with strong research capabilities have accumulated

1. _____

   _____

2. _____

   _____

3. _____

   _____

C

Based on the three situations in this unit, write three questions beginning with *What*, and answer them. The questions do not need to come directly from these situations.

Examples

What do human factor engineering applications in automotive safety testing heavily rely on?

advanced driving simulation systems

What can the interactive fixed-based driving simulator analyze?

an individual's driving behavior

1. _____

_____

2. _____

_____

3. _____

_____

D

Based on the three situations in this unit, write three questions beginning with **Why**, and answer them. The questions do not need to come directly from these situations.

Examples

Why did the National Health Insurance Bureau (NHIB) begin issuing IC cards in January 2004?

to streamline administrative procedures and reduce unnecessary medical expenses

Why do IC cards greatly accelerate the rate at which services are provided?

to maintain an efficient information database system

1. _____

   _____

2. _____

   _____

3. _____

   _____

E Write questions that match the answers provided.

1. _____

_____

five

2. _____

_____

to control their speed

3. _____

_____

an individual's medical history

F Listening Comprehension I

1. How does GameQ strive to enhance on-line games?

   A. by upgrading existing technologies

   B. strengthening its 3D animation skills

   C. both A and B

2. What country dominates the Asian Pacific market in online games?

   A. Taiwan

   B. Japan

   C. Korea

3. In what area will GameQ continuously upgrade its technology expertise to improve its market position?

   A. in 3D animation

   B. in its annual operational budget to R&D

   C. state-of-the-art facilities and the latest commercially available equipment and software

4. What does the on-line gaming sector rely heavily on?

   A. the larger Chinese on-line gaming market

   B. the knowledge and skills of its staff

   C. an Object-Oriented server system with dynamic program module loading

5. How can one characterize Taiwan's on-line gaming sector?

   A. Increasingly stagnant

   B. increasingly redundant

   C. increasingly competitive

Situation 2

1. How is virtual reality technology a convenient means of gathering data using scientific means?

   A. by analyzing an individual's driving behavior as it can efficiently accumulate the results of repetitive experiments

   B. by increasing the comfort of a driving environment through necessary improvements

   C. by simulating a real environment without causing harm to drivers

2. What do advanced driving simulation systems heavily rely on?

   A. appropriate roadway patterns and useful traffic control measures

   B. human factor engineering applications in automotive safety testing

   C. necessary improvements such as the installation of warning or reflective signs along roadways

3. How can one further reduce traffic accidents?

   A. by the alignment of freeway with buffer zones

   B. by creating a virtual environment that convinces individuals that they are actually driving in a real environment

   C. by not turning too late and colliding into traffic islands

4. How can the driving simulation system help to increase the comfort of a driving environment?

   A. by reducing the likelihood of a traffic accident if a convenient and comfortable driving environment can be provided

   B. analyze an individual's driving behavior as it can efficiently accumulate the results of repetitive experiments

   C. by making necessary improvements such as the installation of warning or reflective signs along roadways

5. How are drivers able to avoid accidents from turning too late and colliding into traffic islands?

   A. owing to the ability to identify danger areas that drivers encounter

   B. owing to the interactive fixed-based driving simulator developed at the Intelligent Transportation System Center

   C. owing to reflective warning signs that can remind them of potential roadway danger

Situation 3

1. What is a unique feature of the IC card system developed at the National Health Insurance Bureau?

   A. It greatly simplifies the processing of very large amounts of patient-related data.

B. Individuals can choose whether to list specific ailments on their IC card.

C. It strictly protects the confidentiality of patient information.

2. How is confidentiality of patient information ensured?

A. by registering medical data on an individual's IC card

B. by legislation on the protection thereof

C. by recording organ donor information to inform medical staff

3. What does the IC card NOT contain?

A. an individual's medical history

B. organ donor information

C. the latest information security measures

4. Why did the IC card begin recording organ donor information?

A. to greatly simplify the processing of very large amounts of patient-related data

B. to maintain an efficient information database system

C. to inform medical staff whether a certain organ is available in emergency situations

5. Why do IC cards exploit the latest information security measures?

A. to prevent counterfeiting or information theft

B. to streamline administrative procedures and reduce unnecessary medical expenses

C. to access this information through patients' confidential IC cards

G Reading Comprehension I

Pick the work or expression whose meaning is closest to the meaning of the underlined word or expression in the following passages.

Situation 1

1. GameQ On-line Gaming Company has <u>pioneered</u> the development of digital context technology in Taiwan.

   A. retrogress

   B. ebb

   C. instigated

2. Besides providing online services, GameQ strives to enhance on-line games by upgrading existing technologies and strengthening its 3D animation skills to become <u>competitive</u> in an Asian Pacific market that is dominated by Korean firms.

   A. lethargic

   B. emulous

   C. indolent

3. Beyond the Asian Pacific region, <u>sights</u> are set on the larger Chinese on-line gaming market, as well as on North American and European consumers. Of GameQ's nearly 35 employees, 75% have a bachelor's degree or higher, with an average of five years' professional experience in the field.

   A. pipe dreams

   B. objectives

   C. chicanery

4. These figures reflect a <u>wealth</u> of experience that GameQ staff with strong research capabilities have accumulated, as evidenced by the company's commitment of 1/4 of its annual operational budget to R&D.

   A. slim pickings

   B. exiguousness

   C. plethora

5. While aggressively <u>pursuing</u> its missions, GameQ has established five divisions - Game Design, Programming and Coding Design, Artistic Design, Music Design and R&D.

A. allaying

B. striving for

C. receding

6. As the company's largest division, R&D maintains <u>state-of-the-art</u> facilities and the latest commercially available equipment and software.

A. obsolete

B. old hat

C. precocious

7. As part of the information technology industry, the on-line gaming sector relies heavily on the knowledge and skills of its staff. GameQ is no <u>exception</u>, constantly encouraging staff to pursue further education and frequently attend training sessions on the latest technological developments in the field.

A. boiler plate

B. anomaly

C. garden variety

8. The strong technical capabilities that GameQ has developed so far include an Object-Oriented server system with dynamic program module loading, a stream (TCP/IP)-based communication model in systems operations, data-driven game development capabilities, high-performing 2D rendering capabilities based on the incorporation of 3D <u>accelerated</u> hardware and a message based communication protocol with error tolerance.

A. velocious

B. plodding

C. banausic

185

9. Furthermore, the company applies <u>multidisciplinary</u> approaches to its technical support services.

A. heterogeneous

B. undeviating

C. homogeneous

10. In summary, as Taiwan's on-line gaming sector becomes increasingly competitive, GameQ will continuously <u>upgrade</u> its technology expertise in 3D animation to improve its market position.

A. disparage

B. denigrate

C. boost

Situation 2

1. Human factor engineering applications in automotive safety testing heavily rely on advanced driving <u>simulation</u> systems.

A. divergence

B. deviation

C. replication

2. A notable example is the <u>interactive</u> fixed-based driving simulator developed at the Intelligent Transportation System Center of National Cheng Kung University.

A. desolate

B. requited

C. eremitic

3. This simulator can analyze an individual's driving behavior as it can efficiently accumulate the results of <u>repetitive</u> experiments.

A. sporadic

B. incessant

C. spasmodic

4. Performing repetitive experiments can identify <u>danger</u> areas that drivers encounter.

A. impregnability

B. sanctuary

C. precipice

5. Additionally, the driving simulator system creates a <u>virtual</u> environment that convinces individuals that they are actually driving in a real environment.

A. tacit

B. veritable

C. incarnate

6. Virtual reality technology can thus simulate a real environment without causing harm to drivers, making it a <u>convenient</u> means of gathering data using scientific means ultimately to enhance automotive safety.

A. accommodating

B. malapropos

C. incongruous

7. This simulation system helps drivers to control their speed, as well as reduces the likelihood of a traffic accident if a convenient and <u>comfortable</u> driving environment can be provided through appropriate roadway patterns and useful traffic control measures.

A. grieving

B. vexatious

C. snug

8. Traffic accidents can be further reduced by the <u>alignment</u> of freeway with buffer zones to allow rapid traffic flow without exceeding the speed limit.

A. asymmetry

B. calibration

C. disparity

9. Some accidents caused by braking or turning too slowly can be prevented if the curb radius is further increased. Reflective warning signs can remind drivers of potential roadway danger, enabling them to <u>avoid</u> accidents from turning too late and colliding into traffic islands.

   A. flout

   B. desist

   C. repel

10. In summary, the driving simulation system can help increase the <u>comfort</u> of a driving environment by making necessary improvements such as the installation of warning or reflective signs along roadways.

    A. repose

    B. inquietude

    C. nuisance

Situation 3

1. The National Health Insurance Bureau (NHIB) began issuing IC cards in January 2004 to <u>streamline</u> administrative procedures and reduce unnecessary medical expenses.

   A. intersperse

   B. strew

   C. converge

2. The IC card system greatly <u>simplifies</u> the processing of very large amounts of patient-related data.

   A. obscure

   B. elucidates

C. convolutes

3. To maintain an efficient information database system, IC cards greatly <u>accelerate</u> the rate at which services are provided.

A. slacken

B. impede

C. rev up

4. The NHIB strictly protects the <u>confidentiality</u> of patient information, ensured by legislation on the protection thereof.

A. veracity

B. fraternization

C. frankness

5. For individuals who are concerned with <u>infringement</u> of their privacy through the IC card system, the IC card does not contain an individual's medical history.

A. compliance

B. contravention

C. acquiescence

6. Additionally, IC cards <u>exploit</u> the latest information security measures to prevent counterfeiting or information theft.

A. renounce

B. vacate

C. beguile

7. With medical data registered on an individual's IC card, physicians must <u>access</u> this information through their own confidential IC card, further ensuring security.

A. extirpate

B. expunge

C. corral

8. As a unique feature of this system, individuals can choose whether to list specific <u>ailments</u> on their IC card.

   A. characteristics

   B. maladies

   C. attributes

9. As of November, 2004, the IC card began recording organ donor information to <u>inform</u> medical staff whether a certain organ is available in emergency situations.

   A. illuminate

   B. hoodwink

   C. delude

H

Common elements in describing recent technical accomplishments in a company include the following elements:

1. Briefly describe the role of a company in a particular sector.
   描述公司在特定領域或部門的角色
2. Describe a unique feature of the organization in developing a particular technology.
   描述一個研發特殊科技公司的特色
3. Cite an example of a recent endeavor. 舉一個最近的實例
4. Summarize the technical accomplishments of the organization in a particular sector.
   總結公司研發的特殊科技對特定領域的貢獻

1. Briefly describe the role of a company in a particular sector. 描述公司在特定領域或部門的角色

 Among the commercial enterprises already involved in establishing housing developments for the elderly include RUENTEX Group, Formosa Plastics Group and

CHI MEI Corporation. In particular, the RUENTEX Group has, since 1977, developed strong capabilities in construction, machinery and instrumentation, interior and exterior design, as well as sound management practices.

◎ Located inside of National Chiao Tung University near Hsinchu Science-based Industrial Park, National Nano Device Laboratories (NDL) belongs to a framework of six National Science Council-sponsored research facilities.

◎ As a leading cord blood bank in Taiwan and the safest cord blood cryopreservation facility in Asia, Sino Cell Technologies (SCT) derives its name from "regenerative destiny". Established in 2001, SCT provides advanced processing of cord blood stem cells and storage facilities. Headed by a board of directors comprising renowned physicians, bioscience experts and corporate leaders, SCT is headquartered in Taipei, along with fully-staffed branch offices island wide in Taipei, Hsinchu, Taichung and Kaohsiung. Additionally, SCT's laboratories inside of the Food Industry Research and Development Institute (FIRDI) receive, process, test, and store cord blood stem cell specimens.

2. Describe a unique feature of the organization in developing a particular technology. 描述一個研發特殊科技公司的特色

◎ As the architectural sector for real estate purposes has a vertically and horizontally integrated enterprise structure, the RUENTEX Group utilizes its rich professional and technical expertise in designing luxury residential accommodations with special considerations for the elderly.

◎ Originally established in 1988 as National Sub Micrometer Element Laboratory, NDL trains professionals for careers in the semiconductor industry, facilitates academic research in semiconductor materials and manufacturing as well as develops novel nano-element technologies. For instance, in 1992, construction of a 6 inch silicon wafer clean room provided academic researchers with a novel environment for researching semiconductor materials. The institution was later renamed NDL to avoid confusion with the recently established Submicrometer Electronics Corporation of the Industrial Technology Research Institute.

◎ In addition to providing laboratory testing services to local and overseas Chinese communities, the company actively engages in research of cord blood stem cells. Commercial operations involve collecting and preserving umbilical cord blood (CB) stem cells from newborns in cryostorage. Only the original owner or assignee of the original owner has access to use the stored CB stem cells.

3. Cite an example of a recent endeavor. 舉一個最近的實例

◎ For instance, RUENTEX Group has signed a technology cooperative agreement with Zhong Yin Joint Stock Company, which is responsible for managing the elderly housing authority in Japan. Out of this cooperation, Ruenfu Life Limited Liability Company was formed in 1991, with the aim of providing high quality residential housing island wide for the elderly. Having received a strong favorable response from both the public and governmental authorities, Ruenfu strives to infuse vitality into an elderly retirement community for individuals living independent of their families.

◎ As semiconductor manufacturing technologies have entered the nano era, NDL closely collaborates with academic institutions and private enterprises to remain abreast of the latest advances in this challenging field. Specifically, the emergence of new generation nano materials and applications reflects a global trend in semiconductor manufacturing technologies that requires extensive knowledge of multidisciplinary fields, a long term commitment and international exchange opportunities.

◎ The company's standard operating procedures strictly adhere to AABB guidelines; each CB specimen is treated with the utmost care.

4. Summarize the technical accomplishments of the organization in a particular sector. 總結公司研發的特殊科技對特定領域的貢獻

◎ In sum, the RUENTEX Group represents innovativeness in the growing market for senior citizen housing in Taiwan. Strengthened by technological transfers of expertise from abroad and rich management experience, RUENTEX remains optimistic about its future prospects in the elderly housing market island wide.

◎ As a resource for nano scientists island wide to upgrade Taiwan's nanotechnology capabilities, NDL is a vibrant research environment that enables academic research personnel such as graduate and post doctoral students to fully utilize the latest software and hardware resources to advance nano technology in line with global standards.

◎ Staffed by highly qualified laboratory personnel who stringently follow guidelines for processing and testing cord blood stem cell specimens, SCT is equipped with advanced laboratory equipment to ensure the quality of services provided. Of priority concern is to control the plasticity mechanisms and maximize the regenerative potential of stem cells.

In the space below, describe recent technical accomplishments in a company with respect to developing or promoting a particular product or service.

_____

_____

_____

_____

_____

_____

_____

_____

Look at the following examples of describing recent technical accomplishments in a company or organization.

The Taipei Municipal Government has actively promoted the digitalization of public information, enabling its e-citizens to freely access information in line with global trends in order to sustain the city's international competitiveness. For instance, with the promotion of wireless network use, the city government offers WIFLY wireless wide band services in public spaces. With this hi-quality transmission service, dial-up connections are no longer required to browse the Internet or access one's e-mail account. With its rapid transmission capability, a wireless network system allows individuals to communicate with each other cordially and conveniently, thus stimulating e-commerce opportunities and streamlining many governmental services. The wireless regional network, or wireless local area network (WLAN), transmits information through a wireless signal without the need for bulky cable equipment. The WLAN environment enables online computer users to roam without constraints or restricted access, thus increasing efficiency and productivity through enhanced communication capabilities — whether for work, study or on-line amusement. Coffee shops, fast food restaurants, airports, railway stations and hotels are among the increasing number of establishments that offer wireless network environments. As Taipei aspires to become a globally leading wireless city, WIFLY offers an inexpensive, reliable and pluralistic wireless wide-band network service, with a strong emphasis on maintaining user confidentiality and facilitating economic, humanistic and social activities. Unrestricted information access throughout Taipei City offers its citizens a sense of renewed confidence in undertaking many of life's daily activities.

●

Following the discovery of deoxyribonucleic acid (DNA) in 1953, the mapping of the human genome was recently completed, in which all genes in the human DNA sequence were identified. Genomics will undoubtedly transform the entire structure of commerce and society in the near future. Sectors to be directly impacted include medical treatment and diagnosis, criminology and genetic profiling, cancer research and anti-aging methodologies. The economy is currently investing billions of dollars into DNA—related fields. DNA technology provides an almost incomprehensible array of short-term commercial opportunities. The challenge is to accurately forecast timely advances in DNA research; a company should then position itself advantageously. The six major areas of DNA developmental trends are DNA fingerprinting, genetic testing, anti-aging procedures, DNA and the cure for cancer, cloning and stem cell research and genetic therapy. For example, 400,000,000 of the earth's population has B type hepatitis carrier, with 5%~10% of all infected individuals becoming a carrier. According to Industrial Technology Research Institute, hepatitis-B medication revenues will surpass $US700,000,000 in 2009. Moreover, DNA and the cure for cancer represent a newly emerging and highly promising area of commercial interest and biotechnology development.

●

The Applied Radiation and Isotope Society of Taiwan (ARIST) actively encourages the radiation protection sector to become involved in radiation detection and development of a locally produced CVD diamond detector. As the largest nonprofit organization of its kind in Taiwan, ARIST conducts radiation application-related research, provides technical services to upgrade radiation-related sectors, (including the semiconductor, photoelectronic and electronics industries) and fosters the research capabilities of the newly emerging applied radiation sector in Taiwan. Given the extensive applications of radiation in medicine, industry and agriculture, multidisciplinary approaches are integrated with basic research capabilities to enhance the level of radiation detection technologies. CVD diamond is a new generation radiation detector with many promising applications in medicine. With the growing importance of proton beams in radiation therapy for cancer, the CVD diamond for measuring proton dose has become increasingly important, especially for measuring dosages at the Bragg peak. Previous investigations have already measured the CVD diamond to protons with energies ranging from 0.7 to 3.0 MeV and 15 to 30 MeV. The CVD Diamond Detector may confer benefits over a high energy photon. For instance, CVD has a higher sensitivity in TLD detection for a high energy photon. Potential benefits include an enhanced resolution and reduced signal noise. CVD will occasionally benefit from the more accurate control of photon energy and absorption dose. Additionally, CVD is less expensive and more effective than TLD. Ultimately, ARIST is striving for commercialization of CVD, which requires prioritizing market-orientation as the primary strategy. ARIST already has a highly skilled and experienced staff in the semiconductor, photoelectronic and medicine-related industries. Obviously, a larger market implies greater potential for commercial success. Strategic emphasis is on entering not only the radiation detector market, but also other radiation-related sectors.

Situation 4

waste-treatment equipment, including rubbish compressors, medical waste treatment

the burning method produces dioxins and heavy metal contaminants

upgrading its research capabilities continuously to ensure technological innovation

Situation 5

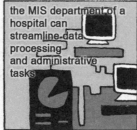

integrating the standards and practices of various information systems

the MIS department of a hospital can streamline data processing and administrative tasks

adopt innovative technologies to facilitate the access and use by system users

Situation 6

teaching and a research facilityStrongly financially supported by the National Health Research Institute

encouraging patients to seek sound medical advice

contain patient data that can be conveniently accessed by physicians and nursing staff

I

Write down the key points of the situations on the preceding page, while the instructor reads aloud the script from the Answer Key. Alternatively, students can listen online at www.chineseowl.idv.tw

Situation 4

_____

_____

_____

Situation 5

_____

_____

_____

Situation 6

_____

_____

_____

J Oral practice II

Based on the three situations in this unit, write three questions beginning with ***What***, and answer them. The questions do not need to come directly from these situations.

Examples

What organization manufactures various waste-treatment equipment?

Shilebaida International Science Technologies Corporation

What provides a more secure means of processing waste than conventional burning?

heat decomposition technology

1. _____

   _____

2. _____

   _____

3. _____

   _____

K

Based on the three situations in this unit, write three questions beginning with **Why**, and answer them. The questions do not need to come directly from these situations.

Examples

Why is it extremely difficult to circulate internal information and prevent administrative errors?

because Taiwanese hospitals have had difficulty in integrating the standards and practices of various information systems adopted at their facilities

Why is it possible to improve the medical services and management capabilities of a hospital?

because information technology has potential for eliminating these obstacles in daily operations

1. _____

_____

2. _____

_____

3. _____

L

Based on the three situations in this unit, write three questions beginning with *How*, and answer them. The questions do not need to come directly from these situations.

Examples

How is Wanfang Hospital classified?

as both a teaching and a research facility

How is Wangfang Hospital supported financially?

by the National Health Research Institute

1. _____

   _____

2. _____

   _____

3. _____

   _____

M Write questions that match the answers provided.

1. _____

_____

It occupies limited space, minimizes overhead costs and is efficient.

2. _____

_____

in determining whether a hospital's information systems satisfy user requirements

3. _____

_____

since the first of May

N Listening Comprehension II

Situation 4

1. Where does the burning method produce dioxins and heavy metal contaminants?

   A. in a closed environment

   B. in a closely monitored environment

   C. in the open air

2. Where is heat decomposition technology unable to release dioxins or heavy metal contaminants?

    A. in a closed environment

    B. in the open air

    C. in a closely monitored environment

3. What is capable of processing decomposed waste and handling gas emissions safely?

    A. various waste treatment equipment

    B. medical waste treatment instrumentation

    C. heat decomposition technology

4. What provides a more secure means of processing waste than conventional burning?

    A. baling press compression machinery

    B. heat decomposition technology

    C. resource recovery barrels

5. Why is Shilebaida International Science Technologies Corporation committed to upgrading its research capabilities?

    A. to protect operating staff and meet environmental concerns

    B. to ensure technological innovation in medical waste treatment

    C. to provide a more secure means of processing waste than conventional burning

Situation 5

1. Why are training courses essential to orienting older employees?

    A. because of enormous amounts of clinical and administrative-related data

    B. because of their reluctance and lack of information technology skills

    C. because of patient waiting time and administrative errors

2. Why can one implement administrative policies efficiently and with a high success rate?

    A. because of the role of information technology in lowering a hospital's operational expenses

B. because of the ability to improve the quality of its medical services

C. both A and B

3. Why must the MIS department continuously adopt innovative technologies?

A. to integrate the standards and practices of various information systems adopted

B. to facilitate the access and use by system users

C. to increase patient satisfaction and simplify the remittance of national health insurance premiums

4. What do daily operations in a hospital produce?

A. advanced support capabilities with extensive throughput and large storage capacities

B. enormous amounts of clinical and administrative-related data

C. the further integration of information technologies into daily work routine

5. How is productivity increased and time saved?

A. through further integration of information technologies into daily work routine

B. through the ability to determine whether a hospital's information systems satisfy user requirements

C. through the streamlining of data processing and administrative tasks

Situation 6

1. Which organization strongly supports Wangfang Hospital financially?

A. the Patient Safety Information Center

B. the National Health Research Institute

C. the National Science Council

2. How many medical centers does Taiwan have?

A. 15

B. 20

205

C. 17

3. Why does the PSI Center place a notebook computer in each hospital ward?

   A. to contain patient data that can be conveniently accessed by physicians and nursing staff

   B. to encourage patients to seek sound medical advice

   C. to implement a system that embeds patient data in an IC chip that individuals can wear as a ring

4. How many research centers has Wangfang Hospital established?

   A. 20

   B. 21

   C. 22

5. Which organization does the Patient Safety Information Center collaborate with?

   A. the National Health Administration

   B. the National Health Research Institute

   C. the National Science Council

O Reading Comprehension II

Select the word or expression whose meaning is closest to the meaning of the underlined word or expression in the following passages.

Situation 4

1. Shilebaida International Science Technologies Corporation manufactures various waste-treatment equipment, including rubbish compressors, medical waste treatment instrumentation, baling press compression machinery, kitchen waste treatment machinery and resource <u>recovery</u> barrels.

   A. retrieval

B. forfeiture

C. squandering

2. Medical waste treatment instrumentation utilizes heat decomposition technology, which provides a more <u>secure</u> means of processing waste than conventional burning does.

A. susceptible

B. liable

C. unassailable

3. In the open air, the burning method produces dioxins and heavy metal contaminants, subsequently <u>harming</u> humans.

A. expediting

B. impairing

C. walking through

4. In a closed environment, heat decomposition technology does not release dioxins or heavy metal <u>contaminants</u>, thus protecting operating staff and addressing environmental concerns.

A. supplicants

B. toxic substances

C. nutrients

5. Capable of processing decomposed waste and handling gas emissions safely, heat decomposition technology <u>occupies</u> limited space, minimizes overhead costs and ensures efficient operations.

A. monopolizes

B. abnegates

C. relinquishes

6. Shilebaida International Science Technologies Corporation is <u>committed</u> to upgrading its research capabilities continuously to ensure technological

innovation in medical waste treatment.

A. refraining

B. neutral

C. devoted

Situation 5

1. Previously, Taiwanese hospitals had difficulty in <u>integrating</u> the standards and practices of various information systems adopted at their facilities, making it extremely difficult to circulate internal information and prevent administrative errors.

A. dissecting

B. incorporating

C. extracting

2. Information technology has potential for <u>eliminating</u> these obstacles in daily operations, thereby improving the medical services and management capabilities of a hospital.

A. extracting

B. initiating

C. promulgating

3. The MIS department of a hospital can streamline data processing and administrative tasks, improve the efficiency and quality of medical care, <u>increase</u> patient satisfaction and simplify the remittance of national health insurance premiums.

A. alter

B. mitigate

C. augment

4. Given the role of information technology in lowering a hospital's operational

expenses while <u>improving</u> the quality of its medical services, administrative policies can be implemented efficiently and successfully.

A. alleviating

B. upgrading

C. reducing

5. As daily operations in a hospital produce <u>enormous</u> amounts of clinical and administrative-related data, internal information systems must have advanced support capabilities with extensive throughput and large storage capacities.

A. miniscule

B. gargantuan

C. slight

6. Additionally, <u>advanced</u> information technologies can increase the efficiency of daily clinical and administrative tasks, thus simplifying many operational procedures and reducing both patient waiting time and administrative errors.

A. archaic

B. remedial

C. progressive

7. However, given the <u>reluctance</u> of older employees and their lack of information technology skills, training courses are essential to orienting them on the further integration of information technologies into their daily work routine, thus increasing productivity and saving time.

A. reticence

B. ardor

C. zeal

8. Outsourced information technology vendors also play a <u>critical</u> role in determining whether a hospital's information systems satisfy user requirements.

A. miniaturized

B. pivotal

C. marginal

9. Therefore, the MIS department must continuously adopt <u>innovative</u> technologies to facilitate the access and use by system users.

A. state-of-the-art

B. obsolescent

C. antiquated

Situation 6

1. As one of Taiwan's 17 medical centers, Wanfang Hospital is both a <u>teaching</u> and a research facility.

A. subordinate

B. complementary

C. pedagogical

2. Strongly <u>supported</u> by the National Health Research Institute financially, Wanfang Hospital has established 22 research centers.

A. agitated

B. facilitated

C. provoked

3. Of these, the Patient Safety Information (PSI) Center collaborates with the National Health Administration in <u>encouraging</u> patients to seek sound medical advice, especially with respect to environmental concerns and the safe use of prescription medicine.

A. diverting

B. repressing

C. invigorating

4. Of these, the Patient Safety Information (PSI) Center collaborates with the National Health Administration in encouraging patients to seek <u>sound</u> medical advice, especially with respect to environmental concerns and the safe use of prescription medicine.

   A. solid

   B. shaky

   C. unreliable

5. Since the first of May, Wanfang Hospital has implemented a system that <u>embeds</u> patient data in an IC chip that individuals can wear as a ring, enabling physicians to access patient information conveniently.

   A. extracts

   B. protracts

   C. instills

6. In addition to <u>developing</u> a system for ordering nursing services, the PSI Center will place a notebook computer in each hospital ward to contain patient data that can be conveniently accessed by physicians and nursing staff.

   A. destabilizing

   B. degrading

   C. nurturing

7. Since the first of May, Wanfang Hospital has implemented a system that embeds patient data in an IC chip that individuals can wear as a ring, enabling physicians to <u>access</u> patient information conveniently.

   A. acquire

   B. retract

   C. allocate

Unit Six

  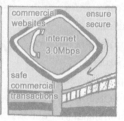

Citing Examples of Product/Service Commercialization

產品／服務銷售實例

1. Introduce the main emphases of a sector or industry.
   簡述特定部門或產業所強調的主要重點
2. Cite specific applications, including examples of commercialization.
   舉出商品化的特定實例
3. Describe the mid-term or long term benefits of such commercialization for a particular field of technology.
   說明產品／服務商品化後對特定領域或部門的中長期利益
4. Describe the mid-term or long term benefits of such commercialization for practical purposes.
   說明產品／服務商品化後在商業實際運用裡的中長期利益

Vocabulary and related expressions

a booming sector	一個景氣好的部門
electronic commerce	電子商業
lag behind	落後於
fully exploit	全面開發
realize the market potential	實現市場潛能
tremendous commercial potential	極大的商業潛能
online entrepreneurs	線上企業家
online auctioning	線上拍賣
unique form of e-commerce	電子商業的獨特形式
markedly exceed	顯著地超過
the most popular venues	最受歡迎的平台
face-to-face interaction	面對面的互動
secure commercial interactions	安全的商業互動
website functionality	網頁機能
credit card transactions	信用卡交易
in collaboration with	跟……合作
population trends	人口趨勢
enhanced living standards	加強生活水準
most appropriate management strategies	最適當的管理策略
appraising potential vendors	估計潛在的賣主
a contracted firm	縮減的公司
collaborative relationship	合作關係
crux	關鍵
a profound role in	深奧的角色
enzyme technology	酵素科技
mitigate	使緩和
genetic defects	遺傳基因造成的缺點

Situation 1

Situation 2

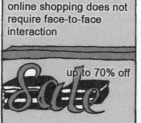

Situation 3

A

Write down the key points of the situations on the preceding page, while the instructor reads aloud the script from the Answer Key. Alternatively, students can listen online at www.chineseowl.idv.tw

Situation 1

_____

_____

_____

Situation 2

_____

_____

_____

Situation 3

_____

_____

_____

B Oral practice I

Based on the three situations in this unit, write three questions beginning with *How*, and answer them. The questions do not need to come directly from these situations.

Examples

How can one demonstrate that electronic commerce is a booming sector?

by its increasing impact on industry

How can online commerce realize its market potential?

by the Internet fully exploiting advanced Web-based technologies

1. _____

_____

2. _____

_____

3. _____

_____

C

Based on the three situations in this unit, write three questions beginning with **Why**, and answer them. The questions do not need to come directly from these situations.

Examples

Why is online auctioning a unique form of e-commerce in the United States?
It combines conventional auctioning practices with advanced information technologies.

Why are Internet users able to access auction websites for bidding or selling without time and location constraints?
owing to the convenience of hi-speed Internet

1. _____

   _____

2. _____

   _____

3. _____

   _____

D

Based on the three situations in this unit, write three questions beginning with *What*, and answer them. The questions do not need to come directly from these situations.

Examples

What must governmental organizations and the private sector do to improve the living environment of the elderly?

coordinate efforts to create an environment in which senior citizens live independently

What did RUENTEX Construction Company in collaboration with Rien Fu Newlife Company establish?

a senior citizens' residential community in Tan-shui

1. _____

   _____

2. _____

   _____

3. _____

   _____

E Write questions that match the answers provided.

1. _____

_____

technological developments and market trends

2. _____

_____

by reinforcing security mechanisms that require credit card or bank account information for identification

3. _____

_____

300

F Listening Comprehension I

Situation 1

1. What happened to the number of Internet users between 2002 and 2006?

    A. It more than tripled.

    B. It more than doubled.

    C. It more than quadrupled.

2. Why are consumers easily discouraged from shopping online?

    A. if any of these technical factors are neglected

B. if product/service strategies are appropriate for electronic commerce

C. if sales growth is continued

3. Why must more incentives be provided for customers?

    A. to successfully implement business strategies

    B. to monitor the consumer growth rate for a particular market niche

    C. to switch their purchasing from traditional retail outlets to the Internet

4. How do many e-business startups look for new customers?

    A. by extending the concept of customer value to Internet-based commercial activities

    B. by striving to protect customer satisfaction and loyalty

    C. by monitoring the consumer growth rate for a particular market niche

5. Why must companies closely scrutinize their product/service strategies?

    A. to realize the market potential of online commerce

    B. to ensure that they are appropriate for electronic commerce

    C. to develop promotional campaigns in order to lure new customers

Situation 2

1. Why does confusion occasionally arise over payment terms?

    A. owing to the lack of potential consumers constantly online

    B. owing to the lack of an escrow service for its customers

    C. owing to the lack of face-to-face interaction

2. What facilitates Internet users' accessing of auction websites for bidding or selling?

    A. the convenience of hi-speed Internet connections

    B. face-to-face interaction

    C. close inspection of a product on the store premises

3. What are *Taiwan Yahoo-Kimo* and *Taiwan E-bay* renowned for?

A. their ability to influence the final product price and sales terms

B. their ability to reinforce security mechanisms that require credit card or bank account information

C. their novel marketing mechanisms and operational models

4. Why is online auctioning a unique form of e-commerce?

A. its ability to combine conventional auctioning practices with advanced information technologies

B. its ability to provide an escrow service for its customers

C. its ability to delay product delivery

5. What is likely to delay product delivery?

A. an expansion in the range of products and services offered

B. a guarantee of confidential and secure commercial interactions

C. poor distribution

Situation 3

1. Who has collaborated with RUENTEX Construction Company in establishing a senior citizens' residential community in Tan-shui?

A. the Department of Health

B. Rien Fu Newlife Company

C. the Taiwanese government

2. What should be the norm rather than the exception?

A. Commercial opportunities are limited.

B. Governmental authorities can evaluate the least appropriate management strategies.

C. Senior citizens can live independently.

3. How was the senior citizens' residential community in Tan-shui established?

A. by providing high-quality comfort with 300 residential units

B. by drawing on the Japanese long term care model to provide residents with hotel-style management

C. by evaluating the most appropriate management strategies

4. Why is the climate for growth opportunities in the long-term care sector in Taiwan favorable?

A. because of the successful operation of senior citizens' residential communities

B. because of the competitiveness level of businesses

C. because of population trends and enhanced living standards

5. What are governmental authorities and industrial planners anxious to do?

A. create numerous commercial opportunities

B. govern the successful operation of senior citizens' residential communities

C. evaluate the most appropriate management strategies

G Reading Comprehension I

Select the word or expression whose meaning is closest to the meaning of the underlined word or expression in the following passages.

Situation 1

1. Electronic commerce is a <u>booming</u> sector, as evidenced by its increasing impact on industry.

   A. inert

   B. putrid

   C. robust

2. As various business strategy models for electronic commerce have emerged, an increasing number of academics have <u>advocated</u> the extension of the concept of

customer value to Internet-based commercial activities.

    A. touted

    B. deprecated

    C. ostracized

3. As revenues from electronic commerce <u>lag</u> behind those of mail-order services, the Internet must fully exploit advanced Web-based technologies to realize the market potential of online commerce.

    A. saunter

    B. coerce

    C. chaperone

4. More <u>incentives</u> must be provided for customers to switch their purchasing from traditional retail outlets to the Internet.

    A. deterrent

    B. hindrance

    C. stimulus

5. E-commerce is growing in terms of marketplace <u>interactions</u> since Internet users number hundreds of millions worldwide.

    A. contradictions

    B. reciprocity

    C. opposition

6. According to the forecasts of eTForecasts and eMarketer, the number of Internet users between 2002 and 2006 more than doubled, <u>reflecting</u> the tremendous commercial potential of the Internet.

    A. absorbing

    B. imbibing

    C. resonating

7. Successful e-commerce strategies rely <u>heavily</u> on technological developments and market trends.

   A. tenuously

   B. tumultuously

   C. subtly

8. Technological developments offer a means by which business strategies are implemented successfully. Such developments include Web design, network transmission performance and product/service representations. Also, the success rate of <u>transactions</u> is important.

   A. rejection

   B. denial

   C. dealings

9. Consumers are easily discouraged from shopping online if any of these technical factors are neglected. Companies must closely <u>scrutinize</u> their product/service strategies to ensure that they are appropriate for electronic commerce.

   A. peruse

   B. glimpse

   C. glance

10. In this area, effective <u>promotional</u> concepts, product price strategy, supply chain systems and the creation of a novel Web environment are all of high priority.

    A. telegenic

    B. interdiction

    C. repudiation

11. Many e-business startups look for new customers by <u>monitoring</u> the consumer growth rate for a particular market niche.

    A. disdaining

    B. overseeing

C. slighting

12. While many companies develop promotional campaigns to <u>lure</u> new customers, they often overlook customer loyalty, which is essential for continued sales growth.

A. dissuade

B. stave

C. inveigle

13. In summary, many online entrepreneurs <u>strive</u> to protect customer satisfaction and loyalty.

A. endeavor

B. cede

C. abjure

Situation 2

1. Online auctioning emerged in the United States as a unique form of e-commerce by combining conventional <u>auctioning</u> practices with advanced information technologies.

A. procuring

B. retailing

C. bartering for

2. The convenience of hi-speed Internet connections facilitates Internet users' <u>accessing</u> of auction websites for bidding or selling without time and location constraints.

A. precluding

B. enjoining

C. scaring up

3. With a seemingly <u>unlimited</u> number of potential consumers constantly online, the

benefits of online auctioning markedly exceed those of conventional auctioning.

A. hemmed in

B. circumscribed

C. unfettered

4. *Taiwan Yahoo-Kimo* and *Taiwan E-bay* are among the most popular venues in Taiwan, <u>renowned</u> for their novel marketing mechanisms and operational models.

A. obscure

B. esteemed

C. remote

5. Websites that offer various service items differ <u>markedly</u> from traditional commercial outlets.

A. barely

B. scarcely

C. appreciably

6. Online shopping does not require face-to-face interaction or close <u>inspection</u> of a product on the store premises.

A. dereliction

B. inquest

C. infraction

7. Therefore, online shopping heavily prioritizes <u>security</u> mechanisms to ensure confidential and secure commercial interactions, website functionality and novel marketing strategies.

A. vulnerability

B. frailty

C. collateral

8. Moreover, online shopping enables consumers to compete with each other on a <u>level playing field</u>, influencing the final product price and sales terms.

A. disparity

B. equanimity

C. divergence

9. Still, online shopping raises several <u>challenges</u>.

A. provocations

B. acquiescence

C. compliance

10. For instance, given the <u>lack</u> of face-to-face interaction, confusion occasionally arises over payment terms.

A. paucity

B. opulence

C. exiguity

11. After a user has purchased a product, poor distribution is likely to <u>delay</u> product delivery.

A. precipitate

B. impede

C. facilitate

12. Additionally, a <u>breach</u> of confidence in personal data, such as that found in credit card transactions, can lead to identity theft. In summary, commercial websites must ensure secure and safe commercial transactions by reinforcing security mechanisms that require credit card or bank account information for identification.

A. juncture

B. alliance

C. fissure

13. Online <u>auction</u> websites should also provide an escrow service for its customers.

A. tender

B. donation

C. charity

14. Once these obstacles are resolved, online auctioneers can <u>expand</u> the range of products and services offered.

A. diminish

B. retract

C. explicate

Situation 3

1. To improve the living environment of the elderly, governmental organizations and the private sector must coordinate efforts to create an environment in which senior citizens living independently is the <u>norm</u> rather than the exception.

A. anomaly

B. barometer

C. perquisite

2. To improve the living environment of the elderly, governmental organizations and the private sector must coordinate efforts to create an environment in which senior citizens living independently is the norm rather than the <u>exception</u>.

A. deviation

B. paradigm

C. archetype

3. In so doing, numerous commercial <u>opportunities</u> will arise.

A. interdiction

B. repudiation

C. potential

4. For instance, RUENTEX Construction Company in collaboration with Rien Fu

Newlife Company has established a senior citizens' residential community in Tan-shui by <u>drawing on</u> the Japanese long term care model to provide residents with hotel-style management.

A. excoriate

B. reprobate

C. referencing to

5. The facilities provide high-quality <u>comfort</u> with 300 residential units, all of which have already been leased.

A. malaise

B. repose

C. nuisance

6. Given population trends and enhanced living standards, the climate for growth opportunities in the long-term care sector in Taiwan is <u>favorable</u>.

A. contentious

B. eristic

C. benign

7. Identifying factors that <u>govern</u> the successful operation of senior citizens' residential communities is thus essential to the competitiveness of the businesses, explaining why governmental authorities and industrial planners are anxious to evaluate the most appropriate management strategies.

A. kowtow

B. hold dominion

C. accede

8. Identifying factors that govern the successful operation of senior citizens' residential communities are thus essential to the competitiveness of businesses, explaining why governmental authorities and industrial planners are <u>anxious</u> to evaluate the most appropriate management strategies.

A. debonair

B. effervescent

C. spooked

H

Common elements in citing examples of product/ service commercialization include the following contents:

1. Introduce the main emphases of a sector or industry.
   簡述特定部門或產業所強調的主要重點
2. Cite specific applications, including examples of commercialization.
   舉出商品化的特定實例
3. Describe the mid-term or long term benefits of such commercialization for a particular field of technology.
   說明產品／服務商品化後對特定領域或部門的中長期利益
4. Describe the mid-term or long term benefits of such commercialization for practical purposes.
   說明產品/服務商品化後在商業實際運用裡的中長期利益

1. Introduce the main emphases of a sector or industry. 簡述特定部門或產業所強調的主要重點

◎ The global biotechnology industry has recently switched its focus to developing biochips. The Taiwanese government has aggressively pursued a biotechnology development strategy since 1998, with domestic output valued at $500 US million in 2002.

◎ The continuous development of nanotechnologies in Taiwan has led to the discovery of physical and chemical properties of certain compounds and elements. The properties of nanometer materials play a significant role in metals and semiconductors of nano colloid particles used in optics and photo electronics.

◎ Hospitals devote a significant amount of their annual operating budgets to upgrading information network capacity through the purchase of advanced hardware and software. Adopting the latest information technologies can greatly enhance a hospital's administrative and managerial capabilities.

2. Cite specific applications, including examples of commercialization. 舉出商品化的特定實例

◎ For clinical purposes, biotechnology also provides an efficient and accurate means of diagnosing illnesses while, simultaneously, conserving a tremendous amount of personnel and material resources. Besides DNA, receptor of a protein and cellular medicines can be placed in biochips. Biochips can also reduce much time in clinical examination. For instance, biochip development can monitor various functions of medicines, including gene induction, cytoxicity and genotoxicity, leading to a change of pathology and reduced treatment time in diagnosing diseases.

◎ Nano particles can be used to modify the chemical composition on the surface of a metal with nucleic acid to form nano particles of nucleic acid. A biochip can subsequently be developed using conventional flat scanner read signals. This biochip system can detect signals to make a single DNA match for use in conjugated phosphor materials under microscopic detection. The Industrial Technology Research Institute has already achieved a gold nano particle through the use of a compound technique based on semiconductor nano particles (CdS and CdSe), CdSe nanorods and magnetism nano particles (ion oxide).

◎ Through the encouragement of Taiwan's National Health Insurance Bureau, many hospitals incorporate a medical information system (MIS) in daily operations to increase the efficiency of physicians in examining patients, diagnosing their illnesses and prescribing therapeutic treatment. However, most MISs consist of many smaller systems that are not integrated with each other. With national development strategies heavily focused on the output value on the island's medical sector, the Taiwanese government is developing a medical health care scheme that, in addition to closely inspecting the health services of domestic medical institutions, aims to devise and implement a nationwide health information system by 2009.

3. Describe the mid-term or long term benefits of such commercialization for a particular field of technology. 說明產品／服務商品化後對特定領域或部門的中長期利益

◎ Given advances in 2000 regarding mapping of the human gene, the importance of biochip technology is more imperative given its ability to combine three conventional steps of medical science: treating samples, responding to chemical reactions and examining results through assaying. In clinical practice, biochip technology can be extensively adopted in medical diagnosis and treatment, gene mapping, medicinal extraction, identification of Chinese herbal medicines, forensic science, food hygiene, environmental monitoring and even national defense.

◎ Additionally, organic modification of nano particles makes possible the further combination of -NH2 and —COOH functional groups with bio-substances. Specifically, gold nano particles in a nucleic acid probe can be used to detect biochips for use in the scanner reading of signals. Already, gold nano-particles labeled as nucleic acid probe can be used in biochips for scanner reading signals and discriminating between SNP signals. Moreover, the use of nano-particle techniques and applications involving the molecular combination of nucleic acid can enhance the sensitivity of detection methods for gene chips.

◎ Specifically, the government will orient hospitals on how to conserve available resources in order to avoid duplication during medical examinations. Meanwhile, hospitals should accelerate the computerization of information-based needs in daily operations, subsequently creating an island wide information network for health institutions to exchange data and form closer collaborative ties. Moreover, information technology vendors can contribute to advances in Taiwan's MIS capabilities by offering state-of-the-art hardware and software that comply with international standards and promoting the island's competitiveness in the intensely competitive global medical sector.

4. Describe the mid-term or long term benefits of such commercialization for practical purposes. 說明產品／服務商品化後在商業實際運用裡的中長期利益

◎ More importantly, biochip technology will enable humans to more thoroughly understand the origins of life, heredity and evolution of human diseases, along with their diagnosis, treatment and prevention. In the near future, biochip technology will lead to the development of a gene database containing genetic information of individuals in a chip form to facilitate the diagnosis and treatment of diseases.

◎ Furthermore, nanoparticle technology can be adopted to increase the accuracy in detecting single nucleic acid variations that lead to genetic diseases.

◎ The active involvement of information technology vendors in the Six Year National Development Strategy will facilitate market expansion of Taiwan's medical sector owing to its assistance in incorporating MISs into local hospitals, subsequently increasing their administrative efficiency and ability to provide quality medical care.

In the space below, cite an example of product/service commercialization.

_____

_____

_____

_____

_____

_____

_____

_____

_____

Look at the following examples of citing examples of product/service commercialization

The Personal Handy-phone System, or commonly known as PHS, is characterized by its lower electromagnetic wave than in other mobile phones. After taking the lead in the PHS market, First International Telecom of Japan began offering services in Taiwan's mobile phone sector in June 2001. 2005 marks the tenth anniversary of the launch of PHS in Japan. From only a few million subscribers in a single country just a few years ago, PHS use has expanded nearly 20 times to over 70 million subscribers in China, Japan, Taiwan, Thailand and Vietnam. According to recent estimates, that figure will reach 110 million subscribers across an even more extended area by the end of this decade. While PHS belongs to the electronic communications sector in Taiwan, the local market scale is small owing to limited success in penetrating the lower electromagnetic wave market, as evidenced by the lack of advertising and technology commercialization capabilities. To foster its competitiveness, the domestic electronic communications sector must strengthen its research capabilities, develop lower electromagnetic wave technologies and attract technology professionals with expertise in multidisciplinary fields. In addition to its low electromagnetic wave and relatively inexpensive per call rate, the PHS mobile phone can function in a wireless network environment. In terms of a marketing strategy, First International Telecom offers PHS services with no monthly fee, no installation payment and an inexpensive per call rate. As for developmental trends of a lower electromagnetic wave, more effective installation of station antenna in the near future may provide reliable communication via telephone and a wireless network link. Given its low electromagnetic wave, the PHS mobile phone can be used in sensitive areas such as hospitals and filling stations without posing a major health risk.

●

According to the Ministry of Communications, in 2003, over 2,000,000 Taiwanese made plans to travel, but were unaware of the sights to see once they reached their travel destination. Given this statistic, several companies in the tour sector view this as an enormous commercial opportunity, especially given the diverse functions of portable-sized global positioning systems (GPS). The Mio pocket GPS facilitates those travelers without a clear destination by helping them plan trip routes and provide trip-related information. The conventionally adopted GPS in cars is light weight and prone to theft when a motor vehicle is stolen. Besides use in a car, the Mio pocket GPS can be used in a car, while traveling at working, during recreation and even during shopping. Given its lightness and small weight, customers can carry it in a pocket, use it anytime and significantly reduce the risk of theft. The Global Positioning System is in its early stage of development in Taiwan; although having not yet reached global standards, the potential applications are infinite. Given the emphasis on use for leisure activities, the GPS can guide tours to scenic spots, thus satisfying consumer demand for a reliable travel companion. Once reaching commercialization, at least 30,000 units are expected to be sold in a six month period, with anticipated revenues of US$ 12,000,000.

●

Liquid crystal display technology has recently emerged in Taiwan as an alternative means of enhancing conventionally adopted cathode ray tube displays. As an advantage, liquid crystal displays do not emit as much radiation as cathode ray tube displays do. Liquid crystal displays also enable individuals to more closely interact with computers by functioning as an output device that displays enhanced picture and text quality, enabling individuals to more succinctly express their intended meaning in a computer environment. Liquid crystal displays reflect the current technology trend that information products should consume less power than previously, remain compact in size, emit little or no radiation and ensure that users enjoy the best visual access in a computer environment available. Successfully adopting liquid crystal displays has increased revenues for many information products, as evidenced by the reported profits of $US 1,300,000,000 in the United States; the compound annual growth rate for the same market was 23.7% from 2000 to 2006. In sum, liquid crystal display technology is a highly promising area for digital content applications, with commercial strategies for its further promulgation under closer scrutiny. Successful commercialization requires prioritizing market orientation, in which technological applications and research design are vital to enhancing global competitiveness. Liquid crystal display products must adopt the latest high technologies by integrating the efforts of multidisciplinary professionals in research design, marketing and product design. As current market trends point towards a larger market potential, liquid crystal display products manufactured locally should be channeled to the Greater China market.

Situation 4

hospital clinics' tendency to outsource their medical information needs

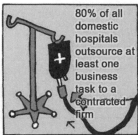

80% of all domestic hospitals outsource at least one business task to a contracted firm

hospitals must overcome great challenges in selecting the most appropriate software package to meet their needs

Situation 5

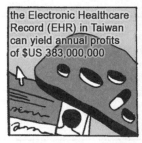

the Electronic Healthcare Record (EHR) in Taiwan can yield annual profits of $US 383,000,000

outsourcing of information systems in America's medical services sector has increased

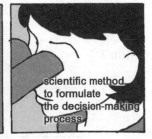

scientific method to formulate the decision-making process

Situation 6

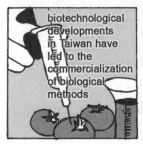

biotechnological developments in Taiwan have led to the commercialization of biological methods

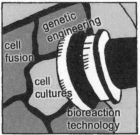

genetic engineering

cell fusion

cell cultures

bioreaction technology

the demand for biotechnology applications that prevent disease is increasing

| I |

Write down the key points of the situations on the preceding page, while the instructor reads aloud the script from the Answer Key. Alternatively, students can listen online at www.chineseowl.idv.tw

Situation 4

_____

_____

_____

Situation 5

_____

_____

_____

Situation 6

_____

_____

_____

J Oral practice II

Based on the three situations in this unit, write three questions beginning with **Why**, and answer them. The questions do not need to come directly from these situations.

Examples

Why is appraising potential vendors extremely difficult?

because of Taiwan's unique National Health Insurance scheme and hospital clinics' tendency to outsource their medical information needs to information technology vendors

Why does outsourcing intend to take advantage of human resources and the technologies of vendors?

to provide quality services

1. _____

   _____

2. _____

   _____

3. _____

   _____

K

Based on the three situations in this unit, write three questions beginning with *How*, and answer them. The questions do not need to come directly from these situations.

Examples

How much in commercial opportunities from the development of the Electronic Healthcare Record (EHR) in Taiwan can annual profits yield?
$US 383,000,000

How much did the American information industry outsource to the medical services sector in 2001?
over $US 1,755,000,000

1. _____

   _____

2. _____

   _____

3. _____

L

Based on the three situations in this unit, write three questions beginning with *What*, and answer them. The questions do not need to come directly from these situations.

Examples

What factors have led to the commercialization of biological methods?
recent biotechnological developments in Taiwan

What area has attracted considerable interest more recently?
the application of cell fusion and cell culture approaches to human cell signal transduction

1. _____

   _____

2. _____

   _____

3. _____

   _____

M Write questions that match the answers provided.

1. _____

   _____

   80%

2. _____

   _____

   the National Health Insurance Bureau

3. _____

   _____

   a medical one

N Listening Comprehension II

Situation 4

1. What percentage of all domestic hospitals outsource at least one business task to
   a contracted firm?

   A. 65%

   B. 80%

   C. 45%

2. What do hospital clinics in Taiwan tend to do?

   A. select the most appropriate software package to meet their needs

B. establish collaborative relationships with the National Health Insurance scheme

C. outsource their medical information needs to information technology vendors

3. How could one characterize the collaborative relationship between the purchaser and provider of outsourcing?

    A. independent of each other

    B. mutually beneficial

    C. mutually exclusive

4. When was the National Health Insurance scheme in Taiwan established?

    A. in 1992

    B. in 1993

    C. in 1995

5. What has been extensively adopted in clinical practice since the establishment of National Health Insurance?

    A. medically oriented information technology

    B. high quality software packages

    C. computer systems

Situation 5

1. How much did the American information industry outsource to the medical services sector in 2001?

    A. over $US 2,809,000,00

    B. $US 383,000,000

    C. over $US 1,755,000,000

2. How much did the American information industry outsource to the medical services sector in 2005?

    A. $US 383,000,000

B. $US 2,809,000,00

C. nearly $US 1,755,000,000

3. What do information technology-related applications play a profound role in?

A. the decision-making process

B. the operational planning of hospitals

C. both A and B

4. What necessitates the adoption of a scientific method to formulate the decision-making process?

A. the fact that the decision-making process faces many uncertainties

B. the fact that the average compound growth rate is 12.5%

C. the fact that commercial opportunities have arisen from the development of the Electronic Healthcare Record

5. What sort of views do managers often adopt in decision making?

A. objective ones

B. optimistic ones

C. subjective ones

Situation 6

1. What application has attracted considerable interest?

A. that of cell fusion and cell culture approaches to human cell signal transduction

B. that of human cell signal transduction to cell fusion and cell culture approaches

C. that of biotechnology to agriculture, genetically modified food and other industrial sectors

2. What can mitigate many genetic defects to enhance human health and provide employment opportunities?

    A. embryo transplantation technology

    B. gene recombination technology

    C. DNA technology

3. What is an emerging trend worldwide?

    A. nucleus transplantation

    B. fermentation technology

    C. biotechnology

4. What perspective is adopted in determining that the demand for biotechnology applications that prevent disease is increasing?

    A. a holistic one

    B. a medical one

    C. a financial one

5. What have recent biotechnological developments in Taiwan led to?

    A. design of highly effective medical procedures

    B. exporting of biotechnology methods developed locally

    C. commercialization of biological methods

O Reading Comprehension II

Select the word or expression whose meaning is closest to the meaning of the underlined word or expression in the following passages.

Situation 4

1. With Taiwan's unique National Health Insurance scheme and hospital clinics' <u>tendency</u> to outsource their medical information needs to information technology vendors, appraising potential vendors is extremely difficult, especially given the current ability of medical information systems operators under the National

Health Insurance scheme to select the most reliable information technology supplier.

A. oddity

B. aberration

C. predilection

2. With Taiwan's unique National Health Insurance scheme and hospital clinics' tendency to outsource their medical information needs to information technology vendors, <u>appraising</u> potential vendors is extremely difficult, especially given the current ability of medical information systems operators under the National Health Insurance scheme to select the most reliable information technology supplier.

A. abating

B. depreciating

C. valuating

3. With Taiwan's unique National Health Insurance scheme and hospital clinics' tendency to outsource their medical information needs to information technology vendors, appraising potential vendors is extremely difficult, especially given the current ability of medical information systems operators under the National Health Insurance scheme to select the most <u>reliable</u> information technology supplier.

A. implausible

B. veracious

C. dubious

4. 80% of all domestic hospitals outsource at least one business task to a contracted firm. Outsourcing intends to <u>take advantage of</u> human resources and the technologies of vendors to provide quality services.

A. vacate

B. abdicate

C. exploit

5. Outsourcing intends to take advantage of human resources and the technologies of vendors to provide <u>quality</u> services.

   A. surpassing

   B. mediocre

   C. tawdry

6. Therefore, both the purchaser and provider of outsourcing can establish a collaborative relationship that is mutually <u>beneficial</u>.

   A. incendiary

   B. propitious

   C. virulent

7. Since the establishment of the National Health Insurance scheme in 1995 and the National Health Information Network (HIN), medically oriented information technology has been <u>extensively</u> adopted in clinical practice.

   A. capaciously

   B. scantily

   C. scarcely

8. As software is the <u>crux</u> of computer systems, hospitals must overcome great challenges in selecting the most appropriate software package to meet their needs.

   A. facade

   B. trivia

   C. core

Situation 5

1. According to National Health Insurance Bureau <u>estimates</u>, commercial opportunities from the development of the Electronic Healthcare Record (EHR)

in Taiwan can yield annual profits of $US 383,000,000.

A. ambiguities

B. projections

C. obscurities

2. According to National Health Insurance Bureau estimates, commercial opportunities from the development of the Electronic Healthcare Record (EHR) in Taiwan can <u>yield</u> annual profits of $US 383,000,000.

A. repudiate

B. exclude

C. accrue

3. In an economics study, Zhou (2004) noted that, according to IDC statistics, the American information industry outsourced over $US 1,755,000,000 to the medical services <u>sector</u> in 2001; the figure was $US 2,809,000,00 in 2005.

A. stratum

B. pandemonium

C. ataxia

4. As <u>evidenced</u> by the average compound growth rate of 12.5%, outsourcing of information systems in America's medical services sector has increased.

A. hypothesized

B. conjectured

C. attested

5. Given technological advances, regardless of local or overseas investment in the medical sector, information technology-related applications play a <u>profound</u> role in the decision-making process and the operational planning of hospitals.

A. peripheral

B. sagacious

C. glib

6. Given technological advances, regardless of local or overseas investment in the medical sector, information technology-related applications play a profound role in the decision-making process and the <u>operational</u> planning of hospitals.

   A. downtime

   B. viable

   C. inoperable

7. Managers often adopt their <u>subjective</u> views or apply previous experience in decision making.

   A. introspective

   B. impartial

   C. candid

8. However, the decision making process faces many <u>uncertainties</u>, necessitating the adoption of a scientific method to formulate the decision-making process.

   A. credence

   B. shoo-in

   C. misgivings

9. However, the decision making process faces many uncertainties, necessitating the adoption of a scientific method to <u>formulate</u> the decision-making process.

   A. disconcert

   B. concoct

   C. bemuse

Situation 6

1. Recent biotechnological developments in Taiwan have led to the commercialization of biological methods in such <u>diverse</u> areas as a) genetic engineering, b) cell fusion, c) bioreaction technology, incorporating fermentation technology, enzyme technology and bioreactors, d) cell cultures, e) gene

recombination, f) embryo transplantation and g) nucleus transplantation.

A. homogeneous

B. congruous

C. multifarious

2. Recent biotechnological developments in Taiwan have led to the commercialization of biological methods in such diverse areas as a) genetic engineering, b) cell fusion, c) bioreaction technology, <u>incorporating</u> fermentation technology, enzyme technology and bioreactors, d) cell cultures, e) gene recombination, f) embryo transplantation and g) nucleus transplantation.

A. demarcating

B. extricating

C. coalescing

3. More recently, the application of cell fusion and cell culture approaches to human cell signal transduction has attracted <u>considerable</u> interest.

A. trifling

B. ample

C. scanty

4. The Taiwanese biotechnology market includes many aspects of DNA technology, which can <u>mitigate</u> many genetic defects to enhance human health and provide employment opportunities.

A. escalate

B. mollify

C. augment

5. The Taiwanese biotechnology market includes many aspects of DNA technology, which can mitigate many genetic <u>defects</u> to enhance human health and provide employment opportunities.

A. glitches

B. merits

C. strong points

6. As an emerging trend worldwide, biotechnology will provide novel medical treatment approaches and can be used to design <u>highly</u> effective medical procedures.

   A. imperceptibly

   B. scantily

   C. eminently

7. As an emerging trend worldwide, biotechnology will provide novel medical treatment approaches and can be used to design highly <u>effective</u> medical procedures.

   A. cogent

   B. emasculate

   C. null

8. Taiwan has many potential markets for the application of biotechnology, including agriculture, genetically <u>modified</u> food and other industrial sectors.

   A. unvarying

   B. constant

   C. renovated

9. Additionally, from a medical perspective, the demand for biotechnology applications that <u>prevent</u> disease is increasing.

   A. thwart

   B. expedite

   C. facilitate

Unit Seven

the Personal Handy-phone System (PHS) for cellular phones initially covered the greater Taipei region

PHS is ranked first among those offered by Taiwan's mobile phone service providers

select various songs or dialogues to replace monotonous ring tones

in recent years has led to high outputs of consumer electronics products

various innovative designs or marketing strategies to stimulate consumers and expand markets

hi-tech
over 50% of all sales come from new products

Identifying Future Directions and Challenges in Developing a Product or Service

產品／服務開發的未來動向及挑戰

1. Introduce a sector or industry concerned with the development of a specific product or service.
   簡述部門或產業對特定產品／服務的關注
2. Describe product or service development in detail.
   針對特定產品／服務的發展詳細說明
3. Cite a specific application.
   舉一個特定應用實例
4. Describe future directions or potential applications of this product or service.
   說明該產品／服務未來的發展方向及其發展潛能

Vocabulary and related expressions

mobile phone users	手機的使用者
bandwidth	頻寬
accelerated the delivery of new information products	加速資訊產品的傳送
innovative designs	創新的設計
still in its infancy	仍在初期發展階段
product innovation	產品創新
technological restrictions	科技的限制
mergers and alliances	合併和結盟
inevitably	不可避免地
in a manner consistent with globalization trends	和全球趨勢一致
tremendous amounts of capital invested in R&D and design	花費在創新及設計上的巨大成本投資
expended considerable effort	花費相當多的努力
to stake a claim in	標出界限
traditional brick-and-mortar industries	傳統的有廠房和店舖的工業
highly talented staff of professionals from multidisciplinary fields	有關各種學問的出色專業人才
striving to satisfy consumer demand	努力的要滿足客戶的需求
aggressively striving	有野心的奮鬥
devote its efforts to	將努力奉獻於……
a patented technology	取得專利權的科技
positioning itself as a leader in	把自己視為主導
a non profit foundation	非營利事業的基金會
functions autonomously	獨立自主地運作
under the auspices of	在……贊助下
become pivotal in	變為重要的
facilitating information exchanges	促進資訊交換
domestic and international cooperative ventures	國內及國際合作企業

Situation 1

the Personal Handy-phone System (PHS) for cellular phones initially covered the greater Taipei region

PHS is ranked first among those offered by Taiwan's mobile phone service providers

select various songs or dialogues to replace monotonous ring tones

Situation 2

in recent years has led to high outputs of consumer electronics products

various innovative designs or marketing strategies to stimulate consumers and expand markets

hi-tech

over 50% of all sales come from new products

Situation 3

the Taiwanese automotive industry is limited not only by its rather small market

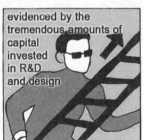
evidenced by the tremendous amounts of capital invested in R&D and design

research to develop high-quality models at competitive prices

automotive manufacturers

A

Write down the key points of the situations on the preceding page, while the instructor reads aloud the script from the Answer Key. Alternatively, students can listen online at www.chineseowl.idv.tw

Situation 1

_____

_____

_____

Situation 2

_____

_____

_____

Situation 3

_____

_____

_____

B Oral practice I

Based on the three situations in this unit, write three questions beginning with *How*, and answer them. The questions do not need to come directly from these situations.

Examples

How did First International Telecom effectively respond to the increasing number of mobile phone users and frequency range?

by obtaining approval for an additional 500,000 phone numbers with the prefix 0966

How has First International Telecom accommodated the growing number of phone subscribers?

by expanding system capacity, with related software/hardware recently installed to accommodate an additional 1,250,000 phone numbers

1. _____

_____

2. _____

_____

3. _____

_____

C

Based on the three situations in this unit, write three questions beginning with *What*, and answer them. The questions do not need to come directly from these situations.

Examples

What has not only accelerated the delivery of new information products that have replaced the old ones, but also shortened the life cycle of such products?

consumer electronics products

What can create niche markets in an era when digital camera markets are growing rapidly?

repositioning products based on future market demand and product development by creative design

1. _____

   _____

2. _____

   _____

3. _____

   _____

D

Based on the three situations in this unit, write three questions beginning with **Why**, and answer them. The questions do not need to come directly from these situations.

Examples

Why is the Taiwanese automotive industry limited?
owing to its rather small market and technological restrictions imposed by overseas parent manufacturers

Why have mergers and alliances occurred in the global automotive market?
overproduction

1. _____

   _____

2. _____

   _____

3. _____

   _____

E Write questions that match the answers provided.

1. _____

   _____

   an additional 1,500,000

2. _____

   _____

   over 50%

3. _____

   _____

   in a manner consistent with globalization trends

F Listening Comprehension I

Situation 1

1. How did First International Telecom effectively respond to the increasing number of mobile phone users and frequency range?

   A. by developing real-time multimedia services and popularize real-time GPS information transmission

   B. by outperforming all of its competitors

   C. by obtaining approval for an additional 500,000 phone numbers with the prefix 0966

2. How has First International Telecom accommodated the growing number of phone subscribers?

   A. by expanding system capacity

   B. by selecting various songs or dialogues to replace monotonous ring tones

   C. by increasing the diversity of mobile telecommunication services

3. What does First International Telecom plan to develop?

   A. a "Mobile Ring Tone" service

   B. the Personal Handy-phone System for cellular phones

   C. real-time multimedia services and popularization of real-time GPS information transmission

4. What does First International Telecom seek to expand?

   A. its value-added services

   B. its vision of full coverage telecommunications

   C. audio quality online

5. How many mobile phone users subscribe to the "Mobile Ring Tone" service?

   A. more than 15,000

   B. around 10,000

   C. less than 5,000

Situation 2

1. Which countries dominate the global digital camera market?

   A. Taiwan and Korea

   B. Japan and the United States

   C. China and Germany

2. What necessitates the continuous incorporation of advanced technologies in product design to satisfy consumer tastes?

   A. product innovation

B. marketing strategies

C. government investment

3. What does the limited and subjective experience of such designers severely limit?

    A. the delivery of new information products

    B. design quantity and quality

    C. the life cycle of consumer electronics products

4. What percentage of all sales comes from new products that were innovated by hi-tech industries?

    A. over 30%

    B. over 40%

    C. over 50%

Situation 3

1. What evidence suggests that the local automotive industry has reached international quality standards?

    A. ability to conform to available resources

    B. various product innovation strategies

    C. tremendous amounts of capital invested in R&D and design

2. How is the Taiwanese automotive industry limited?

    A. its rather small market

    B. technological restrictions imposed by overseas parent manufacturers

    C. both A and B

3. Why have mergers and alliances occurred?

    A. Taiwan's accession to the World Trade Organization

    B. overproduction in the global automotive market

    C. expansion of the domestic market share

4. What has made up for the previously tarnished image of automotive

manufacturers?

A. half a century of development

B. product differentiation

C. high-quality models at competitive prices

5. How has Taiwan's accession to the World Trade Organization affected local automotive manufacturers?

A. positively

B. neutrally

C. negatively

G Reading Comprehension I

Select the word or expression whose meaning is closest to the meaning of the underlined word or expression in the following passages.

Situation 1

1. While the Personal Handy-phone System (PHS) for cellular phones <u>initially</u> covered the greater Taipei region, First International Telecom expanded PHS coverage to Taoyuan and Hsinchu in the beginning of 2002, followed by Kaoshiung and Taichung in 2004.

A. preliminarily

B. belatedly

C. tardily

2. Plans were <u>subsequently</u> made to service Tainan, Nantou and Pingtung in central and southern parts of the island.

A. ante

B. previously

C. infra

3. To effectively <u>respond</u> to the increasing number of mobile phone users and frequency range, First International Telecom obtained approval for an additional 500,000 phone numbers with the prefix 0966.

   A. scorn

   B. reciprocate

   C. discount

4. To <u>accommodate</u> the growing number of phone subscribers, system capacity has expanded, with related software/hardware recently installed to accommodate an additional 1,250,000 phone numbers.

   A. estrange

   B. domicile

   C. disaffect

5. Moreover, an <u>additional</u> 1,500,000 phone numbers will be added by the end of December.

   A. scrimpy

   B. scant

   C. appended

6. Furthermore, to <u>cope</u> with call congestion and an insufficient number of channels given the increasing number of users, First International Telecom has applied to the government to increase its bandwidth to 3 MHz for the northern region, ultimately increasing online audio quality.

   A. contend

   B. bungle

   C. muff

7. In terms of value-added services, PHS is <u>ranked</u> first among those offered by

Taiwan's mobile phone service providers.

A. categorized

B. dispersed

C. diluted

8. MiMi Thumb Information has a sales growth rate of around 10% and a subscription <u>growth</u> rate of 60%, outperforming all of its competitors.

A. constriction

B. proliferation

C. shriveling

9. First International Telecom plans to develop real-time multimedia services and <u>popularize</u> real-time GPS information transmission, integrate information and voice services, as well as introduce corporate services.

A. quell

B. resurrect

C. subjugate

10. First International Telecom has recently launched a "Mobile Ring Tone" service, which enables users to select various songs or dialogues to replace <u>monotonous</u> ring tones.

A. prosaic

B. stimulating

C. enchanting

11. Currently around 10,000 mobile phone users <u>subscribe</u> to this service monthly.

A. expunge

B. annul

C. register

12. First International Telecom seeks to expand its vision of full coverage telecommunications, hopefully providing more <u>innovative</u> and convenient

mobile communications services.

A. dormant

B. avant-garde

C. brackish

13. Given the increasing <u>diversity</u> of mobile telecommunication services and the fiercely competitive nature of the telecom industry, the PHS sector has a bright future.

A. heterogeneity

B. similitude

C. congruity

Situation 2

1. The <u>rapid</u> development of the information industry in recent years has led to high outputs of consumer electronics products, which have not only accelerated the delivery of new information products that have replaced the old ones, but also shortened the life cycle of such products.

A. indolent

B. mercurial

C. lethargic

2. The rapid development of the information industry in recent years has led to high outputs of consumer electronics products, which have not only <u>accelerated</u> the delivery of new information products that have replaced the old ones, but also shortened the life cycle of such products.

A. precipitated

B. deterred

C. stonewalled

3. Therefore, manufacturers engaged in the R&D of such products have attempted

various innovative designs or marketing strategies to <u>stimulate</u> consumers and expand markets.

   A. deprecate

   B. disparage

   C. galvanize

4. However, in an era when digital camera markets are growing rapidly, only repositioning products based on future market demand and developing new products by <u>creative</u> design can create niche markets.

   A. prolific

   B. insipid

   C. trite

5. The digital camera sector in Taiwan is still in its <u>infancy</u>.

   A. archaicism

   B. venerableness

   C. adolescence

6. While Japan and the United States <u>dominate</u> the global market in this area, Japan controls production of the major components.

   A. cave in

   B. dictate

   C. succumb

7. During conceptual development, industrial designers often lack a goal-oriented and <u>systematic</u> approach.

   A. topsy-turvy

   B. helter skelter

   C. methodical

8. The limited and <u>subjective</u> experience of such designers severely limits design quantity and quality.

A. biased

B. impartial

C. forthright

9. Given increasingly diverse consumer preferences, creating innovative concepts in product redesign is extremely challenging. In the future, most Taiwanese manufacturers will either compete with others in the digital camera sector or <u>ally</u> with them to yield mutually beneficial results.

A. sever

B. confederate

C. sunder

10. Product innovation necessitates the <u>continuous</u> incorporation of advanced technologies in product design to satisfy consumer tastes.

A. intermittent

B. perpetual

C. sporadic

11. According to the Product Development and Management Association, over 50% of all sales come from new products that were <u>innovated</u> by hi-tech industries.

A. eviscerated

B. debilitated

C. fostered

12. While product research may prove <u>costly</u> to manufacturers, the hi-tech sector must accurately predict consumer trends and preferences.

A. exorbitant

B. dog cheap

C. real steal

Situation 3

1. Following half a century of development, the Taiwanese automotive industry is <u>limited</u> not only by its rather small market, but also by technological restrictions imposed by overseas parent manufacturers.

   A. infinite

   B. hemmed in

   C. inexhaustible

2. This <u>dilemma</u> has been further exacerbated by overproduction in the global automotive market, resulting in mergers and alliances.

   A. explication

   B. quandary

   C. band-aid

3. Additionally, Taiwan's <u>accession</u> to the World Trade Organization has negatively affected local automotive manufacturers.

   A. repudiation

   B. renunciation

   C. acquiescence

4. The restrictions have definitely limited the ability of Taiwanese automotive manufacturers to compete with multinational corporations, <u>inevitably</u> forcing local enterprises to conform to available resources and adopt various product innovation strategies.

   A. God willing

   B. perchance

   C. inexorably

5. Despite this unfavorable environment, domestic automotive manufacturers have <u>strived</u> aggressively to enter the export market in a manner consistent with globalization trends.

A. endeavored

B. ceded

C. abnegated

6. Following several years of development in this direction, the local automotive industry has reached international quality standards, as evidenced by the <u>tremendous</u> amounts of capital invested in R&D and design.

A. nondescript

B. gargantuan

C. trifling

7. Such efforts have <u>culminated</u> in product differentiation to adhere to local consumer demand.

A. embarked

B. climaxed

C. derived

8. Local <u>acceptance</u> of domestically manufactured automobiles has gradually increased the market share.

A. compliance

B. repulse

C. declension

9. However, <u>expanding</u> the domestic market share has been extremely challenging, prompting local manufacturers to establish production facilities in China and other southeastern Asian countries to offset high labor costs.

A. receding

B. constriction

C. accrual

10. In summary, domestic automotive manufacturers have <u>expended</u> considerable effort in research to develop high-quality models at competitive prices, making

up for their previously tarnished image.

A. replenished

B. dissipated

C. restocked

H

Common elements in identifying future directions and challenges in developing a product or service 產品／服務開發的未來動向及挑戰 include the following elements:

1. Introduce a sector or industry concerned with the development of a specific product or service.
   簡述部門或產業對特定產品／服務的關注
2. Describe product or service development in detail.
   針對特定產品／服務的發展詳細說明
3. Cite a specific application.
   舉一個特定應用實例
4. Describe future directions or potential applications of this product or service.
   說明該產品／服務未來的發展方向及其發展潛能

1. Introduce a sector or industry concerned with the development of a specific product or service. 簡述部門或產業對特定產品／服務的關注

◎ Taiwan's biotechnology sector has rapidly evolved in line with global trends. Given the increased profits of medical-oriented biotechnology firms, a growing number of seemingly unrelated market sectors have expressed much interest in biotechnology applications. Traditional Chinese medicine is no exception.

◎ Cancer often occurs long before diagnosis, making it difficult to treat and cure. Therapeutic treatment is occasionally so extensive that patients fear it as much as the disease itself.

◎ With the rapid evolution of global medical technologies in recent years, radiation oncology departments have developed technologies to keep in pace with technological innovations, such as those involving radiation pharmaceuticals and linear accelerators.

2. Describe product or service development in detail. 針對特定產品／服務的 發展詳細說明

◎ Traditional Chinese medicine and other traditional medical treatments have already received considerable attention in the new millennium, as evidenced by the availability of commercial medicinal herb-based products. Having significantly contributed to restoring human health and treating diseases, traditional Chinese medicine and Western medicine differ mainly in drug design and functional use. Preparing traditional Chinese medicine involves complex treatment procedures, in which crude drugs are derived from many chemical compounds; plants constitute more than 80% of the contents as well.

◎ Positron Emission Tomography (PET) has been extensively adopted in theoretical and clinical experiments for diagnosing cancer in its early stages. For diagnostic purposes, PET acquires physiological images by detecting positrons. Positrons are miniaturized particles emitted from a radioactive substance administered to patients.

◎ With the increasing incidence of cancer in the general population, the health profession has aggressively implemented cancer preventive measures. As the market demand for radiation technology-based cancer treatments increases along with available product innovations, a recent National Science Council study indicated that revenues from the radiation oncology sector ranged from $NT 500 million to 1 billion in Taipei in 2004. Given the large market potential, radiation oncology departments in Taiwanese hospitals have expressed much interest in radiation oncology technology applications, which have received strong governmental support.

3. Cite a specific application. 舉一個特定應用實例

◎ Medicinal herb products became popular in the United States around 1994 owing to their relaxing effects, with related products including ginseng, Chinese angelica, garlic and ginkgo. Recent developments in medicinal herbal products heavily draw upon the practices of traditional Chinese medicine. In 1882, an investigation of the role of Chinese ephedra in traditional Chinese medicine led to the discovery of ephedrine. Additionally, chemical compounds and many synthetic derivatives used in traditional Chinese medicine are highly beneficial to the human respiratory system. Given the numerous beneficial results obtained from the study of traditional Chinese medicine, therapeutic treatment has been developed to treat tumors, resist the artemisine found in malaria, resist the DDB found in hepatitis, as well as utilize Huperzine A and Anisodamine to treat nervous system disorders.

◎ The most useful positron emission originates from stable parent isotopes that can not be produced in a generator, only the cyclotron. In the cyclotron, stable nuclei are bombarded with protons or deuterons to create the positron proton rich state necessary for positron emission. Given their relatively short half-lives, the cyclotron must be constructed close to the PET scanner. For instance, carbon-11 half lives last only 20.3 minutes. Therefore, a PET Center without a cyclotron is inefficient. Unfortunately, National Tsing Hua University has the only center that specializes in producing nuclear medicine (commonly referred to as a tracer), providing this medicine for all PET centers in southern Taiwan.

◎ As an effective means of understanding this market sector, the five-point based market strategy can provide an effective means for radiation oncology departments to equip management professionals with appropriate and efficient marketing policies. The five-point based marketing strategy consists of product, price function, accuracy and promotion. The product strategy focuses on technology differentiation, in which hospital physicists emphasize how their product line differs from that of other hospitals. The price strategy emphasizes setting prices based on competitive products while considering quality control and efficacy of those products.

4. Describe future directions or potential applications of this product or service.說明該產品／服務未來的發展方向及其發展潛能

◎ Moreover, traditional Chinese medicine has much potential for the health food market. Given strong governmental support for research and the rapid development of the biotechnology sector, the potential applications for traditional Chinese medicine appear to be limitless.

◎ The accelerated growth of nuclear medicine worldwide has greatly enhanced clinical practice. To keep pace with global trends in nuclear medicine, Taiwan must establish a Cyclotron Center that specializes in producing tracers. Taichung would be the ideal location for providing tracers to PET Centers in central and southern Taiwan. While satisfying the market demand for tracer medicine in PET centers such as Shin Kong Hospital, China Medical University Hospital, Chung Shan Medical University Hospital and National Cheng Kung University Hospital, the Cyclotron Center is also a forum for scholars and clinicians to conduct PET-related research. Additional benefits may include entrepreneurial investment in real estate, schools and hospitals near the Center. Moreover, the Cyclotron Center would operate under the auspices of the Atomic Energy Council to avoid environmental pollution caused by nuclear medicine. Despite the large initial investment to keep the surrounding environment free of pollution, entrepreneurs may find investment in the Cyclotron Center as rewarding as industrial parks such as the Hsinchu Science-based Industrial Park.

◎ For successful implementation, radiation oncology departments must exercise careful control in adopting new technologies. The promotional aspect of the five-point strategy emphasizes the role of a company's product given intense competition in the medical sector. Finally, the place aspect of the five-point strategy stresses the role of qualified agent for marketing purposes. In sum, the five-based marketing strategy can greatly facilitate radiation oncology departments in remaining abreast of the latest trends of this rapidly evolving technology sector.

In the space below, identify future directions and challenges in developing or promoting a particular product or service.

_____

_____

_____

_____

_____

_____

_____

_____

Look at the following examples of identifying future directions and challenges
in developing a product or service

Given a growing public health consciousness in Taiwan, overseas entrepreneurs have
concentrated heavily on Taiwan's health fitness sector since 1999. Whereas only 26
independently owned health fitness centers operated island wide in 1996, that figure
rose to 138 in 2002, which does not include franchises of large chain groups. Health
fitness centers adopt diverse strategies to attract members in an already intensely
competitive market. More than just attracting new clients, fitness centers are also
concerned with customer retention by offering follow-up services to ensure customer
satisfaction. Customer satisfaction often leads to positive referrals that generate even
more clients. In this area, marketing personnel obviously play an influential role.
Increasing customer satisfaction and ensuring renewed memberships largely depend
on the following service-related factors: service quality, management structure with
respect to offering quality services, customer relations and pursuit of client referrals,
measures to remedy the company's breach of contact or customer dissatisfaction,
proposals to continuously improve service quality, continuous efforts to improve
customer satisfaction and strengthening of relations between members and the health
fitness center. Fitness center club members in Taipei fit the following profile:
females (56.7%), an age range of 21 to 30 years old (66.1%), university-educated
(44.1%), unmarried (85.5%), no children (89.8%), full-time employment (41.2%)
and a monthly income ranging between ＄NT 20,001 - 40,000 (43.1%). Given the
increasing economic contribution of women to families, their expendable income is
a positive developmental trend for the fitness center sector in Taiwan.

●

Taiwan's biotechnology industry has rapidly evolved in recent years, subsequently
increasing marketing efforts in the local cosmetics sector. As the market and

technology for biotechnology-based cosmetics develop continuously, the Industrial Technology Research Institute indicated that revenues from the local cosmetics sector ranged from $US 1,700,000,000 - 1,800,000,000 in 2002. Given this enormous market potential, the local cosmetics industry in Taiwan has expressed much interest in biotechnology applications, with substantial governmental subsidy in support. As an effective means of understanding this market sector, the 4P-based marketing strategy can provide Taiwan's biotech industry with clear guidelines to equip management professionals with appropriate and efficient marketing policies. The 4P-based marketing strategy consists of product, price, promotion and place. The product strategy focuses on product differentiation, in which company personnel stress how their product line differs from that of its competitors. The price strategy emphasizes setting prices based on competitive products and, more difficult, customers' cognition, psychology towards and awareness of competitive products. Additionally, the promotion strategy involves promoting a company's product through the electronic media. Finally, the place strategy stresses meeting the most appropriate agent for marketing purposes. Company personnel should expand their logistic channels to increase brand awareness and ease in purchasing products. In sum, the 4P-based marketing strategy can greatly facilitate the biotechnology industry in clarifying consumer behavioral patterns in the cosmetics sector.

●

The product insurance sector has remained under closely scrutinized governmental controls for more than four decades. Not large in scale, the island's product insurance sector has largely been influenced by protectionist governmental policies and a few operators dominating the market unfairly. Such restraints have prevented Taiwan from keeping pace with counterparts in Europe and North America. Taiwan's entry into the World Trade Organization (WTO) in 2002 marked the opening of the financial insurance market to overseas competition. To coordinate efforts to liberalize the market, Taiwan's Ministry of Finance began implementing the transition in three stages last April with the launching of tariff liberalization. Income generated from insurance premiums in Taiwan has maintained stable growth in recent years, surpassing the NT$100,000,000,000 mark in 2002; of which, 51.23% came from commercial banks. This figure reflects the continuous development of the bank-sponsored life insurance segment. Conversely, with income generated from insurance premiums in the commercial property sector reaching NT$73,513,000,000 in 2000, only NT$287,000,000 came from the bank insurance segment, i.e., approximately 0.39% of the total amount. Tariff liberalization has subsequently accelerated product diversification. Insurance companies must depend on their previous experiences, available market data, obstacles to entry, responsiveness to governmental legislation and awareness of pending commercial opportunities. With market liberalization, governmental protection of regulation fee rates no longer exists, necessitating the need to classify risks in the market. By adopting customer data to categorize risks incrementally, insurance operators can effectively respond to perceived risks and, simultaneously, diversify its insurance policy offerings.

Situation 1

as the service sector in Taiwan gradually matures to a level

TSC strives to lead the cosmetics sector by addressing global concerns

TSC aggressively pursues large capital investment

Situation 2

Elsa Bedding

research and development division to advance product technology

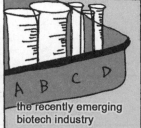
A B C D

the recently emerging biotech industry

increase its productivity through innovative products and services

Situation 3

non-profit foundation

created out of law enacted from Taiwan's Legislative Yuan in 1995

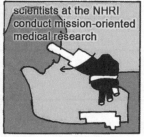
scientists at the NHRI conduct mission-oriented medical research

coordinate, integrate and support research activities undertaken by medical institutions

I

Write down the key points of the situations on the preceding page, while the instructor reads aloud the script from the Answer Key. Alternatively, students can listen online at www.chineseowl.idv.tw

Situation 4

_____

_____

_____

Situation 5

_____

_____

_____

Situation 6

_____

_____

_____

J Oral practice II

Based on the three situations in this unit, write three questions beginning with *How*, and answer them. The questions do not need to come directly from these situations.

Examples

How do numerous service-oriented franchisers in Taiwan aspire to stake a claim in the island's increasingly competitive market?

by offering differentiated products, services and forms of technical support.

How do conventional marketing strategies of traditional brick-and-mortar industries differ from the new approach?

They largely depend on a particular mode that has evolved over time.

1. _____

_____

2. _____

_____

3. _____

_____

K

Based on the three situations in this unit, write three questions beginning with **Why**, and answer them. The questions do not need to come directly from these situations.

Examples

Why did Elsa Bedding Franchise in Taiwan establish a research and development division?

to advance product technology

Why must a company incorporate innovation?

to identify customers' needs

1. _____

_____

2. _____

_____

3. _____

L

Based on the three situations in this unit, write three questions beginning with **What**, and answer them. The questions do not need to come directly from these situations.

Examples

What was created as a non-profit foundation out of law enacted from Taiwan's Legislative Yuan in 1995?

the National Health Research Institute (NHRI)

What organization does NHRI function autonomously under the auspices of?

the Department of Health

1. _____

   _____

2. _____

   _____

3. _____

   _____

M Write questions that match the answers provided.

1. _____

   _____

   Collagen toner water, Collagen body lotion, Ocean spirit cleansing, Collalife
   bone fixer, Ocean spirit body shampoo and Collalife slim magic

2. _____

   _____

   to satisfy customers

3. _____

   _____

   coordinate, integrate and support research activities undertaken by medical
   institutions

N Listening Comprehension II

Situation 4

1. What drives TSC?

   A. the island's increasingly competitive market

   B. a highly talented staff of professionals from multidisciplinary fields

   C. effective and inexpensive beauty products

2. What are conventional marketing strategies aimed at?

    A. service-oriented franchisers

    B. various information sources

    C. traditional brick-and-mortar industries

3. How does TSC strive to lead the cosmetics sector?

    A. by addressing global concerns over aging prevention and treatment

    B. by attempting to transform the cosmetics sector with safe, effective and inexpensive beauty products

    C. by aggressively pursuing large capital investment, state-of-the-art technologies

4. Why has TSC aggressively pursued large capital investment, state-of-the-art technologies and various information sources?

    A. to further strengthen its core competence

    B. to become a globally competitive leader in this intensely competitive sector

    C. both A and B

Situation 5

1. What is a source of innovation in Taiwan's bedding sector?

    A. government investment

    B. the biotechnology industry

    C. innovative products and services

2. Why has Elsa Bedding Franchise in Taiwan established a research and development division?

    A. to advance product technology

    B. to receive an additional 30% of base salary

    C. to receive a bonus if results of their research lead to a patented technology

3. Why must a company incorporate innovation?

    A. to increase productivity through innovative products and services

B. to integrate its efforts with the recently emerging biotech industry

C. to identify customers' needs

4. How will ELSA employees receive a bonus?

A. if results of their research lead to a patented technology

B. if the company can successfully integrate its efforts with the recently emerging biotech industry

C. if the company can position itself as a leader in Taiwan's bedding sector

5. When do R&D employees receive on-the-job training?

A. every other weekend

B. each Saturday morning

C. each Sunday morning

Situation 6

1. How was the National Health Research Institute created?

A. out of a mandate promulgated by the Department of Health

B. out of law enacted from Taiwan's Legislative Yuan in 1995

C. out of law enacted from the National Health Insurance Bureau

2. How many research divisions and departments does the NHRI comprise?

A. five and three, respectively

B. ten and four, respectively

C. six and two

3. What do scientists at the NHRI investigate?

A. overall directions of national science and technology development in medical care

B. a transparent system for reviewing and assessing research projects

C. many aspects of biomedical sciences

4. Knowledge expertise and facilities at the NHRI will become pivotal in doing

what?

    A. planning the overall directions of national science and technology development in medical care

    B. understanding, preventing and curing diseases nationwide

    C. coordinating, integrating and supporting research activities undertaken by medical institutions

5. How does the NHRI facilitate information exchanges?

    A. by training young scientists and physicians

    B. by dedicating itself to the enhancement of medical research and healthcare island wide

    C. through domestic and international cooperative ventures

O Reading Comprehension II

Select the word or expression whose meaning is closest to the meaning of the underlined word or expression in the following passages

Situation 4

1. As the service sector in Taiwan gradually matures to a level comparable with that found in other industrialized countries, numerous service-oriented franchisers aspire to stake a <u>claim</u> in the island's increasingly competitive market by offering differentiated products, services and forms of technical support.

    A. retraction

    B. assertion

    C. abjuration

2. As the service sector in Taiwan gradually matures to a level comparable with that found in other industrialized countries, numerous service-oriented franchisers

aspire to stake a claim in the island's increasingly competitive market by offering <u>differentiated</u> products, services and forms of technical support.

A. ossified

B. monolithic

C. demarcated

3. They do so in contrast to conventional marketing strategies of traditional brick-and-mortar industries, which largely depend on a particular <u>mode</u> that has evolved over time.

A. dearth

B. vein

C. omission

4. Under the mottos of *Vision, Mission* and *Core Value*, TSC strives to <u>lead</u> the cosmetics sector by addressing global concerns over aging prevention and treatment.

A. coerce

B. supersede

C. postdate

5. While attempting to transform the cosmetics sector with safe, effective and inexpensive beauty products, TSC is driven by a highly talented staff of professionals from multidisciplinary fields that integrate their efforts <u>synergistically</u> in a spirit of mutual respect.

A. cooperatively

B. autonomously

C. independently

6. While attempting to transform the cosmetics sector with safe, effective and inexpensive beauty products, TSC is driven by a highly <u>talented</u> staff of professionals from multidisciplinary fields that integrate their efforts

synergistically in a spirit of mutual respect.

A. oafish

B. all thumbs

C. endowed

7. <u>Notable</u> brand name products in the TSC product line include Collagen toner water, Collagen body lotion, Ocean spirit cleansing, Collalife bone fixer, Ocean spirit body shampoo and Collalife slim magic.

A. rubric

B. obscure

C. cryptic

8. To enhance its competitive edge, TSC <u>aggressively</u> pursues large capital investment, state-of-the-art technologies and various information sources to further strengthen its core competence and become a globally competitive leader in this intensely competitive sector.

A. indifferently

B. inertly

C. intrusively

9. To enhance its competitive edge, TSC aggressively pursues large capital investment, <u>state-of-the-art</u> technologies and various information sources to further strengthen its core competence and become a globally competitive leader in this intensely competitive sector.

A. vintage

B. anachronous

C. ultramodern

10. To enhance its competitive edge, TSC aggressively pursues large capital investment, state-of-the-art technologies and various information sources to further strengthen its core <u>competence</u> and become a globally competitive leader

in this intensely competitive sector.

A. ineptness

B. savvy

C. amateurishness

Situation 5

1. While striving to <u>satisfy</u> consumer demand for quality sleep, Elsa Bedding Franchise in Taiwan established a research and development division to advance product technology.

A. perturb

B. gratify

C. dismay

2. According to management <u>guru</u> Peter Drucker, a company's purpose is to satisfy customers.

A. groupie

B. sage

C. disciple

3. More than just marketing, a company must <u>incorporate</u> innovation to identify customers' needs.

A. obviate

B. sideline

C. imbibe

4. <u>Innovation</u> is to be attained in the present, not the future.

A. Docility

B. Conformity

C. Contrivance

5. One source of innovation is the biotechnology industry. Taiwan's information

technology sector is aggressively striving to integrate its efforts with the recently <u>emerging</u> biotech industry.

A. emanation

B. receding

C. abridgement

6. Biotech products such as cosmetics have been widely <u>commercialized</u> by local manufacturers such as the Taiwan Sugar Corporation.

A. monopolized

B. marketed

C. oligopoly

7. Given the increasing public demand for health care products, Elsa's R&D Department will <u>devote</u> its efforts to this area of development.

A. renounce

B. apostatize

C. consecrate

8. First, Elsa will <u>recruit</u> three employees with undergraduate or graduate training in biotechnology.

A. subdue

B. muster

C. pacify

9. Previous employees of the Industrial Technology Research Institute will receive an additional 30% of base <u>salary</u>.

A. recompense

B. mulct

C. amercement

10. Next, R&D employees will receive on-the-job training each Sunday morning. Finally, <u>employees</u> will receive a bonus if results of their research lead to a

patented technology.

A. clientele

B. patronage

C. personnel

11. Despite <u>mounting</u> competition, Elsa is determined to increase its productivity through innovative products and services, positioning itself as a leader in Taiwan's bedding sector.

A. precipitating

B. ascending

C. cascading

Situation 6

1. As a non-profit foundation created out of law enacted from Taiwan's Legislative Yuan in 1995, the National Health Research Institute (NHRI) functions autonomously under the <u>auspices</u> of the Department of Health.

A. incursion

B. encroachment

C. aegis

2. As a non-profit foundation created out of law enacted from Taiwan's Legislative Yuan in 1995, the National Health Research Institute (NHRI) functions <u>autonomously</u> under the auspices of the Department of Health.

A. exclusive of

B. facilitated

C. co opted

3. While <u>dedicating</u> itself to the enhancement of medical research and healthcare island wide, the NHRI comprises ten research divisions and four departments (Administration, Intramural Research, Extramural Research, and Research

Resources).

A. refraining

B. consigning

C. abjuring

4. Scientists at the NHRI conduct mission-oriented medical research and investigate many aspects of biomedical sciences, as well as <u>specific</u> diseases.

A. prevalent

B. unambiguous

C. non descript

5. Clinical disorders range from aging, cancer, infectious diseases, mental <u>disorders</u> and occupational diseases.

A. maladies

B. placebos

C. elixirs

6. Hopefully, knowledge expertise and facilities at the NHRI will become <u>pivotal</u> in understanding, preventing and curing diseases nationwide.

A. cardinal

B. evanescent

C. trifling

7. Besides planning the overall directions of national science and technology development in medical care, the NHRI strives to <u>coordinate</u>, integrate and support research activities undertaken by medical institutions.

A. embroil

B. confound

C. mesh

8. Besides planning the overall directions of national science and technology development in medical care, the NHRI strives to coordinate, <u>integrate</u> and

support research activities undertaken by medical institutions.

A. dichotomize

B. assimilate

C. dissect

9. Furthermore, in addition to training young scientists and physicians, the NHRI also focuses on establishing a <u>transparent</u> system for reviewing and assessing research projects, as well as facilitating information exchanges through domestic and international cooperative ventures.

A. forthright

B. dubious

C. paradoxical

10. Furthermore, in addition to training young scientists and physicians, the NHRI also focuses on establishing a transparent system for reviewing and <u>assessing</u> research projects, as well as facilitating information exchanges through domestic and international cooperative ventures.

A. deferring

B. valuating

C. protracting

Answer Key

Answer Key
Unit One Making Inferences from Statistics
統計結果的推論及應用

A

Situation 1

According to market forecasts by Communications Industry Researchers and iSuppli, the global production value of LEDs and LED displays grew 78% between 2004 and 2008. China and Taiwan will probably pave the way as manufacturers with production bases in the Asia Pacific region, as evidenced by the fact that China and Taiwan account for over 25% of the global production of LED and LED displays, with output in the former expected to reach 65 billion units by 2007. Production in China, Hong Kong and Taiwan is expected to rise markedly in the next few years, driven mainly by portable electronic devices, such as mobile phones, PDAs, digital cameras, as well as applications in indoor and outdoor lighting and illumination, automotive electronics, navigation, aviation, railway and traffic systems. In China alone, production output reached roughly 50 billion units in 2004. Spurred on by large-scale governmental initiatives, output is expected to reach a record 65 billion units in 2006 or 2007. Meanwhile, Taiwan is strengthening its market position in the global LED industry. According to the Industrial Technology Research Institute, the Asia Pacific region's global market share for LEDs increased to 25% - second only to that of Japan at 50%. HB LEDs used in the automotive industry are more cost efficient and longer lasting than fluorescent lights. While Chinese, Taiwanese and Hong Kong companies can produce HB LEDs, Taiwan leads global production, followed by China and Japan. However, given the influx of overseas LED manufacturers, China is widely expected to become the global leader, with nearly 30% of global production. HB LEDs already account for 1/3 of LEDs produced by Chinese manufacturers, and are used particularly for backlighting, and in portable devices and automobiles. Moreover, Chinese and Taiwanese manufacturers are aligning their chip LED production to the strong market demand from the portable devices sector. The production of LEDs and LED displays is also concentrated in Jiangsu, Zhejiang, Shandong, Shanghai, Fujian and Guangdong. At least 500 manufacturers produce LEDs and LED displays. In 2004, while domestic suppliers produced 25 billion of the LEDs and LED displays produced in China, overseas companies that were operating locally produced at least 20 billion units. In contrast, 30 manufacturers in Taiwan comprise the supplier base, reflecting a tremendous potential for expansion given the above statistics and trends.

Situation 2

The World Health Organization defines a country as an aging society when 7% of the population exceeds 65 years old. With most industrialized countries having attained this status, aggressive policies have been implemented to ensure the welfare of the elderly. Having become an aging society in 1993, Taiwan lacks clear legislation and policies to ensure the welfare of the elderly, by comparison with other industrialized countries. According to population trend estimates from Taiwan's Council for Economic Planning and Development and the Ministry of the Interior, a widely anticipated surge in the elderly population will increase the demand for care. For instance, in the next two to three decades, 1/3 of Taipei's population will become elderly. In 1990, the elderly populations of northern and eastern townships in Taiwan outside of central business districts surpassed 7 %, as they did in some western townships in 1996 and in some southern townships in 2001. Consistent with this trend, senior citizen housing was one of the ten leading building structures in 2003. Already a mature market, senior citizen housing in the United States is estimated to be able to expand in the next two decades. Given increased demand for elderly care and tax incentive policies, private enterprises in Taiwan have significantly expanded investments into the senior citizen housing sector, reflecting public concern over meeting the accommodation and special needs of this population. Effective marketing policies are an effective means of forecasting trends in this housing market. The above statistics reflect not only strong market growth for senior citizen housing and acceptance by consumers of this trend, but also the importance of product, price, promotion and place to marketing strategies in this area.

Situation 3

Taiwan's hospital sector is unique in that it includes private, non-profit and government-owned facilities - all occasionally competing for the same patients. While patients account for only 5% of revenue in the health care sector, governmental subsidies through the National Health Insurance Scheme (54%) and private insurers (34%) account for the majority of revenues, with 7% from other sources. This unique situation requires that the hospital sector develop strategic models that resemble those applied in industry. Empirical evidence suggests that some environmental issues normally considered in analyzing organizations are irrelevant to analyzing the financial accountability of hospitals, while others are very relevant. For instance, the unemployment rate and per capita income of the local population can accurately predict whether a hospital will close. Other environmental factors only slightly affect hospital performance. Since the implementation of Taiwan's national health insurance scheme in 1995, medical institutions have often cited difficulty in continuing operations, given increasing competition in the health sector. In particular, the Taiwanese healthcare market faces several challenges. (1) The average size of hospitals has increased. (2) The geographical positions of hospitals are not distributed uniformly around the island. (3) Hospitals fiercely compete with clinics for patients. (4) Medical organizations are either extremely small or large. According to the Department of Health, Executive Yuan, Taiwan (DOH), the number of hospitals in Taiwan declined by 231 or 29.35%, from 787 in 1989 to 556 in 2004. Additionally, the number of public hospitals declined by five or 5.38%, from 93 in 1989 to 88 in 2004; correspondingly, the number of private hospitals declined by 126 or 32.56%, from 694 in 1989 to 468 in 2004 (DOH, 2005). Obviously, this reduction in hospitals will negatively affect the medical sector.

Additionally, the global aging phenomenon is evident in Taiwan, with the island officially becoming a "rapidly aging society" in 1993, as defined by the World Health Organization. Therefore, from a market demand perspective, Taiwan has enormous growth potential, as evidenced by the establishment of many hospitals and increasing competitiveness in the medical care sector. Given the saturated and fiercely competitive medical service sector, selecting the wrong location for a new hospital could significantly increase operational costs and stymie future growth. Selecting the location of a hospital to maximize competitiveness involves devising appropriate evaluation criteria.

B

When is output of LEDs and LED displays expected to reach a record 65 billion units in China?
in 2006 or 2007

When is output of LEDs and LED displays in China expected to reach 65 billion units?
by 2007

When is production of LEDs and LED displays in China, Hong Kong and Taiwan expected to rise markedly?
in the next few years

C

How does Taiwan know that it lacks clear legislation and policies to ensure the welfare of the elderly?
by comparison with other industrialized countries

How have private enterprises in Taiwan significantly expanded investments into the senior citizen housing sector?
increased demand for elderly care and tax incentive policies

How does one know that a widely anticipated surge in the elderly population will increase the demand for care?
according to population trend estimates from Taiwan's Council for Economic Planning and Development and the Ministry of the Interior

D

Why could selecting the wrong location for a new hospital significantly increase operational costs and stymie future growth?
Owing to the saturated and fiercely competitive medical service sector

Why is the global aging phenomenon evident in Taiwan?
Because the island officially became a "rapidly aging society" in 1993

Why does Taiwan have enormous growth potential from a market demand perspective
The establishment of many hospitals and increasing competitiveness in the medical care sector

E

Which country is widely expected to become the global leader in LED manufacturing, with nearly 30% of global production?

What proportion of Taipei's population will become elderly in the next two to three decades?

What factors can accurately predict whether a hospital will close?

F

Situation 1

1.B   2. C   3.B   4. A   5. A

Situation 2

1. C   2. C   3. B   4. C   5. A

Situation 3

1. B   2. B   3. A   4. C   5. C

G

Situation 1

1. B   2. C   3. A   4. B   5. A   6. C   7. B   8. B   9.A
10. C   11. C   12. B   13. A   14. C

Situation 2

1. A   2. A   3. C   4. B   5. A   6. C   7. C   8. A   9. B   10. B

Situation 3

1. B   2. C   3. A   4. C   5. C   6. B   7. A   8. C   9. A
10. C   11. B   12. B   13. C   14. C   15. B   16. C   17. A

I

Situation 4

Since the National Health Insurance scheme was established in 1995, medical expenditures have been recorded electronically as the Taiwanese government has promoted the use of the National Health Information Network (HIN), which enables medical institutions island-wide to make data accessible and transparent in digital form. In 1996, The National Health Insurance Journal addressed the status of computerization in clinical practice, revealing that before the implementation of the National Health Insurance scheme, computerization of medical records in clinical practice was below 20%. However, according to current statistics, this proportion now exceeds 60%. In 1996, a hospital survey of computerization and on-line impetus groups noted a rapid increase in the number of clinics that were computerized. From 1994-1996, computerization increased from 28% to 57%. In 1997, 76.3% (6977) of all clinics had computerized their operations, representing a significant increase of 25.7% (4666) in 1994 and 54.9% (6509) in 1996. Moreover, 92.9% of all hospitals in Taiwan that applied to the National Health insurance for reimbursement of service processing had computerized their operations. According to the results of an analysis of clinical software sources, software represented approximately 84.6% of purchases from contracted information vendors. 35.3% of all hospitals had invested under $100,000 in computers for clinical use; 32% had invested $100,000-$200,000, and 25.1% had invested above $200,000; 7.5% did not reply. As most hospitals experience difficulty in adjusting to changes in National Health Insurance laws, 8.7% of them expressed a desire to provide computer education and training. Many hospitals can outsource their medical information system requirements, reduce the costs of developing medical software, as well as those of maintenance and personnel, receive governmental subsidies for medical expenses and, in doing so, increase the efficiency and effectiveness of staff.

Thus, advances in information systems have greatly facilitated administrative operations, pricing strategies and bookkeeping.

Situation 5

Taiwan's biotech sector has invested considerable resources in adopting traditional Chinese medicine in a diverse array of health-oriented products. Globally, traditional Chinese medicine generated revenues of $US 15 billion in 1997. A forecasted $US 30.5 billion by 2006 reflects its increasing societal acceptance. With 195 Taiwanese manufacturers' developing traditional Chinese medicine, domestic output probably exceeds 4 billion New Taiwanese (NT) dollars. This sector employs more than 4,000 individuals, and products are sold in a wide array of fields on a relatively small scale. Despite an abundance of pharmaceutical firms that manufacture Chinese herbal medicines, the sector lacks a global development strategy. More importantly than developing new medicine and pricing competitively, the sector must effectively address the abundance of low-quality Chinese herbal medicine. The clinical curative effect of components in traditional Chinese medicine requires further evaluation of existing patent laws and scope of application. Notably, several collaborative efforts are being made by experts across many disciplines to develop Chinese herbal medicine, as evidenced by the growing number of technology transfers from research institutes, teaching hospitals and clinical testing centers to local industry for commercialization. Given these efforts, breakthroughs are widely anticipated in the near future.

Situation 6

The Taiwanese government relaxed financial market regulations in 1980 for overseas firms, resulting in the establishment of 16 new banks, each with its own approach to improving customer service. Such measures have not only enhanced the overall quality of financial services island wide, but have also led to strong market competition. While striving to gain customer loyalty, each bank develops unique financial services to gain a competitive edge. However, lending services are often offered via more established banks, and new banks are confronted with the challenge of creating their own unique market niche to provide innovative financial services. Current low interest rates, increased local consumption and extended credit through the pervasive use of credit cards have dramatically transformed consumption trends — as individuals have become less frugal and are concerned with cultivating personal tastes. In summary, Taiwan is becoming a more credit-based than cash-based society in terms of purchasing habits. Given such changes in local purchasing habits, the credit card market has become almost saturated, as evidenced by the large number of credit card-issuing banks. For instance, Taiwanese banks such as Fubon Bank and Chinatrust Commercial Bank aggressively strive to build upon their existing market share with numerous customer-tailored services. While Fubon increased its number of issued credit cards by 50% in 2002, Chinatrust had approximately 5 million card holders by March of the same year. Such consumer trends appear to be positive: more credit cards in the market will boost consumer spending, ultimately generating bank revenues. However, such an assumption does not consider some of the potential risks that lending banks face. Whereas market growth is driven by competition with other lending institutions rather than by consumer demand, an economic recession or stalled personal income growth could lead to high defaulted credit card debt if banks lack adequate credit rating standards and qualified lending practices.

J

Why do 8.7% of Taiwanese hospitals express a desire to provide computer education and training?
Because they experience difficulty in adjusting to changes in National Health Insurance laws

Why are many hospitals able to increase the efficiency and effectiveness of staff?
They can outsource their medical information system requirements and reduce the

costs of developing medical software.

Why have administrative operations, pricing strategies and bookkeeping been greatly facilitated?
advances in information systems

K

How can one improve the clinical curative effect of components in traditional Chinese medicine?
by further evaluation of existing patent laws and scope of application.

How could one anticipate breakthroughs in the near future?
by the growing number of technology transfers from research institutes, teaching hospitals and clinical testing centers to local industry for commercialization

How are traditional Chinese medicine products sold?
in a wide array of fields on a relatively small scale

L

What do more established banks often offer?
lending services

What factors have dramatically transformed consumption trends?
Current low interest rates, increased local consumption and extended credit through the pervasive use of credit cards

What do Taiwanese banks such as Fubon Bank and Chinatrust Commercial Bank aggressively strive to do?

build upon their existing market share with numerous customer-tailored services

.

M

Which publication addressed the status of computerization in clinical practice?

How many Taiwanese manufacturers are developing traditional Chinese medicine?

How is Taiwan becoming a more credit-based than cash-based society?

N

Situation 4

1.C   2.B   3.A   4.C   5.B

Situation 5

1. C   2. B   3. A   4. C   5. C

Situation 6

1. C   2. A   3.C   4. B   5. A

O

Situation 4

1.A   2.C   3.A   4.C   5.C   6.B   7.B   8.A   9.C   10.C   11.B

Situation 5

1.B   2.B   3.A   4.C   5.A   6.B   7.B   8.A   9.C   10.A

Situation 6

1.B   2.C   3.A   4.C   5.B   6.C   7.A   8.B   9.B   10.A   11.C   12.A

Answer Key
Describing Organizational or Technical Needs
描述組織或科技需求

A

Situation 1

The finance sector in Taiwan has undergone tremendous changes in recent years, as evidenced by the availability of Internet-based financial data that enable customers to remain abreast of the latest market trends and opportunities. Given the gradual increase in consumer demand for such information, customer relationship management (CRM) has been greatly emphasized in the organizational strategies of banks to increase their competitiveness. While banking is a traditional business, many newly established banks have difficulty in distinguishing their financial services from those of well-established banks. To increase their competitive advantage, banks must identify those success factors that are essential to retaining customers and identifying new ones. Analyzing transaction data is a complex task, and obtaining such data is difficult. Nevertheless, such an analysis can help banks to draw up guidelines and promotional strategies to lure new customers. For instance, Taiwanese banks actively promote wealth management banking. Given the relative inflexibility of strategies that banks offer in this area, each bank must highlight the unique features of its program to strengthen its competitiveness by encouraging customer loyalty and seeking new clients. With a lack of research on wealth management practices in the banking sector, major success factors have not been identified nor has its potential contribution to bank revenues been determined, limiting the scope of not only banking management strategies but also available services. The large number of banks in Taiwan explains the slow growth rate of 5% among individual banks. Given the emphasis on the lifetime value of consumers and long-term transaction fees, banks fiercely compete with each other in the wealth management market. Financial specialists must not only be able to attract new customers, but also provide satisfactory wealth management strategies that are consistent with banking practices. In the intensely competitive financial market, financial specialists must carefully balance effective marketing strategies with efforts to earn the long-term loyalty of customers. The inability of banks to adopt CRM and employ effective financial planners negatively affects their competitive edge in the wealth management market.

Situation 2

Market liberalization since the 1980s has increased commercial activity between China and Taiwan. China's accession to the World Trade Organization in 2002 and its hosting of the 2008 Olympic Games have further spurred economic growth. Moreover, as globalization trends encourage foreign direct investment, many multinational corporations intend to move some of their operations to China. With increasing direct investment in China by overseas companies in recent years, international business centers offer overseas investors resources such as hardware and software, and in so doing are following global economic trends. While helping small and medium-sized overseas firms to invest in China and increase the level of their investments, international business centers can increase domestic and international trade, create employment opportunities and promote economic growth. Market liberalization and export-oriented markets have enabled China's economy to grow at an annual rate of more than 9%, with external trade increasing by nearly 15% annually. International business centers help small and medium-sized overseas firms that are uncertain of the investment climate and laws, and are unfamiliar with the local language and constraints on capital. International business centers can arrange transportation, hold business functions, help expatriates adjust to daily life and provide business premises for rent; they can also help companies reduce operational costs, exchange information, hire secretarial staff and contribute to the development of emerging markets. An international business center in China typically disseminates information through the mass media to attract foreign investment, acts as a liaison between the overseas investor and governmental officials, helps overseas investors to adjust to Chinese culture by providing information on such topics as food, clothing and lifestyle. While performing these functions, an international business center must adhere to local governmental regulations. Identifying the factors that influence the location of an international business center is vital to commercial success. Selecting sites where overseas firms can operate can be a complex task. Selecting a site model to meet investors' concerns is especially important. The inability to locate an international business center efficiently will increase operating costs and reduce the profit margin. Therefore, the factors that influence the choice of location model to be adopted by an international business center must be identified using the decision making statistical method of AHP.

Situation 3

Given the stagnant Taiwanese economy and increasing unemployment in recent years, growing crime rates and related convictions have led to a high prisoner population on the island. As individuals strive to cope with the rapidly transforming global economy, the accelerating growth of China has adversely affected Taiwan in terms of lost production and loss of foreign investment. The unemployment rate in Taiwan stands at 5.5%. Often contradictory political policies have sought to remedy this negative trend, only to have exacerbated the situation. Increasing unemployment and lost production have continuously reduced tax revenues, necessitating that the government reduce funding for public projects. Consequently, loss of employment has had dire consequences for many families, as Taiwan finds itself in transition from a manufacturing-based economy to a knowledge-based one, and has been partially responsible for high incarceration rates. However, the conventional means of locating correctional facilities is not objective, and depends often on the subjective judgment of decision makers. The conventional approach is associated with high public funding, especially for long-term prisoners in correctional facilities. Despite strict governmental controls on the management or construction of other publicly funded facilities, such measures have been ineffective for correctional facilities. The conventional approach involves selecting a large piece of land away from the general population. However, doing so often requires that the government spend tremendous amounts of capital to maintain the facilities and prevent crime, since a conventionally chosen location is not close to service providers. The expansion of, or maintenance of materials for, correctional facilities often involves high handling costs. Hesitancy among the general population to live near such high-risk facilities, often referred to as not-in-my-backyard (or NIMBY), results in increased operational costs and societal unease. For instance, the number of inmates in the 53 correctional facilities in Taiwan increased from 37,000 to 43,000 from September, 2005 until now, with that figure continually increasing. Moreover, the ratio of correctional facility staff to prisoners is a dangerously low 1 : 20 - far below the prescribed standard. Such a dangerous imbalance makes effective management almost impossible, as evidenced by the recent jail rioting in Brazil. Regaining control and repairing that facility cost that government hugely in capital and human resources. Not only Brazil, but many industrialized countries devote considerable resources to preventing prison rebellions. The inability to solve this problem in Taiwan's correctional facilities will extract many unforeseen societal costs in the future, ultimately overburdening governmental finances. Additionally, the location of such facilities affects the convenience of the supply of materials and services; a limited number of service providers that can deliver severely restrict the ability of administrators to control the prisoner population. Therefore, factors that affect the infrastructure and safety of correctional facilities in Taiwan must be identified via the analytic hierarchy process (AHP) to optimize the target population and location of such facilities.

B

Why have the organizational strategies of banks greatly emphasized customer relationship management (CRM)?

to increase their competitiveness

Why is it difficult to obtain transaction data?

Because analyzing it is a complex task

Why do banks fiercely compete with each other in the wealth management market?

Because of the emphasis on the lifetime value of consumers and long-term transaction fees

C

How does an international business center in China typically disseminate information to attract foreign investment?

through the mass media

By helping small and medium-sized overseas firms to invest in China and increase the level of their investments

How has China's economy been able to grow at an annual rate of more than 9%?

Market liberalization and export-oriented markets

How can international business centers help small and medium-sized overseas firms that are uncertain of the investment climate and laws?

They can arrange transportation, hold business functions, help expatriates adjust to daily life and provide business premises for rent; they can also help companies reduce operational costs, exchange information, hire secretarial staff and contribute to the development of emerging markets.

D

What factors have continuously reduced tax revenues?
Increasing unemployment and lost production

What does Taiwan finds itself in?
transition from a manufacturing-based economy to a knowledge-based one

What has resulted in increased operational costs of Taiwanese correctional facilities and societal unease?
Hesitancy among the general population to live near such high-risk facilities, often referred to as not-in-my-backyard (or NIMBY)

E

What have many newly established banks in Taiwan had difficulty in doing?

How much is external trade in China increasing annually?

What depends often on the subjective judgment of decision makers?

F

Situation 1
1. C 2. A 3. C 4. C 5. B

Situation 2
1. C 2. A 3. C 4. A 5. B

Situation 3
1. B 2. A 3. C 4. B 5. C

G

Situation 1

1.B 2.B 3.C 4.A 5.C 6.B 7.A 8.C 9.B 10.B 11.C 12.B 13.A
14.C

Situation 2

1.B 2.C 3.A 4.C 5.B 6.B 7.C 8.A 9.C 10.C 11.B 12.B 13.C
14.C

Situation 3

1.B 2.A 3.C 4.C 5.B 6.C 7.A 8.C 9.B 10.C 11.A 12.B
13.B 14.C 15.B 16.A 17.C 18.B 19.A

I

Situation 4

The Global Budget System implemented by the National Health Insurance Bureau in Taiwan poses a major challenge for hospitals as they seek to create a budgetary balance in their daily operations. Increasingly fierce competition among hospitals and the need for sustainable development have forced administrators to scrutinize closely business models applied to daily operations. Such initiatives include organizational rearrangement, personnel layoffs, operational cost reductions, lowering of operational risks, outsourcing and the making of investments to enhance the quality of medical care and competitiveness. Medical administrators have focused heavily on constructing a deluxe health examination center to outsource diagnosis operations. By outsourcing to companies that provide health care, medical institutions do not require additional budgeting for construction equipment, materials and personnel management, helping to maintain the quality of medical treatment without increasing hospital revenues. Given the uniqueness of medical operations, outsourcing such operations differs from outsourcing the general affairs of administrative units. Effectively controlling overhead and, more importantly, establishing a mechanism for sharing in capital and business-related risks are essential to enhancing the division of both labor and management among specialized departments, to ensure medical quality and provide a competitive edge over other medical facilities with respect to operations, expanded market share and advanced technologies. However, when hospitals examine the feasibility of outsourcing the operations of a medical unit, the analytic hierarchy process and extension theory are seldom applied to evaluate the weights of the assessment criteria and ensure objectivity. Of the 34 public hospitals that operate under the Department of Health, three offer advanced health examinations that are outsourced to private medical units and more than 15 hospitals will contract with outside companies to provide such operation within three years. Outsourcing reduces expenditure on machines, equipment, medical supplies, renovation and utilities, as well as the numbers of doctors, nurses, medical technicians and administrators. Outsourcing also reduces the annual investment by more than 10%. However, the inability of public hospitals that outsource general operations to examine thoroughly the feasibility of generating revenue from such outsourcing under the Global Budget System severely restricts their competitiveness, increasing operating expenses. Therefore, the factors influencing the operational expenses of a hospital, including investment in equipment, personnel costs and costs of utilities, must be identified.

Situation 5

The relationship between trends in the global semiconductor market and Taiwan's semiconductor industry has received increasing attention. The electronics industry is an integral part of the Taiwanese economy, and local semiconductor manufacturers play a leading role in global production. The revenues of the semiconductor industry increase, following economic trends, and its business cycle is highly volatile. A strong market demand increases industrial output and revenues, causing suppliers to invest heavily in facilities, land and equipment. Although total capital investment of the industry has significantly increased, the average sales price (ASP) of integrated circuits has decreased since the recent construction of mass production facilities has markedly increased the available supply. As Japan and the United States have gradually lost market share, Taiwan has met strong competition from Asian chipmakers such as those from China and Korea that have gained a competitive advantage using low-price strategies. Taiwanese semiconductor manufacturers are thus concerned with how to enhance production. Moreover, governmental authorities, enterprise managers and investors must understand how industrial development and management performance are related. Having expanded over the past two decades, the semiconductor industry in Taiwan has significantly affected the island's economy, as evidenced by generated revenues of US$18.65 billion in 2002. As of 2001, Taiwan's semiconductor industry comprised more than 100 design companies, 20 wafer manufacturers, over 40 packaging firms and 30 testing firms. However, conventional methods apply both quantitative and qualitative means to evaluate productivity. While qualitative evaluation methods include the expert system and the Delphi method, quantitative evaluation methods include time series analysis, exponential smoothing and neural networks. Although the global billings and bookings (B/B ratio) of North American semiconductor equipment producers are used to forecast market trends in the global semiconductor industry, exactly how such trends are related to Taiwan's semiconductor industry has not been addressed. Prior to 1998, Europe and the United States accounted for 60% of the semiconductor market, reflecting their previous dominance in this area. However, in recent years, capital expenditure by the Asian semiconductor industry has increased - from 25% in 1999 to 38% in 2003, with a forecasted 40% in 2006. Although the annual revenues of the Taiwanese semiconductor industry have risen, such increases have not seen economies of scale in production. Although previous marketing research to understand Taiwan's semiconductor industry have contributed to economic growth, administrators find that further increasing economic growth without a clear marketing strategy is almost impossible. Taiwanese information technology and electronics firms face fierce competition from multinational corporations when they enter export markets. Maintaining a competitive advantage depends on the ability of Taiwanese firms to invest continuously in research and development. Exactly how global market trends in the semiconductor industry influence the operating performance of Taiwan's semiconductor industry can be analyzed based on an index of semiconductor equipment producers in Japan.

Situation 6

Taiwanese living standards have dramatically increased in recent years, as evidenced by the availability of consumer goods, the pursuit of cultural interests and strong health consciousness. Media emphasis on maintaining one's health and the wide acceptance of nutritional supplements have paved the way for a health food products market, which is promoted by an increase in the popularity of genetically modified foods. The growth in daily consumption of health food products explains why, according to governmental statistics, medical and healthcare expenditures account for an increasing share of household consumption in Taiwan and, correspondingly, a rise in the number of recently established local pharmacies. A recent study of consumer trends in the health food products sector in Taiwan revealed not only that consumers prefer retail outlets over direct selling channels, but also that consumers most often purchase health food products at pharmacies. While local pharmacies play a vital role in the island's healthcare system, continuous changes in retail trends, commercial practices and the national health insurance scheme necessitate that pharmacists remain abreast of marketing and promotional strategies to increase profits.

J

What are some of the initiatives that hospitals have adopted to create a budgetary balance?
organizational rearrangement, personnel layoffs, operational cost reductions, lowering of operational risks, outsourcing and the making of investments to enhance the quality of medical care and competitiveness

What must be done to enhance the division of both labor and management among specialized departments, to ensure medical quality and provide a competitive edge over other medical facilities with respect to operations, expanded market share and advanced technologies?
effectively controlling overhead and, more importantly, establishing a mechanism for sharing in capital and business-related risks

What severely restricts their competitiveness of public hospitals that outsource general operations?
their inability to examine thoroughly the feasibility of generating revenue from such outsourcing under the Global Budget System

K

Why are Taiwanese semiconductor manufacturers concerned with how to enhance production?
Because it has met strong competition from Asian chipmakers

Why must Taiwanese firms invest continuously in research and development?
To maintain a competitive advantage

Why do Taiwanese information technology and electronics firms face fierce competition when they enter export markets?

Because of pressure from multinational corporations

Why do conventional methods apply both quantitative and qualitative means?

To evaluate productivity

Why has previous marketing research attempted to understand Taiwan's semiconductor industry?

To contribute to economic growth

L

How can one demonstrate that consumers prefer retail outlets over direct selling channels?

through a recent study of consumer trends in the health food products sector in Taiwan

How has daily consumption of health food products grown?

through an increasing share of household consumption in Taiwan and, correspondingly, a rise in the number of recently established local pharmacies.

How are pharmacists motivated to remain abreast of marketing and promotional strategies to increase profits?

through continuous changes in retail trends, commercial practices and the national health insurance scheme

M

How many public hospitals operate under the Department of Health?

How long has the semiconductor industry in Taiwan expanded?

What has the media emphasized?

N

Situation 4

1.B   2.C   3.A   4.B   5.C

Situation 5

1.C   2.A   3.A   4.C   5.B

Situation 6

1.B   2.A   3.C   4.A   5.C

O

Situation 4

1.C   2.A   3.A   4.C   5.B   6.A   7.B   8.C   9.B   10.A   11.C

Situation 5

1.B   2.B   3.C   4.A   5.C   6.B   7.C   8.A   9.B   10.C

Situation 6

1.B   2.A   3.A   4.B   5.A   6.A   7.C   8.B   9.B

A

Situation 1

A rapidly growing elderly population poses a major challenge for long-term care management, requiring immediate solutions, given changing family structures and the frequency of chronic illnesses. Employees in hospital-subsidized respiratory care centers, respiratory care wards and nursing homes are nearly all nursing care attendants. They are members of a sub-specialized field and do not hold specialized license certification nor have reached a particular level of academic attainment. These workers simply require basic healthcare training skills and the necessary knowledge of hospital or governmental infrastructure to enable them to perform their tasks efficiently. Playing an important role in Taiwanese society, nursing care attendants accompany disabled individuals and help them in their daily activities, such as taking baths and eating meals. They also monitor urinary or stool specimens, change the posture of incapacitated stroke victims and provide general comfort. Despite their contributions, most nursing care attendants lack a uniform management approach to ensure the quality of service. These workers have no restrictions of age, education or experience, save for their being mentally and physically sound. Despite the abundance of outsourcing agencies for nursing care attendants, the lack of standardized training makes controlling the quality of service provided island-wide impossible. Moreover, changes in Taiwan's National Health Insurance scheme have led to an emphasis on controlling personnel costs while maintaining high-quality services, further contributing to the outsourcing of nursing care attendants. Generally, relatives of the patient directly employ nursing care attendants without adequate evaluative criteria to select the most appropriate care provider. Additionally, outsourcing firms lack objective criteria in selecting nursing care attendants, leading to widespread customer dissatisfaction and increasing management difficulty.

Situation 2

Credit cooperatives have played a pivotal role as financial institutions in Taiwan's economic development. The market liberalization policies of the Taiwanese government since 1992 have led to the emergence of several banks, and financial organizations have sprung up quickly, intensifying market competition. The rapid growth of this market sector has had some adverse effects, such as banks' lowering their criteria for loan approvals to remain competitive, increasing the incidence of loan defaults. An increasing number of financial organizations, especially credit cooperatives, have run into this problem. Given turbulent political and economic situations worldwide, financial institutions in Taiwan must adopt dramatic reform measures to maintain their competitiveness. Only banks, and not credit cooperatives, have benefited from governmental initiatives such as the nationwide Financial Reform Project, explaining the low competitiveness of the latter in Taiwan's financial market. Although attempting to reform the financial market, financial research does not directly focus on market developments. In practice, while financial organizations draw on their personal experiences to improve their competitiveness, doing so often leads to poor investments and subsequent defaulted loans. This situation is especially prevalent among credit cooperatives, explaining their inability to reform and lower the rate of defaulted loans. The survival of credit cooperatives as financial institutions in Taiwan is at great risk, necessitating improved understanding of their importance and unique features. The inability of the Experience Rule and financial research to reduce the risk of defaulted loans will lead to further corporate loss among Taiwan's financial organizations. Under these circumstances, Taiwanese financial organizations will become less competitive. Their number has already decreased: only 30 credit cooperatives are currently operating in Taiwan, in contrast to the 72 that used to operate. Even following their elimination, many credit cooperatives leave behind several unresolved financial problems, creating a serious financial crisis domestically.

Situation 3

The Taiwanese government has implemented separate frameworks for the medical and pharmaceutical sectors since 1997, and the rate of hospital prescription drugs filled by pharmacies is extremely low. This fact explains why over-the-counter drug purchases, along with sanitary and other related medical products, have become the major source of revenue for pharmacies. Local pharmacies have thus adopted a business model of one-stop shopping in recent years, according to which customers can purchase a wide array of medical and health food products. Although empirical analysis of pharmacies in the field of business management has focused on management strategies, the orientation of pharmacists toward marketing practices, consumer purchasing behavior and pricing strategies, studies have not developed a forecasting model to help pharmaceutical managers increase their effectiveness. The inability to forecast accurately either the share of household income spent on medical and health car or the number of local pharmacies to be established makes almost impossible an accurate analysis by managers of market competition and the development of effective strategies.

B

What do nursing care attendants require to perform their tasks efficiently?
basic healthcare training skills and the necessary knowledge of hospital or governmental infrastructure

What are some of the tasks that nursing care attendants perform in Taiwan when accompanying disabled individuals?
They monitor urinary or stool specimens, change the posture of incapacitated stroke victims and provide general comfort.

What has led to an emphasis on controlling personnel costs while maintaining high-quality services?

changes in Taiwan's National Health Insurance scheme

C

How have turbulent political and economic situations worldwide influenced financial institutions in Taiwan?

They must adopt dramatic reform measures to maintain their competitiveness.

How do poor investments and subsequent defaulted loans often occur?

Financial organizations draw on their personal experiences to improve their competitiveness

How could a serious financial crisis domestically evolve?

if many credit cooperatives leave behind several unresolved financial problems

D

Why is it ironic that previous studies have not developed a forecasting model to help pharmaceutical managers increase their effectiveness?

Because empirical analysis of pharmacies in the field of business management has focused on management strategies, the orientation of pharmacists toward marketing practices, consumer purchasing behavior and pricing strategies

Why is it almost impossible an accurate analysis by managers of market competition and the development of effective strategies?

Owing to the inability to forecast accurately either the share of household income spent on medical and health car or the number of local pharmacies to be established

Why has the Taiwanese government implemented separate frameworks for the medical and pharmaceutical sectors since 1997?

to ensure that over-the-counter drug purchases, along with sanitary and other related medical products, become the major source of revenue for pharmacies

E

What do most nursing care attendants lack?

How many credit cooperatives are currently operating in Taiwan?

How long has the Taiwanese government implemented separate frameworks for the medical and pharmaceutical sectors?

F

Situation 1

1.C 2.A 3.B 4.B 5.C

Situation 2

1.C 2.B 3.B 4.A 5.C

Situation 3

1.C 2.A 3.B 4.B 5.A

G

Situation 1

1.C 2.A 3.C 4.C 5.B 6.C 7.C 8.A 9.B 10.B

Situation 2

1.A 2.C 3.C 4.B 5.B 6.C 7.B 8.A 9.C 10.C

Situation 3

1.C 2.B 3.B 4.A 5.C 6.C 7.B 8.A 9.A

Situation 4

Intellectual capital is a significant resource in creating wealth. Although tangible assets such as property, facilities and equipment continue to play a vital role in the manufacture of products and the provision of services, their relative importance has declined with the increasing importance of knowledge-based assets. Although able to measure the value of tangible assets that can be quantified in a company, conventional accounting methods do not include knowledge-based assets, leading to the underrating of a company's value. Additionally, scientific and technological advances have increased the importance of intellectual capital. For instance, on-line gaming companies emphasize the ownership of intellectual capital rather than tangible assets. Accordingly, the value of on-line gaming companies has seldom been measured in previous studies. Online gaming is the most important part of the gaming industry, with generated revenues of US$ 1 billion in 1999, skyrocketing to US$ 2 billion dollars in 2002. According to the International Data Corporation (2003), in 2002, the number of on-line game players was 533,000,000 in the Asian Pacific region, with South Korea and Taiwan leading the way, accounting for 54% and 26%, respectively. The inability to measure the value of companies without incorporating intellectual capital not only leads to an underrating of their value, but also makes impossible an understanding of the effect of intellectual capital on the on-line gaming market.

Situation 5

Complex administrative procedures associated with Taiwan's National Health Insurance (NHI) scheme have led to errors in insurance claims and much inefficiency. For instance, adhering to all NHI regulations would require a patient to fill out more than 30 forms, relating to insurance claims, salary readjustment, and the insurer's/claimant's name. With errors caused by confusion over forms, the NHI staff spends much time in handling errors and requesting insurers and claimants to correct erroneous information. Despite the enormous amount of administrative time and cost involved in handling these errors, this growing concern and its larger implications have not been addressed in the literature. The inability to gradually reduce the amount of human resources involved in handling insurer and claimant errors and simplify administrative procedures as well as NHI forms, will lead to higher operational costs. In practice, telephone, fax or mail is used to correct such errors, creating substantial overhead and increasing the time spent by human resources.

Situation 6

A young soldier with a high fever brought about by a widespread common cold presented himself to a physician, being otherwise physiologically healthy. However, after his condition suddenly deteriorated after six days in the sickbay, he died in the intensive care unit (ICU) despite three days of emergency rescue procedures by medical personnel. The coroner's autopsy cited heart palsy as the cause of death. The actual cause of death remains unknown, and the coroner's report is merely a formality for family members in completing procedures to receive compensation for death incurred from military duty. Medical institutions must be responsible for instilling in physicians a sense of professional ethics so that medical professionals can assume responsibility without the assigning of fault to a particular party. Moreover, medical treatment involves a degree of risk such that even some management approaches cannot be applied. Professional health care administrators not only encounter resistance from medical consumers, but also pose a potential threat to a patient's rights. Under such circumstances, these administrators must occasionally make choices without conferring with many others.

J

How much in revenues did on-line gaming generate in 1999?

US$ 1 billion

How is intellectual capital a significant resource?

in creating wealth

How is it impossible to understand the effect of intellectual capital on the on-line gaming market?

owing to the inability to measure the value of companies without incorporating intellectual capital

K

What does the NHI staff spend much time in doing?

handling errors and requesting insurers and claimants to correct erroneous information.

What will lead to higher operational costs?

the inability to gradually reduce the amount of human resources involved in handling insurer and claimant errors and simplify administrative procedures as well as NHI forms

What creates substantial overhead and increases the time spent by human resources?

using telephone, fax or mail to correct insurer and claimant errors

L

Why must professional health care administrators occasionally make choices without conferring with many others?
because they not only encounter resistance from medical consumers, but also pose a potential threat to a patient's rights

Why did an otherwise physiologically healthy and young soldier present himself to a physician?
because he had a high fever brought about by a widespread common cold

Why is the coroner's report merely a formality for family members in completing procedures?
to receive compensation for death incurred from military duty

M

How many on-line game players were there in the Asian Pacific region in 2002?
What has the literature not addressed?
What did the coroner's autopsy cite?

N

Situation 4

1.B   2.A   3.B   4.C   5.A

Situation 5

1.C   2.A   3.C   4.C   5.B

Situation 6

1.C   2.B   3.A   4.C   5.A

O

Situation 4

1.C 2.B 3.B 4.C 5.B 6.A 7.C 8.B 9.B

Situation 5

1.C 2.A 3.B 4.B 5.B 6.A 7.C 8.A 9.C 10.B

Situation 6

1.C 2.B 3.A 4.C 5.B 6.A 7.B 8.B 9.C 10.A

A

Situation 1

Based on an index of semiconductor equipment producers in Japan, our recent project analyzed exactly how global market trends in the semiconductor industry influence the operating performance of Taiwan's semiconductor industry. Semiconductor equipment producers in Japan announce their B/B ratio on a monthly basis. Publicly listed Taiwanese semiconductor manufacturers in information technology and electronics industries from 2002 to 2004 were selected as the sample in this study. The operating performance of Taiwan's semiconductor industry was then analyzed using statistical software. Next, the operating performance of the Taiwanese semiconductor industry was determined by factor analysis. Additionally, the relationships between the B/B ratio and leading indicators of the composite index of Taiwan, the operational performance of the Taiwanese semiconductor industry and the semiconductor sector in Philadelphia were determined by regression analysis. Moreover, whether or not business cycle and operational performance influence each other was explored. The proposed index enables the semiconductor equipment producers in Japan to assess more accurately the global B/B ratio of semiconductor equipment producers in North America based on the operational performance of Taiwan's semiconductor industry. Additionally, the proposed index can determine whether semiconductor equipment producers in Japan can exceed 20% of the global B/B ratio of semiconductor equipment producers in North America. Moreover, in addition to enabling entrepreneurs to understand more thoroughly the global ranking of Taiwan's semiconductor industry, the proposed index can provide a valuable reference not only for stock market investors, but also for enterprise managers who are devising appropriate strategies for various economic cycles. A significantly positive relation between the sales growth rate and the net profit after tax growth rate indicates a significantly positive relationship between management performance and fluctuations of the business cycle in the semiconductor industry.

Situation 2

Our most recent collaboration developed a customer ranking model for analyzing the dynamic purchasing behavior of customers and identifying potential generators of bank revenues. The behavioral results can be used to devise diverse promotional strategies or to customize products or services to meet consumer needs, achieving market differentiation and effective management of customer relations. Based on numerous available customer data, a data mining method, CRISP-DM, was employed, combining conventional means of data exploration with two mathematical calculations (decision tree and category nerve) to determine how various purchasing activities are related and how many factors can be used to rank the value of a customer's relationship. Factors associated with customer relations and the customer life-cycle were then combined to construct an enhanced management model. According to our results, the proposed customer ranking model can be adopted to manage effectively customer relations, significantly reducing promotional costs and allowing sales staff to concentrate on identifying potential customers. By incorporating CRIPS-DM, the proposed model can efficiently analyze current customer data, enabling marketing staff to understand customers more closely; identify potential niche markets, and optimize the relationship between the customer and the institution. The proposed model can be used to verify and adjust factors of the ranking module to ensure that a company continues to provide quality services. While the customer's value in the customer relationship management system can be determined, this model can significantly enhance the ability to attract new customers. Furthermore, it can be used in other business sectors to enhance the ability to identify, acquire and retain the loyalty and profitability of customers.

Situation 3

Our recent project developed a novel index based on the analytic hierarchy process (AHP) to measure the value of the intellectual capital of on-line gaming companies. Content analysis was performed to devise questionnaires on the components of intellectual capital. The questionnaires were sent to the managers of on-line gaming companies and banks to find out which factors should be considered in measuring the intangible capital of their companies. Next, AHP was used to understand which factors are deemed most important by the managers of on-line gaming companies and banks in determining the intellectual capital of on-line gaming companies. Using AHP, the weight (relative importance) of each intellectual capital variable was evaluated, based on the perceptions of managers of on-line gaming companies and banks. The results were considered based on the criteria applied by banks to measure the intellectual capital of a business. Moreover, exactly how banks and on-line game companies differ when measuring intellectual capital was determined using Principal Component Analysis. Based on the results, the proposed index provides on-line gaming companies with criteria to determine their intellectual capital, providing a valuable reference for banks when determining whether to grant commercial loans. The ability to measure the actual value of an on-line gaming company will significantly reduce the likelihood of defaulted loans. Additionally, on-line gaming companies will have clear guidelines regarding how banks measure intellectual capital, enhancing their competitiveness. Moreover, the proposed index of intellectual capital in this growth sector can enhance the conventionally used indexes and increase their accuracy. The results of this study provide a valuable reference for banking institutions that need to understand how on-line gaming companies measure their intangible capital.

B

What was analyzed using statistical software?

the operating performance of Taiwan's semiconductor industry

What was explored?
whether or not business cycle and operational performance influence each other

What indicates a significantly positive relationship between management performance and fluctuations of the business cycle in the semiconductor industry?
a significantly positive relation between the sales growth rate and the net profit after tax growth rate

C

Why were factors associated with customer relations and the customer life-cycle combined?
to construct an enhanced management model.

Why can the proposed customer ranking model significantly reduce promotional costs and allow sales staff to concentrate on identifying potential customers?
owing to its ability to manage effectively customer relations,

Why can a company continue to provide quality services?
because the proposed model can be used to verify and adjust factors of the ranking module

D

How was the intellectual capital of on-line gaming companies determined?
by using AHP to understand which factors are deemed most important by the managers of on-line gaming companies and banks

How was the weight (relative importance) of each intellectual capital variable evaluated?

based on the perceptions of managers of on-line gaming companies and banks

How can one significantly reduce the likelihood of defaulted loans?

by measuring the actual value of an on-line gaming company

E

How were the operational performance of the Taiwanese semiconductor industry and the semiconductor sector in Philadelphia determined?

How can one use the model in other business sectors?

What does the proposed index provide on-line gaming companies with?

F

Situation 1

1.C 2.C 3.B 4.A 5.C

Situation 2

1.B 2.C 3.A 4.C 5.B

Situation 3

1.B 2.C 3.B 4.C 5.B

G

Situation 1

1.C 2.B 3.A 4.B 5.C 6.C 7.A 8.B 9.C

Situation 2

1.B 2.A 3.C 4.B 5.B 6.A 7.C 8.B 9.A

Situation 3

1.C 2.C 3.B 4.B 5.C 6.C 7.A 8.A 9.C 10.B 11.A 12.C

I

Situation 4

Our research group recently developed a novel evaluation method to identify target credit card customers. The method incorporates characteristics associated with the lifestyles of such customers and the factors that contribute to their incurring of debts. Pertinent literature was reviewed to identify the characteristics of credit card customers and the effect of their lifestyles on their purchasing behavior. Questionnaires were sent to customers to determine their personality and lifestyle, and their relationships to their purchasing behavior. Based on the results, cluster analysis was used to classify credit card customers into different categories. The proposed evaluation method provides a valuable reference for banking institutions that are attempting to identify desirable credit card customers, eventually leading not only to the development of a marketing strategy to attract such target customers, but also to the lowering of operating costs and credit risk.

Situation 5

Our most recent project developed a credit risk assessment model by analyzing a mass of data or by detecting concealed purchasing models, to reduce the defaulted loan burden of small financial institutions. A database of customer data was constructed, to which highly effective data mining approaches were applied to identify the attributes of each customer account, including overdraft records, outstanding loans and income level. Credit ranking criteria based on a decision tree were then established for all customers in the bank database. In addition to greatly facilitating the decision of a banking officer on whether to grant a loan, the credit risk assessment model also reduces operating costs by enhancing process flow. Moreover, the proposed model paves the way for other potential data mining applications in financial institutions, such as more thoroughly satisfying customers through more effective marketing strategies based on acquired data. The proposed model is highly promising for other industrial applications.

Situation 6

Our group recently developed an investment risk model that analyzes the features of credit cooperatives in Taiwan. A questionnaire was designed for loan officers at credit cooperatives to accumulate relevant loan information and background information about credit cooperatives. Features of credit cooperatives were then analyzed using factor analysis. Next, factors that influence whether or not financial officers approve loans were analyzed using SPSS statistical software. Additionally, potential defaulted loans are identified using MDS. Moreover, factors that distinguish credit cooperatives from banks were analyzed using cluster analysis. According to our results, the proposed investment risk model can enable loan officers in banks and credit cooperatives to identify potentially defaulting loans, since the method is derived by directly focusing on market developments that previous financial research neglected. Additionally, whereas previous studies have not addressed the financial problems of credit cooperatives, the proposed model can more thoroughly elucidate the features and the role of credit cooperatives by identifying factors that enhance their performance. In addition to compensating for limitations of previous financial research and the Experience Rule, the proposed model provides a valuable means of understanding current developments in financial markets, and helps credit cooperatives to make good loan decisions to maintain their market competitiveness. Moreover, the proposed method provides a valuable reference for the Taiwanese Government to initiate timely financial reforms that will enhance the role of cooperatives in the financial market.

J

Why were questionnaires sent to customers?
to determine their personality and lifestyle, and their relationships to their purchasing behavior.

Why was cluster analysis used in the research?
to classify credit card customers into different categories

Why does the proposed evaluation method provide a valuable reference for banking institutions that are attempting to identify desirable credit card customers?
because it will eventually lead not only to the development of a marketing strategy to attract such target customers, but also to the lowering of operating costs and credit risk.

K

How has the credit risk assessment model reduced operating costs?
by enhancing process flow

How can the proposed model pave the way for other potential data mining applications in financial institutions?
by more thoroughly satisfying customers through more effective marketing strategies based on acquired data

How does the credit risk assessment model benefit the banking sector?
It greatly facilitates the decision of a banking officer on whether to grant a loan,

L

What can the proposed investment risk model enable loan officers in banks and credit cooperatives to do?
identify potentially defaulting loans

What area did previous studies not address?
the financial problems of credit cooperatives

What does the proposed method provide the Taiwanese Government with?
a valuable reference when initiating timely financial reforms that will enhance the role of cooperatives in the financial market.

M

What does the method incorporate?

Why was a credit ranking criteria based on a decision tree established?

How is the method derived?

N

Situation 4

1.C   2.B   3.C   4.B   5.C

Situation 5

1.C   2.B   3.C   4.B   5.C

Situation 6

1.C   2.C   3.C   4.A   5.A

○

Situation 4

1.B   2.A   3.C   4.C   5.B   6.B   7.C   8.A   9.B   10. C

Situation 5

1.B   2.C   3.B   4.B   5.C   6.A   7.C   8.C   9.A   10.A

Situation 6

1.C   2.A   3.C   4.B   5.B   6.B   7.B   8.C   9.A   10.A

Answer Key
Describing Recent Technical Accomplishments in a Company
描述公司最新的科技成就

A

Situation 1

GameQ On-line Gaming Company has pioneered the development of digital context technology in Taiwan. Besides providing online services, GameQ strives to enhance on-line games by upgrading existing technologies and strengthening its 3D animation skills to become competitive in an Asian Pacific market that is dominated by Korean firms. Beyond the Asian Pacific region, sights are set on the larger Chinese on-line gaming market, as well as on North American and European consumers. Of GameQ's nearly 35 employees, 75% have a bachelor's degree or higher, with an average of five years' professional experience in the field. These figures reflect a wealth of experience that GameQ staff with strong research capabilities have accumulated, as evidenced by the company's commitment of 1/4 of its annual operational budget to R&D. While aggressively pursuing its missions, GameQ has established five divisions - Game Design, Programming and Coding Design, Artistic Design, Music Design and R&D. As the company's largest division, R&D maintains state-of-the-art facilities and the latest commercially available equipment and software. As part of the information technology industry, the on-line gaming sector relies heavily on the knowledge and skills of its staff. GameQ is no exception, constantly encouraging staff to pursue further education and frequently attend training sessions on the latest technological developments in the field. The strong technical capabilities that GameQ has developed so far include an Object-Oriented server system with dynamic program module loading, a stream (TCP/IP)-based communication model in systems operations, data-driven game development capabilities, high-performing 2D rendering capabilities based on the incorporation of 3D accelerated hardware and a message based communication protocol with error tolerance. Furthermore, the company applies multidisciplinary approaches to its technical support services. In summary, as Taiwan's on-line gaming sector becomes increasingly competitive, GameQ will continuously upgrade its technology expertise in 3D animation to improve its market position.

Situation 2

Human factor engineering applications in automotive safety testing heavily rely on advanced driving simulation systems.　A notable example is the interactive fixed-based driving simulator developed at the Intelligent Transportation System Center of National Cheng Kung University.　This simulator can analyze an individual's driving behavior as it can efficiently accumulate the results of repetitive experiments.　Performing repetitive experiments can identify danger areas that drivers encounter. Additionally, the driving simulator system creates a virtual environment that convinces individuals that they are actually driving in a real environment. Virtual reality technology can thus simulate a real environment without causing harm to drivers, making it a convenient means of gathering data using scientific means ultimately to enhance automotive safety. This simulation system helps drivers to control their speed, and reduces the likelihood of a traffic accident if a convenient and comfortable driving environment can be provided through appropriate roadway patterns and useful traffic control measures. Traffic accidents can be further reduced by the alignment of freeway with buffer zones to allow rapid traffic flow without exceeding the speed limit .　Some accidents caused by braking or turning too slowly can be prevented if the curb radius is further increased. Reflective warning signs can remind drivers of potential roadway danger, enabling them to avoid accidents from turning too late and colliding into traffic islands. In summary, the driving simulation system can help increase the comfort of a driving environment by making necessary improvements such as the installation of warning or reflective signs along roadways.

Situation 3

The National Health Insurance Bureau (NHIB) began issuing IC cards in January

2004 to streamline administrative procedures and reduce unnecessary medical expenses. The IC card system greatly simplifies the processing of very large amounts of patient-related data. To maintain an efficient information database system, IC cards greatly accelerate the rate at which services are provided. The NHIB strictly protects the confidentiality of patient information, ensured by legislation on the protection thereof. For individuals who are concerned with infringement of their privacy through the IC card system, the IC card does not contain an individual's medical history. Additionally, IC cards exploit the latest information security measures to prevent counterfeiting or information theft. With medical data registered on an individual's IC card, physicians must access this information through their own confidential IC card, further ensuring security. As a unique feature of this system, individuals can choose whether to list specific ailments on their IC card. As of November, 2004, the IC card began recording organ donor information to inform medical staff whether a certain organ is available in emergency situations.

B

How is the on-line gaming sector a part of the information technology industry?
It relies heavily on the knowledge and skills of its staff.

How are GameQ's nearly 35 employees qualified?
75% have a bachelor's degree or higher, with an average of five years' professional experience in the field.

How will GameQ strive to improve its market position?
by continuously upgrading its technology expertise in 3D animation

C

What can performing repetitive experiments identify?

danger areas that drivers encounter

What is a convenient means of gathering data using scientific means ultimately to enhance automotive safety?

virtual reality technology

What can remind drivers of potential roadway danger?

reflective warning signs

D

Why do IC cards exploit the latest information security measures?

to prevent counterfeiting or information theft

Why is this system unique?

Individuals can choose whether to list specific ailments on their IC card.

Why did the IC card begin recording organ donor information as of November, 2004?

to inform medical staff whether a certain organ is available in emergency situations

E

How many divisions as GameQ established?

How does this simulation system help drivers?

What does the IC card not contain?

F

Situation 1

1.C   2.C   3.A   4.B   5.C

Situation 2

1.C   2.B   3.A   4.C   5.C

Situation 3

1.B   2.B   3.A   4.C   5.A

G

Situation 1

1.C   2.B   3.B   4.C   5.B   6.C   7.B   8.A   9.A   10.C

Situation 2

1.C   2.B   3.B   4.C   5.A   6.A   7.C   8.B   9.B   10.A

Situation 3

1.C   2.B   3.C   4.B   5.B   6.C   7.C   8.B   9.A

I

Situation 4

Shilebaida International Science Technologies Corporation manufactures various waste-treatment equipment, including rubbish compressors, medical waste treatment instrumentation, baling press compression machinery, kitchen waste treatment machinery and resource recovery barrels. Medical waste treatment instrumentation utilizes heat decomposition technology, which provides a more secure means of processing waste than conventional burning. In the open air, the burning method produces dioxins and heavy metal contaminants, harming humans. In a closed environment, heat decomposition technology does not release dioxins or heavy metal contaminants, protecting operating staff and addressing environmental concerns. Capable of processing decomposed waste and handling gas emissions safely, heat decomposition technology occupies limited space, minimizes overhead costs and is efficient. Shilebaida International Science Technologies Corporation is committed to upgrading its research capabilities continuously to ensure technological innovation in medical waste treatment.

Situation 5

Previously, Taiwanese hospitals had difficulty in integrating the standards and practices of various information systems adopted at their facilities, making extremely difficult the circulation of internal information and the prevention of administrative errors. Information technology has potential for eliminating these obstacles in daily operations, thereby improving the medical services and management capabilities of a hospital. The MIS department of a hospital can streamline data processing and administrative tasks; improve the efficiency and quality of medical care; increase patient satisfaction and simplify the remittance of national health insurance premiums. Given the role of information technology in lowering a hospital's operational expenses while improving the quality of its medical services, administrative policies can be implemented efficiently and with a high success rate. As daily operations in a hospital produce enormous amounts of clinical and administrative-related data, internal information systems must have advanced support capabilities with extensive throughput and large storage capacities. Additionally, advanced information technologies can increase the efficiency of daily clinical and administrative tasks, simplifying many operational procedures and reducing both patient waiting time and administrative errors. However, given the reluctance of older employees and their lack of information technology skills, training courses are essential to orienting them on the further integration of information technologies into their daily work routine, thus increasing productivity and saving time. Outsourced information technology vendors also play a critical role in determining whether a hospital's information systems satisfy user requirements. Therefore, the MIS department must continuously adopt innovative technologies to facilitate the access and use by system users.

Situation 6

As one of Taiwan's 17 medical centers, Wanfang Hospital is both a teaching and a research facility. Strongly supported by the National Health Research Institute financially, Wanfang Hospital has established 22 research centers. Of these, the Patient Safety Information (PSI) Center collaborates with the National Health Administration in encouraging patients to seek sound medical advice, especially with respect to environmental concerns and the safe use of prescription medicine. Since the first of May, Wanfang Hospital has implemented a system that embeds patient data in an IC chip that individuals can wear as a ring, enabling physicians to access patient information conveniently. In addition to developing a system for ordering nursing services, the PSI Center will place a notebook computer in each hospital ward to contain patient data that can be conveniently accessed by physicians and nursing staff.

J

What produces dioxins and heavy metal contaminants?
the burning method

What protects operating staff and addresses environmental concerns?
heat decomposition technology

What is Shilebaida International Science Technologies Corporation committed to?
upgrading its research capabilities continuously to ensure technological innovation in medical waste treatment

K

Why is the MIS department of a hospital valuable to daily operations?
It can streamline data processing and administrative tasks; improve the efficiency and quality of medical care; increase patient satisfaction and simplify the remittance of national health insurance premiums.

Why can administrative policies be implemented efficiently and with a high success rate?
Owing to the role of information technology in lowering a hospital's operational expenses while improving the quality of its medical services

Why is it possible to simplify many operational procedures and reduce both patient waiting time and administrative errors?
because advanced information technologies can increase the efficiency of daily clinical and administrative tasks

L

How does the Patient Safety Information (PSI) Center encourage patients to seek sound medical advice?
by collaborating with the National Health Administration

How are physicians at Wangfang Hospital able to access patient information conveniently?
through an IC chip that individuals can wear as a ring

How can physicians and nursing staff access patient data conveniently?

by placing a notebook computer in each hospital ward

M

What are the merits of heat decomposition technology?

How do outsourced information technology vendors play a critical role?

How long has Wanfang Hospital implemented a system that embeds patient data in an IC chip that individuals can wear as a ring?

N

Situation 4

1.C   2.A   3.C   4.B   5.B

Situation 5

1.B   2.C   3.B   4.B   5.A

Situation 6

1.B   2.C   3.A   4.C   5.A

O

Situation 4

1.A   2.C   3.B   4.B   5.A   6.C

Situation 5

1.B   2.A   3.C   4.B   5.B   6.C   7.A   8.B   9.A

Situation 6

1.C   2.B   3.C   4.A   5.C   6.C   7.A

Answer Key
Citing Examples of Product/Service Commercialization
產品／服務銷售實例

A

Situation 1

Electronic commerce is a booming sector, as evidenced by its increasing impact on industry. As various business strategy models for electronic commerce have emerged, an increasing number of academics have advocated the extension of the concept of customer value to Internet-based commercial activities. As revenues from electronic commerce lag behind those of mail-order services, the Internet must fully exploit advanced Web-based technologies to realize the market potential of online commerce. More incentives must be provided for customers to switch their purchasing from traditional retail outlets to the Internet. E-commerce is growing in terms of marketplace interactions since Internet users number hundreds of millions worldwide. According to the forecasts of eTForecasts and eMarketer, the number of Internet users between 2002 and 2006 more than doubled, reflecting the tremendous commercial potential of the Internet. Successful e-commerce strategies rely heavily on technological developments and market trends. Technological developments offer a means by which business strategies are successfully implemented. Such developments include Web design, network transmission performance and product/service representations. Also, the success rate of transactions is important. Consumers are easily discouraged from shopping online if any of these technical factors are neglected. Companies must closely scrutinize their product/service strategies to ensure that they are appropriate for electronic commerce. In this area, effective promotional concepts, product price strategy, supply chain systems and the creation of a novel Web environment are all of high priority. Many e-business startups look for new customers by monitoring the consumer growth rate for a particular market niche. While many companies develop promotional campaigns to lure new customers, they often overlook customer loyalty, which is essential for continued sales growth. In summary, many online entrepreneurs strive to protect customer satisfaction and loyalty.

Situation 2

Online auctioning emerged in the United States as a unique form of e-commerce by combining conventional auctioning practices with advanced information technologies. The convenience of hi-speed Internet connections facilitates Internet users' accessing of auction websites for bidding or selling without time and location constraints. With a seemingly unlimited number of potential consumers constantly online, the benefits of online auctioning markedly exceed those of conventional auctioning. Taiwan Yahoo-Kimo and Taiwan E-bay are among the most popular venues in Taiwan, renowned for their novel marketing mechanisms and operational models. Websites that offer various service items differ markedly from traditional commercial outlets. Online shopping does not require face-to-face interaction or close inspection of a product on the store premises. Therefore, online shopping heavily prioritizes security mechanisms to ensure confidential and secure commercial interactions, website functionality and novel marketing strategies. Moreover, online shopping enables consumers to compete with each other on a level playing field, influencing the final product price and sales terms. Still, online shopping raises several challenges. For instance, given the lack of face-to-face interaction, confusion occasionally arises over payment terms. After a user has purchased a product, poor distribution is likely to delay product delivery. Additionally, a breach of confidence in personal data, such as that found in credit card transactions, can lead to identity theft. In summary, commercial websites must ensure secure and safe commercial transactions by reinforcing security mechanisms that require credit card or bank account information for identification. Online auction websites should also provide an escrow service for its customers. Once these obstacles are resolved, online auctioneers can expand the range of products and services offered.

Situation 3

To improve the living environment of the elderly, governmental organizations and the private sector must coordinate efforts to create an environment in which senior citizens' living independently is the norm rather than the exception. In so doing, numerous commercial opportunities will arise. For instance, RUENTEX Construction Company in collaboration with Rien Fu Newlife Company has established a senior citizens' residential community in Tan-shui by drawing on the Japanese long term care model to provide residents with hotel-style management. The facilities provide high-quality comfort with 300 residential units, all of which have already been leased out. Given population trends and enhanced living standards, the climate for growth opportunities in the long-term care sector in Taiwan is favorable. Identifying factors that govern the successful operation of senior citizens' residential communities is thus essential to the competitiveness of businesses, explaining why governmental authorities and industrial planners are anxious to evaluate the most appropriate management strategies.

B

How can one encourage customers to switch their purchasing from traditional retail outlets to the Internet?
by providing more incentives for them to do so

How is the tremendous commercial potential of the Internet reflected?
The number of Internet users between 2002 and 2006 more than doubled.

How are business strategies successfully implemented using technological developments?
through developments such as Web design, network transmission performance and product/service representations

C

Why are *Taiwan Yahoo-Kimo* and *Taiwan E-bay* are among the most popular venues for online auctioning. in Taiwan?
They are renowned for their novel marketing mechanisms and operational models.

Why does online shopping heavily prioritize security mechanisms?
to ensure confidential and secure commercial interactions, website functionality and novel marketing strategies

Why does confusion occasionally arise over payment terms?
because of the lack of face-to-face interaction,

D

What long term care model did RUENTEX Construction Company draw upon to provide residents with hotel-style management?
a Japanese one

What factors make the climate for growth opportunities in the long-term care sector in Taiwan a favorable one?
population trends and enhanced living standards,

What is essential to the competitiveness of businesses?
identifying factors that govern the successful operation of senior citizens'
residential communities

E

What do successful e-commerce strategies rely heavily on?

How must commercial websites ensure secure and safe commercial transactions?

How many residential units does the senior citizens' residential community in Tan-shui have?

F

Situation 1

1.B   2.A   3.C   4.C   5.B

Situation 2

1.C   2.A   3.C   4.A   5.C

Situation 3

1.B   2.C   3.B   4.C   5.C

G

Situation 1

1.C   2.A   3.A   4.C   5.B   6.C   7.B   8.C   9.A   10.A   11.B   12.C   13.A

Situation 2

1.B   2.C   3.C   4.B   5.C   6.B   7.C   8.B   9.A   10.C   11.B   12.C   13.A
14.C

Situation 3

1.B   2.A   3.C   4.C   5.B   6.C   7.B   8.C

Situation 4

With Taiwan's unique National Health Insurance scheme and hospital clinics' tendency to outsource their medical information needs to information technology vendors, appraising potential vendors is extremely difficult, especially given the current ability of medical information systems operators under the National Health Insurance scheme to select the most reliable information technology supplier. 80% of all domestic hospitals outsource at least one business task to a contracted firm. Outsourcing intends to take advantage of human resources and the technologies of vendors to provide quality services. Therefore, both the purchaser and provider of outsourcing can establish a collaborative relationship that is mutually beneficial. Since the establishment of the National Health Insurance scheme in 1995 and the National Health Information Network (HIN), medically oriented information technology has been extensively adopted in clinical practice. As software is the crux of computer systems, hospitals must overcome great challenges in selecting the most appropriate software package to meet their needs.

Situation 5

According to National Health Insurance Bureau estimates, commercial opportunities from the development of the Electronic Healthcare Record (EHR) in Taiwan can yield annual profits of $US 383,000,000. In an economics study, Zhou (2004) noted that, according to IDC statistics, the American information industry outsourced over $US 1,755,000,000 to the medical services sector in 2001; the figure was $US 2,809,000,00 in 2005. As evidenced by the average compound growth rate of 12.5%, outsourcing of information systems in America's medical services sector has increased. Given technological advances, regardless of local or overseas investment in the medical sector, information technology-related applications play a profound role in the decision-making process and the operational planning of hospitals.

Managers often adopt their subjective views or apply previous experience in decision making. However, the decision-making process faces many uncertainties, necessitating the adoption of a scientific method to formulate the decision-making process.

Situation 6

Recent biotechnological developments in Taiwan have led to the commercialization of biological methods in such diverse areas as a) genetic engineering, b) cell fusion, c) bioreaction technology, incorporating fermentation technology, enzyme technology and bioreactors, d) cell cultures, e) gene recombination, f) embryo transplantation and g) nucleus transplantation. More recently, the application of cell fusion and cell culture approaches to human cell signal transduction has attracted considerable interest. The Taiwanese biotechnology market includes many aspects of DNA technology, which can mitigate many genetic defects to enhance human health and provide employment opportunities. As an emerging trend worldwide, biotechnology will provide novel medical treatment approaches and can be used to design highly effective medical procedures. Taiwan has many potential markets for the application of biotechnology, including agriculture, genetically modified food and other industrial sectors. Additionally, from a medical perspective, the demand for biotechnology applications that prevent disease is increasing.

J

Why is it especially difficult to do so?

Owing to the current ability of medical information systems operators under the National Health Insurance scheme to select the most reliable information technology supplier.

Why would both the purchaser and provider of outsourcing want to establish a collaborative relationship?

because it would be a mutually beneficial one

Why must hospitals overcome great challenges in selecting the most appropriate software package? to meet their needs given the importance of software in computer systems

K

How much did the American information industry outsourceto the medical services sector in 2005?

$US 2,809,000,00

How much is the average compound growth rate?

12.5%

How do managers often perform in decision making?

They adopt their subjective views or apply previous experience.

L

What can mitigate many genetic defects to enhance human health and provide employment opportunities?

DNA technology

What is an emerging trend worldwide?

biotechnology

What is increasing?

M

What percentage of all domestic hospitals outsource at least one business task to a contracted firm?

Which organization estimates that commercial opportunities from the development of the Electronic Healthcare Record (EHR) in Taiwan can yield annual profits of $US 383,000,000?

From what perspective is the demand for biotechnology applications that prevent disease increasing?

N

Situation 4

1.B   2.C   3.B   4.C   5.A

Situation 5

1.C   2.B   3.C   4.A   5.C

Situation 6

1.A   2.C   3.C   4.B   5.C

O

Situation 4

1.C   2.C   3.B   4.C   5.A   6.B   7.A   8.C

Situation 5

1.B   2.C   3.A   4.C   5.B   6.B   7.A   8.C   9.B

Situation 6

1.C 2.C 3.B 4.B 5.A 6.C 7.A 8.C 9.A

Answer Key

Identifying Future Directions and Challenges in Developing a Product or Service
產品／服務開發的未來動向及挑戰

A

Situation 1

While the Personal Handy-phone System (PHS) for cellular phones initially covered the greater Taipei region, First International Telecom expanded PHS coverage to Taoyuan and Hsinchu in the beginning of 2002, followed by Kaoshiung and Taichung in 2004. Plans were subsequently made to service Tainan, Nantou and Pingtung in central and southern parts of the island. To effectively respond to the increasing number of mobile phone users and frequency range, First International Telecom obtained approval for an additional 500,000 phone numbers with the prefix 0966. To accommodate the growing number of phone subscribers, system capacity has expanded, with related software/hardware recently installed to accommodate an additional 1,250,000 phone numbers. Moreover, an additional 1,500,000 phone numbers will be added by the end of December. Furthermore, to cope with call congestion and an insufficient number of channels given the increasing number of users, First International Telecom has applied to the government to increase its bandwidth to 3 MHz for the northern region, to increase audio quality online. In terms of value-added services, PHS is ranked first among those offered by Taiwan's mobile phone service providers. MiMi Thumb Information has a sales growth rate of around 10% and a subscription growth rate of 60%, outperforming all of its competitors. First International Telecom plans to develop real-time multimedia services and popularize real-time GPS information transmission; integrate information and voice services, and introduce corporate services. First International Telecom has recently launched a "Mobile Ring Tone" service, which enables users to select various songs or dialogues to replace monotonous ring tones. Currently around 10,000 mobile phone users subscribe to this service monthly. First International Telecom seeks to expand its vision of full coverage telecommunications, hopefully providing more innovative and convenient mobile communications services. Given the increasing diversity of mobile telecommunication services and the fiercely competitive nature of the telecom industry, the PHS sector has a bright future.

Situation 2

The rapid development of the information industry in recent years has led to high outputs of consumer electronics products, which have not only accelerated the delivery of new information products that have replaced the old ones, but also shortened the life cycle of such products. Therefore, manufacturers engaged in the R&D of such products have attempted various innovative designs or marketing strategies to stimulate consumers and expand markets. However, in an era when digital camera markets are growing rapidly, only repositioning products based on future market demand and developing new products by creative design can create niche markets. The digital camera sector in Taiwan is still in its infancy. While Japan and the United States dominate the global market in this area, Japan controls production of the major components. During conceptual development, industrial designers often lack a goal-oriented and systematic approach. The limited and subjective experience of such designers severely limits design quantity and quality. Given increasingly diverse consumer preferences, creating innovative concepts in product redesign is extremely challenging. In the future, most Taiwanese manufacturers will either compete with others in the digital camera sector or ally with them to yield mutually beneficial results. Product innovation necessitates the continuous incorporation of advanced technologies in product design to satisfy consumer tastes. According to the Product Development and Management Association, over 50% of all sales come from new products that were innovated by hi-tech industries. While product research may prove costly to manufacturers, the hi-tech sector must accurately predict consumer trends and preferences.

Unit
Seven

Answer Key
Identifying Future Directions and Challenges in Developing a Produc
or Service
產品／服務開發的未來動向及挑戰

Situation 3

Following half a century of development, the Taiwanese automotive industry is limited not only by its rather small market, but also by technological restrictions imposed by overseas parent manufacturers. This dilemma has been further exacerbated by overproduction in the global automotive market, resulting in mergers and alliances. Additionally, Taiwan's accession to the World Trade Organization negatively affected local automotive manufacturers. The restrictions have definitely limited the ability of Taiwanese automotive manufacturers to compete with multinational corporations, inevitably forcing local enterprises to conform to available resources and adopt various product innovation strategies. Despite this unfavorable environment, domestic automotive manufacturers have strived aggressively to enter the export market in a manner consistent with globalization trends. Following several years of development in this direction, the local automotive industry has reached international quality standards, as evidenced by the tremendous amounts of capital invested in R&D and design. Such efforts have culminated in product differentiation to adhere to local consumer demand. Local acceptance of domestically manufactured automobiles has gradually increased the market share. However, expanding the domestic market share has been extremely challenging, prompting local manufacturers to establish production facilities in China and other southeastern Asian countries to offset high labor costs. In summary, domestic automotive manufacturers have expended considerable effort in research to develop high-quality models at competitive prices, making up for their previously tarnished image.

B

How does First International Telecom hope to cope with call congestion and an insufficient number of channels given the increasing number of users?

by increasing audio quality online through applying to the government to increase its bandwidth to 3 MHz for the northern region

How does First International Telecom enable users to select various songs or dialogues to replace monotonous ring tones?

with its recent launch of a "Mobile Ring Tone" service

How does First International Telecom hope to provide more innovative and convenient mobile communications services?

by expanding its vision of full coverage telecommunications

C

What countries dominate the global market in digital cameras?

Japan and the United States

What do industrial designers often lack during conceptual development?

a goal-oriented and systematic approach.

What does product innovation necessitate?

the continuous incorporation of advanced technologies in product design to satisfy consumer tastes

D

Why have local automotive manufacturers been negatively affected?

Taiwan's accession to the World Trade Organization

Why have local enterprises been forced to conform to available resources and adopt

various product innovation strategies?
because of restrictions that have definitely limited the ability of Taiwanese
automotive manufacturers to compete with multinational corporations

Why have local manufacturers established production facilities in China and other
southeastern Asian countries?
to offset high labor costs

E

How many phone numbers will First International Telecom add by the end of
December?

What percentage of all sales come from new products that were innovated by hi-tech
industries?

How have domestic automotive manufacturers strived aggressively to enter the
export market?

F

Situation 1

1.C   2.A   3.C   4.B   5.B

Situation 2

1.B   2.A   3.B   4.C

Situation 3

1.C   2.C   3.B   4.C   5.C

G

Situation 1

1.A   2.C   3.B   4.B   5.C   6.A   7.A   8.B   9.B   10.A   11.C   12.B   13.A

Situation 2

1.B   2.A   3.C   4.A   5.C   6.B   7.C   8.A   9.B   10.B   11.C   12.A

Situation 3

1.B   2.B   3.C   4.C   5.A   6.B   7.B   8.A   9.C   10.B

I

Situation 4

As the service sector in Taiwan gradually matures to a level comparable with that found in other industrialized countries, numerous service-oriented franchisers aspire to stake a claim in the island's increasingly competitive market by offering differentiated products, services and forms of technical support. They do so in contrast to conventional marketing strategies of traditional brick-and-mortar industries, which largely depend on a particular mode that has evolved over time. Under the mottos of Vision, Mission and Core Value, TSC strives to lead the cosmetics sector by addressing global concerns over aging prevention and treatment. While attempting to transform the cosmetics sector with safe, effective and inexpensive beauty products, TSC is driven by a highly talented staff of professionals from multidisciplinary fields that integrate their efforts synergistically in a spirit of mutual respect. Notable brand name products in the TSC product line include Collagen toner water, Collagen body lotion, Ocean spirit cleansing, Collalife bone fixer, Ocean spirit body shampoo and Collalife slim magic. To enhance its competitive edge, TSC aggressively pursues large capital investment, state-of-the-art technologies and various information sources to further strengthen its core competence and become a globally competitive leader in this intensely competitive sector.

Situation 5

While striving to satisfy consumer demand for quality sleep, Elsa Bedding Franchise in Taiwan established a research and development division to advance product technology. According to management guru Peter Drucker, a company's purpose is to satisfy customers. More than just marketing, a company must incorporate innovation to identify customers' needs. Innovation is to be attained in the present, not the future. One source of innovation is the biotechnology industry. Taiwan's information technology sector is aggressively striving to integrate its efforts with the recently emerging biotech industry. Biotech products such as cosmetics have been widely commercialized by local manufacturers such as the Taiwan Sugar Corporation. Given the increasing public demand for health care products, Elsa's R&D Department will devote its efforts to this area of development. First, Elsa will recruit three employees with undergraduate or graduate training in biotechnology. Previous employees of the Industrial Technology Research Institute will receive an additional 30% of base salary. Next, R&D employees will receive on-the-job training each Sunday morning. Finally, employees will receive a bonus if results of their research lead to a patented technology. Despite mounting competition, Elsa is determined to increase its productivity through innovative products and services, positioning itself as a leader in Taiwan's bedding sector.

Situation 6

As a non-profit foundation created out of law enacted from Taiwan's Legislative Yuan in 1995, the National Health Research Institute (NHRI) functions autonomously under the auspices of the Department of Health. While dedicating itself to the enhancement of medical research and healthcare island wide, the NHRI comprises ten research divisions and four departments (Administration, Intramural Research, Extramural Research, and Research Resources). Scientists at the NHRI conduct mission-oriented medical research and investigate many aspects of biomedical sciences, as well as specific diseases. Clinical disorders range from aging, cancer, infectious diseases, mental disorders and occupational diseases. Hopefully, knowledge expertise and facilities at the NHRI will become pivotal in understanding, preventing and curing diseases nationwide. Besides planning the overall directions of national science and technology development in medical care, the NHRI strives to coordinate, integrate and support research activities undertaken by medical institutions. Furthermore, in addition to training young scientists and physicians, the NHRI also focuses on establishing a transparent system for reviewing and assessing research projects, as well as facilitating information exchanges through domestic and international cooperative ventures.

J

How does TSC strive to lead the cosmetics sector?
by addressing global concerns over aging prevention and treatment

How does TSC's highly talented staff of professionals from multidisciplinary fields cooperate with each other?
in a spirit of mutual respect

How does TSC strive to further strengthen its core competence and become a globally competitive leader in this intensely competitive sector?
by aggressively pursuing large capital investment, state-of-the-art technologies and various information sources

Unit
Seven

Answer Key
Identifying Future Directions and Challenges in Developing a Produc
or Service
產品／服務開發的未來動向及挑戰

K

Why will Elsa's R&D Department will devote its efforts to health care products?
given the increasing public demand for them

Why will Elsa employees receive a bonus?
if results of their research lead to a patented technology

Why is Elsa determined to increase its productivity through innovative products and services? To position itself as a leader in Taiwan's bedding sector

L

What kind of research does scientists at the NHRI conduct?
mission-oriented medical research

What will become pivotal in understanding, preventing and curing diseases nationwide?
knowledge expertise and facilities at the NHRI

What does the NHRI focus on establishing?
a transparent system for reviewing and assessing research projects

M

What are some of the notable brand name products in the TSC product line?

What is a a company's purpose?

What does the NHRI strive to do?

N

Situation 4

1.B   2.C   3.A   4.C

Situation 5

1.B   2.A   3.C   4.A   5.C

Situation 6

1.B   2.B   3.C   4.B   5.C

O

Situation 4

1B   2.C   3.B   4.A   5.A   6.C   7.A   8.C   9.C   10.B

Situation 5

1.B   2.B   3.C   4.C   5.A   6.B   7.C   8.B   9.A   10.C   11.B

Situation 6

1.C   2.A   3.B   4.B   5.A   6.A   7.C   8.B   9.A   10.B

About the Author

Born on his father's birthday, Ted Knoy received a Bachelor of Arts in History at Franklin College of Indiana (Franklin, Indiana) and a Master's degree in Public Administration at American International College (Springfield, Massachusetts). He is currently a Ph.D. student in Education at the University of East Anglia (Norwich, England). Having conducted research and independent study in New Zealand, Ukraine, Scotland, South Africa, India, Nicaragua and Switzerland, he has lived in Taiwan since 1989 where he has been a permanent resident since 2000.

Having taught technical writing in the graduate school programs of National Chiao Tung University (Institute of Information Management, Institute of Communications Engineering, Institute of Technology Management, Department of Industrial Engineering Management, Department of Transportation Managment and, currently, in the College of Management) and National Tsing Hua University (Computer Science, Life Science, Electrical Engineering, Power Mechanical Engineering, Chemistry and Chemical Engineering Departments) since 1989, Ted also teaches in the Institute of Business Management at Yuan Pei University. He is also the English editor of several technical and medical journals and publications in Taiwan.

Ted is author of *The Chinese Technical Writers' Series,* which includes An English Style Approach for Chinese Technical Writers, English Oral Presentations for Chinese Technical Writers, A Correspondence Manual for Chinese Technical Writers, An Editing Workbook for Chinese Technical Writers and Advanced Copyediting Practice for Chinese Technical Writers. He is also author of *The Chinese Professional Writers' Series*, which includes Writing Effective Study Plans, Writing Effective Work Proposals, Writing Effective Employment Application Statements, Writing Effective Career Statements, Effectively Communicating

374

Online, <u>Writing Effective Marketing Promotional Materials</u> and <u>Effective Management Communication</u>.

Ted created and coordinates the Chinese On-line Writing Lab (OWL) at www.chineseowl.idv.tw

Acknowledgments

Thanks to the following individuals for contributing to this book:

特別感謝以下人員的貢獻：

國立交通大學工業管理學系 唐麗英教授
魏　源　林姍慧　金新恩　王有志　林麗甄　裴善康　張志偉　蔡志偉

元培科技大學 經營管理研究所
許碧芳（所長）　王貞穎　李仁智　陳彥谷　胡惠眞　陳碧俞　王連慶
蔡玟純　高青莉　賴姝惠　李雅玎　戴碧美　楊明雄　陳皇助　林宏隆
鍾玠融　李昭蓉　許美菁　葉伯彥　林羿君　吳政龍　鄭凱元　黃志斌
郭美萱　李尉誠　陳靜怡　盧筱嵐　鄭彥均　劉偉翔　彭廣興　林宗瑋
巫怡樺　朱建華

元培科技大學 影像醫學研究所
王愛義（所長）　周美榮　顏映君　林孟聰　張雅玲　彭薇莉　張明偉
李玉綸　聶伊辛　黃勝賢　張格瑜　龔慧敏　林永健　呂忠祐　李仁忠
王國偉　李政翰　黃國明　蔡明輝　杜俊元　丁健益　方詩涵　余宗銘
劉力瑛　郭明杰

元培科技大學 生物技術研究所
陳　孃（所長）　范齡文　彭姵華　鄭啓軒　許凱文　李昇憲　陳雪君
鄭凱暹　尤鼎元　陳玉梅　鄭美玲　郭軒中　朱芳儀　周佩穎　吳佳眞

國立交通大學管理學院

Thanks also to Ming-Jay Chen for illustrating this book. My technical writing students in the Department of Computer Science and Institute of Life Science at National Tsing Hua University, as well as the College of Management at National Chiao Tung University are also appreciated. Thanks also to Seamus Harris and Bill Hodgson for reviewing this book.

精通科技論文（報告）寫作之捷徑
An English Style Approach for Chinese Technical Writers （修訂版）

作者：柯泰德（Ted Knoy）

內容簡介

使用直接而流利的英文會話

讓您所寫的英文科技論文很容易被了解

提供不同形式的句型供您參考利用

比較中英句子結構之異同

利用介系詞片語將二個句子連接在一起

萬其超／李國鼎科技發展基金會秘書長

本書是多年實務經驗和專注力之結晶，因此是一本坊間少見而極具實用
價值的書。

陳文華／國立清華大學工學院院長

中國人使用英文寫作時，語法上常會犯錯，本書提供了很好的實例示
範，對於科技論文寫作有相當參考價值。

徐　章／工業技術研究院量測中心主任

這是一個讓初學英文寫作的人，能夠先由不犯寫作的錯誤開始再根據書
中的步驟逐步學習提升寫作能力的好工具，此書的內容及解說方式使讀
者也可以無師自通，藉由自修的方式學習進步，但是更重要的是它雖然
是一本好書，當您學會了書中的許多技巧，如果您還想要更進步，那麼
基本原則還是要常常練習，才能發揮書的精髓。

Kathleen Ford, English Editor, Proceedings(Life Science Divison),

National Science Council

The Chinese Technical Writers Series is valuable for anyone involved with
creating scientific documentation.

※若有任何英文文件修改問題，請直接與柯泰德先生聯絡：（03）5724895

特　　價　新台幣300元
劃　　撥　19419482 清蔚科技股份有限公司
線上訂購　四方書網 www.4Book.com.tw
發 行 所　華香園出版社

作好英語會議簡報
English Oral Presentations for Chinese Technical Writers

作者：柯泰德（Ted Kony）

內容簡介

本書共分十二個單元，涵括產品開發、組織、部門、科技、及產業的介紹、科技背景、公司訪問、研究能力及論文之發表等，每一單元提供不同型態的科技口頭簡報範例，以進行英文口頭簡報的寫作及表達練習，是一本非常實用的著作。

李鍾熙／工業技術研究院化學工業研究所所長

　　一個成功的科技簡報，就是使演講流暢，用簡單直接的方法、清楚表達內容。本書提供一個創新的方法（途徑），給組織每一成員做為借鏡，得以自行準備口頭簡報。利用本書這套有系統的方法加以練習，將必然使您信心備增，簡報更加順利成功。

薛敬和／IUPAC台北國際高分子研討會執行長
　　　　國立清華大學教授

　　本書以個案方式介紹各英文會議簡報之執行方式，深入簡出，為邁入實用狀況的最佳參考書籍。

沙晉康／清華大學化學研究所所長
　　　　第十五屆國際雜環化學會議主席

　　本書介紹英文簡報的格式，值得國人參考。今天在學術或工商界與外國接觸來往均日益增多，我們應加強表達的技巧，尤其是英文的簡報應具有很高的專業水準。本書做為一個很好的範例。

張俊彥／國立交通大學電機資訊學院教授兼院長

　　針對中國學生協助他們寫好英文的國際論文參加國際會議如何以英語演講、內容切中要害特別推薦。

※若有任何英文文件修改問題，請直接與柯泰德先生聯絡：（03）5724895

特　　價　　新台幣250元
劃　　撥　　19419482 清蔚科技股份有限公司
線上訂購　　四方書網 www.4Book.com.tw
發 行 所　　工業技術研究院

英文信函參考手冊
A Correspondence Manual for Chinese Technical Writers

作者：柯泰德（Ted Knoy）

內容簡介

本書期望成為從事專業管理與科技之中國人，在國際場合上溝通交流時之參考指導書籍。本書所提供的書信範例（附磁碟片），可為您撰述信件時的參考範本。更實際的是，本書如同一「寫作計畫小組」，能因應特定場合（狀況）撰寫出所需要的信函。

李國鼎 / 總統府資政

我國科技人員在國際場合溝通表達之機會急遽增加，希望大家都來重視英文說寫之能力。

羅明哲 / 國立中興大學教務長

一份表達精準且適切的英文信函，在國際間的往來交流上，重要性不亞於研究成果的報告發表。本書介紹各類英文技術信函的特徵及寫作指引，所附範例中肯實用，為優良的學習及參考書籍。

廖俊臣 / 國立清華大學理學院院長

本書提供許多有關工業技術合作、技術轉移、工業資訊、人員訓練及互訪等接洽信函的例句和範例，頗為實用，極具參考價值。

于樹偉 / 工業安全衛生技術發展中心主任

國際間往來日益頻繁，以英文有效地溝通交流，是現今從事科技研究人員所需具備的重要技能。本書在寫作風格、文法結構與取材等方面，提供極佳的寫作參考與指引，所列舉的範例，皆經過作者細心的修訂與潤飾，必能切合讀者的實際需要。

※若有任何英文文件修改問題，請直接與柯泰德先生聯絡：（03）5724895

特　　價　新台幣250元
劃　　撥　19419482 清蔚科技股份有限公司
線上訂購　四方書網 www.4Book.com.tw
發 行 所　工業技術研究院

科技英文編修訓練手冊
An Editing Workbook for Chinese Technical Writers

作者：柯泰德（Ted Knoy）

內容簡介

要把科技英文寫的精確並不是件容易的事情。通常在投寄文稿發表前，作者都要前前後後修改草稿，在這樣繁複過程中甚至最後可能請專業的文件編修人士代勞雕琢使全文更為清楚明確。

本書由科技論文的寫作型式、方法型式、內容結構及內容品質著手，並以習題方式使學生透過反覆練習熟能生巧，能確實提昇科技英文之寫作及編修能力。

劉炯明 / 國立清華大學校長

「科技英文寫作」是一項非常重要的技巧。本書針對台灣科技研究人員在英文寫作發表這方面的訓練，書中以實用性練習對症下藥，期望科技英文寫作者熟能生巧，實在是一個很有用的教材。

彭旭明 / 國立台灣大學副校長

本書為科技英文寫作系列之四；以練習題為主，由反覆練習中提昇寫作反編輯能力。適合理、工、醫、農的學生及研究人員使用，特為推薦。

許千樹 / 國立交通大學研究發展處研發長

處於今日高科技時代，國人用到科技英文寫作之機會甚多，如何能以精練的手法寫出一篇好的科技論文，極為重要。本書針對國人寫作之缺點提供了各種清楚的編修範例，實用性高，極具參考價值。

陳文村 / 國立清華大學電機資訊學院院長

處在我國日益國際化、資訊化的社會裡，英文書寫是必備的能力，本書提供很多極具參考價值的範例。柯泰德先生在清大任教科技英文寫作多年，深受學生喜愛，本人樂於推薦此書。

※若有任何英文文件修改問題，請直接與柯泰德先生聯絡：（03）5724895

特　　價　新台幣350元
劃　　撥　19419482 清蔚科技股份有限公司
線上訂購　四方書網 www.4Book.com.tw
發 行 所　清蔚科技股份有限公司

科技英文編修訓練手冊【進階篇】
Advanced Copyediting Practice for Chinese Technical Writers

作者：柯泰德（Ted Knoy）

內容簡介

本書延續科技英文寫作系列之四「科技英文編修訓練手冊」之寫作指導原則，更進一步把重點放在如何讓作者想表達的意思更明顯，即明白寫作。把文章中曖昧不清全部去除，使閱讀您文章的讀者很容易的理解您作品的精髓。

本手冊同時國立清華大學資訊工程學系非同步遠距教學科技英文寫作課程指導範本。

張俊彥 / 國立交通大學校長暨中研院院士

對於國內理工學生及從事科技研究之人士而言，可說是一本相當有用的書籍，特向讀者推薦。

蔡仁堅 / 前新竹市長

科技不分國界，隨著進入公元兩千年的資訊時代，使用國際語言撰寫學術報告已是時勢所趨；今欣見柯泰德先生致力於編撰此著作，並彙集了許多實例詳加解說，相信對於科技英文的撰寫有著莫大的裨益，特予以推薦。

史欽泰 / 工研院院長

本書即以實用範例，針對國人寫作的缺點提供簡單、明白的寫作原則，非常適合科技研發人員使用。

張智星 / 國立清華大學資訊工程學系副教授、計算中心組長

本書是特別針對系上所開科技英文寫作非同步遠距教學而設計，範圍內容豐富，所列練習也非常實用，學生可以配合課程來使用，在時間上更有彈性的針對自己情況來練習，很有助益。

劉世東 / 長庚大學醫學院微生物免疫科主任

書中的例子及習題對閱讀者會有很大的助益。這是一本研究生必讀的書，也是一般研究者重要的參考書。

※若有任何英文文件修改問題，請直接與柯泰德先生聯絡：（03）5724895

特　　　價　新台幣450元
劃　　　撥　19419482 清蔚科技股份有限公司
線上訂購　四方書網 www.4Book.com.tw
發 行 所　清蔚科技股份有限公司

有效撰寫英文讀書計畫
Writing Effective Study Plans

作者：柯泰德（Ted Knoy）

內容簡介

本書指導準備出國進修的學生撰寫精簡切要的英文讀書計畫，內容包括：表達學習的領域及興趣、展現所具備之專業領域知識、敘述學歷背景及成就等。本書的每個單元皆提供視覺化的具體情境及相關寫作訓練，讓讀者進行實際的訊息運用練習。此外，書中的編修訓練並可加強「精確寫作」及「明白寫作」的技巧。本書適用於個人自修以及團體授課，能確實引導讀者寫出精簡而有效的英文讀書計畫。

本手冊同時為國立清華大學資訊工程學系非同步遠距教學科技英文寫作課程指導範本。

于樹偉／工業技術研究院主任

《有效撰寫讀書計畫》一書主旨在提供國人精深學習前的準備，包括：讀書計畫及推薦信函的建構、完成。藉由本書中視覺化訊息的互動及練習，國人可以更明確的掌握全篇的意涵，及更完整的表達心中的意念。這也是本書異於坊間同類書籍只著重在片斷記憶，不求理解最大之處。

王　玫／工業研究技術院、化學工業研究所組長

《有效撰寫讀書計畫》主要是針對想要進階學習的讀者，由基本的自我學習經驗描述延伸至未來目標的設定，更進一步強調推薦信函的撰寫，藉出圖片式訊息互動，讓讀者主動聯想及運用寫作知識及技巧，避免一味的記憶零星的範例；如此一來，讀者可以更清楚表明個別的特質及快速掌握重點。

※若有任何英文文件修改問題，請直接與柯泰德先生聯絡：（03）5724895

特　　價　新台幣450元
劃　　撥　19419482 清蔚科技股份有限公司
線上訂購　四方書網 www.4Book.com.tw
發 行 所　清蔚科技股份有限公司

有效撰寫英文工作提案
Writing Effective Work Proposals

作者：柯泰德（Ted Knoy）

內容簡介

許多國人都是在工作方案完成時才開始撰寫相關英文提案，他們視撰寫提案為行政工作的一環，只是消極記錄已完成的事項，而不是積極的規劃掌控未來及現在正進行的工作。如果國人可以在撰寫英文提案時，事先仔細明辨工作計畫提案的背景及目標，不僅可以確保寫作進度、寫作結構的完整性，更可兼顧提案相關讀者的興趣強調。本書中詳細的步驟可指導工作提案寫作者達成此一目標。 書中的每個單元呈現三個視覺化的情境，提供國人英文工作提案寫作實質訊息，而相關附加的寫作練習讓讀者做實際的訊息運用。此外，本書也非常適合在課堂上使用，教師可以先描述單元情境而讓學生藉由書中練習循序完成具有良好架構的工作提案。書中內容包括：1.工作提案計畫（第一部分）：背景 2.工作提案計畫（第二部分）：行動 3.問題描述 4.假設描述 5.摘要撰寫（第一部分）： 簡介背景、目標及方法 6.摘要撰寫（第二部分）： 歸納希望的結果及其對特定領域的貢獻 7.綜合上述寫成精確工作提案。

唐傳義 / 國立清華大學資訊工程學系主任

　　　　本書重點放在如何在工作計畫一開始時便可以用英文來規劃整個工作提案，由工作提案的背景、行動、方法及預期的結果漸次教導國人如何寫出具有良好結構的英文工作提案。如此用英文明確界定工作提案的程序及工作目標更可以確保英文工作提案及工作計畫的即時完成。對工作效率而言也有助益。

　　　　在國人積極加入WTO之後的調整期，優良的英文工作提案寫作能力絕對是一項競爭力快速加分的工具。

※若有任何英文文件修改問題，請直接與柯泰德先生聯絡：（03）5724895

特　　價　新台幣450元
劃　　撥　19735365 葉忠賢
線上訂購　www.ycrc.com.tw
發 行 所　揚智文化事業股份有限公司

有效撰寫求職英文自傳
Writing Effective Employment Application Statements

作者：柯泰德（Ted Knoy）

內容簡介

本書主要教導讀者如何建構良好的求職英文自傳。書中內容包括：1.表達工作相關興趣；2.興趣相關產業描寫；3.描述所參與方案裡專業興趣的表現；4.描述學歷背景及已獲成就；5.介紹研究及工作經驗；6.描述與求職相關的課外活動；7.綜合上述寫成精確求職英文自傳。

有效的求職英文自傳不僅必須能讓求職者在企業主限定的字數內精確的描述自身的背景資訊及先前成就，更關鍵性的因素是有效的求職英文自傳更能讓企業主快速明瞭求職者如何應用相關知識技能或其特殊領導特質來貢獻企業主。

書中的每個單元呈現三個視覺化的情境，提供國人求職英文自傳寫作實質訊息，而相關附加的寫作練習讓讀者做實際的訊息運用。此外，本書也非常適合在課堂上使用，教師可以先描述單元情境而讓學生藉由書中練習循序完成具有良好架構的求職英文自傳。

黎漢林／國立交通大學管理學院院長

我國加入WTO後，國際化的腳步日益加快；而企業人員之英文寫作能力更形重要。它不僅可促進國際合作夥伴間的溝通，同時也增加了國際客戶的信任。因此國際企業在求才時無不特別注意其員工的英文表達能力。

柯泰德先生著作《有效撰寫求職英文自傳》即希望幫助求職者能以英文有系統的介紹其能力、經驗與抱負。這本書是柯先生有關英文寫作的第八本專書，柯先生教學與編書十分專注，我相信這本書對求職者是甚佳的參考書籍。

※若有任何英文文件修改問題，請直接與柯泰德先生聯絡：（03）5724895

特　　價　新台幣450元
劃　　撥　19735365 葉忠賢
線上訂購　www.ycrc.com.tw
發 行 所　揚智文化事業股份有限公司

有效撰寫英文職涯經歷
Writing Effective Career Statements

作者：柯泰德（Ted Knoy）

內容簡介

本書主要教導讀者如何建構良好的英文職涯經歷。書中內容包括：1.表達工作相關興趣；2.興趣相關產業描寫；3.描述所參與方案裡專業興趣的表現；4.描述學歷背景及已獲成就；5.介紹研究及工作經驗；6.描述與求職相關的課外活動；7.綜合上述寫成英文職涯經歷。

有效的職涯經歷描述不僅能讓再度就業者在企業主限定的字數內精準的描述自身的背景資訊及先前工作經驗及成就，更關鍵性的，有效的職涯經歷能讓企業主快速明瞭求職者如何應用相關知識技能及先前的就業經驗結合來貢獻企業主。

書中的每個單元呈現六個視覺化的情境，經由以全民英語檢定為標準而設計的口說訓練、聽力、閱讀及寫作四種不同功能來強化英文能力。此外，本書也非常適合在課堂上使用，教師可以先描述單元情境而讓學生藉由書中練習循序在短期內完成。

林進財／元培科學技術學院校長

近年來，台灣無不時時刻刻地努力提高國際競爭力，不論政府或企業界求才皆以英文表達能力為主要考量之一。唯有員工具備優秀的英文能力，才足以把本身的能力、工作經驗與國際競爭舞台接軌。

柯泰德先生著作《有效撰寫英文職涯經歷》，即希望幫助已有工作經驗的求職者能以英文有效地介紹其能力、工作經驗與成就。此書是柯先生有關英文寫作的第九本專書，相信對再度求職者是進入職場絕佳的工具書。

※若有任何英文文件修改問題，請直接與柯泰德先生聯絡：（03）5724895

特　　價　新台幣480元
劃　　撥　19735365 葉忠賢
線上訂購　www.ycrc.com.tw
發 行 所　揚智文化事業股份有限公司

有效撰寫專業英文電子郵件
Effectively Communicating Online

作者：柯泰德（Ted Knoy）

內容簡介

本書主要教導讀者如何建構良好的專業英文電子郵件。書中內容包括：1.科技訓練請求信函；2.資訊交流信函；3.科技訪問信函；4.演講者邀請信函；5.旅行安排信函；6.資訊請求信函。

書中的每個單元呈現三個視覺化的情境，經由以全民英語檢定為標準而設計的口說訓練、聽力、閱讀及寫作四種不同功能來強化英文能力。此外，本書也非常適合在課堂上使用，教師可以先描述單元情境而讓學生藉由書中練習循序在短期內完成。

許碧芳／元培科學技術學院經營管理研究所所長

隨著時代快速變遷，人們生活步調及習性也十倍速的演變。舉郵件為例，由早期傳統的郵局寄送方式改為現今的電子郵件（e-mail）系統。速度不但快且也節省費用。對有時效性的訊息傳送更可達事半功倍的效果。不僅如此，電子郵件不受地域性的限制，可以隨地進行溝通，也是生活及職場上一項利器。

柯先生所著《有效撰寫專業英文電子郵件》，乃針對目前對電子郵件寫作需求，配合六種不同情境展示近二百個範例寫作。藉此觀摩他人電子郵件寫作來加強讀者本身的寫作技巧，同時配合書中網路練習訓練英文聽力及閱讀技巧。是一本非常實用且符合網路時代需求的工具書。

※若有任何英文文件修改問題，請直接與柯泰德先生聯絡：（03）5724895

特　　價　新台幣520元
劃　　撥　19735365 葉忠賢
線上訂購　www.ycrc.com.tw
發 行 所　揚智文化事業股份有限公司

有效撰寫行銷英文
Writing Effective Marketing Promotional Materials

作者：柯泰德（Ted Knoy）

內容簡介

本書主要教導讀者如何建構良好的行銷英文。書中內容包括：1.預測市場趨勢；2.產品或服務研發；3.專案描述；4.公司或組織介紹；5.組或部門介紹；6.科技介紹；7.工業介紹。

書中的每個單元呈現六個視覺化的情境，經由以全民英語檢定為標準而設計的口說訓練、聽力、閱讀及寫作四種不同功能來強化英文能力。此外，本書也非常適合在課堂上使用，教師可以先描述單元情境而讓學生藉由書中練習循序在短期內完成。

李鍾熙／工業科技研究院院長

本書特別針對行銷英文加以解說並輔以範例，加深讀者之印象，並以六個視覺化的情境，訓練讀者的口說、聽力、閱讀及寫作能力，是從事國際行銷、管理工作者值得參閱的書籍。

※若有任何英文文件修改問題，請直接與柯泰德先生聯絡：（03）5724895

特　　價　新台幣480元
劃　　撥　19735365 葉忠賢
線上訂購　www.ycrc.com.tw
發 行 所　揚智文化事業股份有限公司

管理英文
Effective Management Communication

作者：柯泰德（Ted Knoy）

內容簡介

本書為「應用英文寫作系列」之第七本書，主要訓練管理人才（管理師）撰寫符合工作場合需要的書面英文。書中內容包括：1.有效撰寫管理英文備忘錄─調查性與建議性報告；2.有效撰寫管理英文備忘錄─說服力的展現；3.有效撰寫管理英文備忘錄─非正式實用管理技術報告；4.有效海外管理英文交流──探討管理師如何有效的與海外專業人士交流英文；5.管理師專業英文工作經歷撰寫；6.有效撰寫英文工作提案；7.管理師學術及專業訓練英文申請撰寫；8.有效進行管理英文口語簡報；9.管理英文寫作上之常見問題；10.求職申請信函；11.專業訓練申請信函；12.求職推荐信函。

書中列出許多範例與練習，主要是幫助讀者糾正常犯寫作格式上錯誤，由反覆練習中，進而熟能生巧提升有關個人管理方面的英文寫作能力。

※若有任何英文文件修改問題，請直接與柯泰德先生聯絡：（03）5724895

特　　價　　新台幣450元
劃　　撥　　19735365 葉忠賢
線上訂購　　www.ycrc.com.tw
發 行 所　　揚智文化事業股份有限公司

The Chinese
Online Writing Lab
【 柯泰德線上英文論文編修訓練服務 】
http://www.cc.nctu.edu.tw/~tedknoy

您有科技英文寫作上的困擾嗎？

您的文章在投稿時常被國外論文審核人員批評文法很爛嗎？以至於被退稿嗎？

您對論文段落的時式使用上常混淆不清嗎？

您在寫作論文時同一個動詞或名詞常常重複使用嗎？

您的這些煩惱現在均可透過柯泰德網路線上科技英文論文編修
服務來替您加以解決。本服務項目分別含括如下：

1. 英文論文編輯與修改
2. 科技英文寫作開課訓練服務
3. 線上寫作家教
4. 免費寫作格式建議服務，及網頁問題討論區解答
5. 線上遠距教學（互動練習）

另外，為能廣為服務中國人士對論文寫作上之缺點，柯泰德亦
同時著作下列參考書籍可供有志人士為寫作上之參考。

＜1.精通科技論文（報告）寫作之捷徑
＜2.做好英文會議簡報
＜3.英文信函參考手冊
＜4.科技英文編修訓練手冊
＜5.科技英文編修訓練手冊（進階篇）
＜6.有效撰寫英文讀書計畫

上部分亦可由柯泰德先生的首頁中下載得到。

如果您對本服務有興趣的話，可參考柯泰德先生的首頁標示。

柯泰德網路線上科技英文論文編修服務
地址：新竹市大學路50號8樓之三
TEL:03-5724895
FAX:03-5724938
網址：http://www.cc.nctu.edu.tw/~tedknoy
E-mail:tedaknoy@ms11.hinet.net

應用英文寫作系列 08

商用英文

作　　者／柯泰德（Ted Knoy）
出 版 者／揚智文化事業股份有限公司
發 行 人／葉忠賢
總 編 輯／閻富萍
執行編輯／胡琡珮
地　　址／台北縣深坑鄉北深路三段 260 號 8 樓
電　　話／(02)86626826
傳　　真／(02)2664-7633
　E-mail ／ service@ycrc.com.tw
印　　刷／鼎易印刷事業股份有限公司
　I S B N ／ 978-957-818-934-8
初版一刷／2009 年 12 月
定　　價／新台幣 480 元

＊本書如有缺頁、破損、裝訂錯誤，請寄回更換＊

國家圖書館出版品預行編目資料

商用英文＝Effective business communication /
　　柯泰德（Ted Knoy）作. -- 初版. -- 臺北縣
　　深坑鄉：揚智文化, 2009.12
　　　面；　公分. --（應用英文寫作系列；8）

　　ISBN 978-957-818-934-8（平裝）

　　1.商業英文　2.讀本

805.18　　　　　　　　　　　　　98020606